MURDERLIZED:
A SHORT STORY COLLECTION

MAX ALLAN COLLINS
AND
MATTHEW V. CLEMENS

Murderlized: A Short Story Collection

Paperback Edition

Wolfpack Publishing
6032 Wheat Penny Avenue
Las Vegas, NV 89122

wolfpackpublishing.com

This book is a work of fiction. Any references to historical events, real people or real places are used fictitiously. Other names, characters, places and events are products of the author's imagination, and any resemblance to actual events, places or persons, living or dead, is entirely coincidental.

Paperback ISBN 978-1-64734-092-6
eBook ISBN 978-1-64734-091-9

MURDERLIZED:
A SHORT STORY COLLECTION

In memory of
Karl Largent,
BJ Elsner
and
David Collins
with fond memories of
the Mississippi Valley Writers conferences.

Contents

INTRODUCTION
by
Max Allan Collins

On April 10, 1992, Matthew V. Clemens quit his job with a company for whom he had mostly been driving truck to go fulltime as a professional writer. His first significant gig was working editorially with Karl Largent on several of the latter's bestselling Tom Clancy-style techno thrillers; Karl was a fine guy and a first-rate writer himself.

I met Matt when I was teaching at the Mississippi Valley Writers Conference at Augustana College in Rock Island, Illinois, in the 1980s, a one-week summer writing program founded by the late David Collins (no relation), a respected and award-winning writer of children's books. David had taken Matt under his wing as a guy with confidence and personality who could get things done. Matt was often assisted by another force of nature, BJ Elsner, who would later help me research *Road to Perdition.*

Matt was one of my students and I chose him to receive the John Locher Award (named for the late son of my *Dick Tracy* collaborator, Dick Locher). We hit it off, and had already met when Matt came to a gig where my band Crusin' was playing at a strip mall bar in Davenport,

Iowa, around 1984. What set Matt apart from other young writers at the time (and he *was* young at the time) was the professional polish of his work. It read like published stuff. My critique of his work mainly consisted of, "Get off your ass and do this."

When I got the assignment in the early '90s to do biographical pieces on both Mickey Spillane and Ian Fleming for some reference book or other, I hired Matt to do a rough draft on Fleming while I took care of Mickey. Matt did well, and by the mid-'90s – when Matt was working as a P.A. on my two independent films, *Mommy* and *Mommy's Day* – I made him unit publicist and he did articles for (among others) *Femme Fatales* and *Fangoria* about me and my little movies.

We did our first short stories together shortly after that, starting with "A Pebble for Papa," collected herein. We had an aborted novel project for a company that went bust before it actually started publishing, although that led to us creating the John Sand character (see "Lie With Me" in this volume), who almost twenty years later we are finally resurrecting for the book series we intended to do all that time ago.

Our larger collaboration began in 2000 when I got a call about writing TV tie-in novels for the new series, *CSI: Crime Scene Investigation*, which was about five episodes into its first season run. I had been writing movie tie-ins – novelizations like *Air Force One* and *Maverick* – and had already done two *NYPD Blue* novels. But I hadn't seen CSI. I called Matt and he had. I enlisted him to help me as a researcher and he reached out to forensics police officers in our home area, one of whom – Chris Kauffman – was the Gil Grissom of the Bettendorf PD, and would be an invaluable resource for years to come.

Matt also co-plotted and prepared a story treatment on the first book, *Double Dealer*, and that quickly evolved into him writing rough drafts for me. The process was that I came up with the basic premise and then we plotted together, and he wrote a short rough draft (heavy on the research) and I did the final draft. We wound up doing eight *CSI* novels and two *CSI: Miami*'s as well, plus video games, graphic novels and even jigsaw puzzles. The books were bestsellers, many of them getting on the *USA Today* list.

While I always did the movie novelizations alone, Matt became my co-writer on the original TV novels, like the three *Dark Angel* books and the trio of *Criminal Minds* tie-ins.

During this same period we began writing short stories together, following much the same pattern of me coming up with the basic idea followed by a co-plotting session and finally Matt doing a short rough draft and me the longer final one. This was during a time when a lot of theme anthologies were being published, often edited by Marty Greenberg and Ed Gorman. I edited a few myself, several times with Jeff Gelb.

Eventually Matt and I wrote some novels together that weren't tie-ins. He researched *USS Powderkeg* and provided a story treatment, and we co-created the J.C. Harrow serial killer series and the Reeder & Rogers political thrillers, with Matt sharing byline.

This volume collects the stories that, over a twenty-year period, Matt and I have collaborated on, which fall into the mystery/suspense area, with a couple venturing into supernatural/horror territory, but always with a crime/detective slant.

We've always had a good time working together, laughing and giving each other shit (sorry, but that's the best way to put it). I smile just thinking about us sitting in a corner booth at Applebee's and discussing murder while other diners looked on in quiet alarm.

You, at least, have been forewarned about what we're up to.

MURDERLIZED

The early lunch crowd at Sardi's seemed thin even for a Monday. Okay, Moe Howard thought, *so it's only two days after Christmas...but where the hell is everybody?*

Sitting alone in a booth near the front, the little man wore a dark suit, white shirt and conservative shades-of-blue tie, his trademark Three Stooges soup-bowl haircut slicked back and parted in the middle. Although the haircut was part of the act, Moe cultivated a different look off stage—when you played an idiot, you had to make sure the role didn't follow you into real life, particularly business.

On the table in front of him rested a four-day old *LA Times* and a cup of coffee from which he sipped only occasionally, to help him maintain this little piece of linen-tablecloth-covered California real estate.

Outside, the morning sun gave Hollywood Boulevard that golden aura that drew the dreamers, schemers, and desperate souls who served as sustenance for the Hollywood dream machine. Traffic glided slowly by, but both the famous Hollywood and Vine intersection and the eatery itself seemed uncharacteristically quiet.

Right now Moe shared the joint only with the staff, a handful of tourists and the array of caricatures famously lining the walls of the restaurant. Nursing his cup of coffee, he glanced idly up at the drawings.

Many, hell, most of them, were friends and acquaintances, none of whom treated Moe and his brother Jerry and their partner Larry like second-class citizens, even if the Stooges were relegated these days to short subjects, not features. Looking at these familiar faces—Crosby, Gable, that sweet kid Shirley Temple and the old standbys like Wallace Beery and Marie Dressler— Moe felt a wave of melancholy nostalgia wash over him.

The Alex Gard-sketched caricature that had summoned these feelings, creating the kind of expression on Moe Howard's face that usually preceded the delivery of a slap to a fellow Stooge—was of Ted Healy, the well-known vaudevillian and film comedian...and the reason Moe found himself in Hollywood occupying a booth in Sardi's this bright December morning.

A Texan transplanted to Brooklyn, Charles Ernest Lee Nash— a mouthful that somehow became the stage name "Ted Healy"—had in his (and their) youth made close friends with the Horovitz brothers, especially Moses and Samuel. The three Show Biz aspirants palled around Coney Island doing anything they could to elicit laughs, and maybe the odd donation, from passersby.

Though the fire for fame already burned in the bellies of Moses and Samuel Horovitz, Nash had fanned those flames, nudging, nagging, encouraging, challenging. Eventually the boys changed their names, Marx Brothers-style, taking family nicknames (Moses and Sam into Moe and Shemp) and changing their last name to Howard. Eventually, the baby of the five Horovitz boys, Jerome, would become Curly Howard and take his turn in the act.

But the real beginnings had been in 1923, when Healy was working a vaudeville show in Brooklyn only to inadvertently change the history of show business by having his two friends Moe and Shemp Howard join him on stage as his foils.

His stooges.

The act had bumped along for a couple of years in various incarnations until they met a young Philadelphia comic/musician named Larry Fine, who joined up and gave Healy a third stooge to slap, providing visual variety with the similarly visaged Howard brothers. Like the rest of them, Fine— who had an unruly wreath of wiry hair giving no quarter to a fast-receding hairline—had shortened his name (from Feinberg).

Healy, however, was always the star of the show, and—friend or not— made sure they all knew that. He paid each stooge a hundred dollars a week while he was making a cool thousand. Known to be a hard-nosed businessman, Healy could be foe more than friend, particularly when, as they traveled on the road together, he turned into a mean, belligerent drunk.

But bastard boss or not, Healy had been the one who got the Stooges to Hollywood—no question, he had almost literally made them. They had shot their first film together, *Soup to Nuts*, in 1930 and, from there, things had simultaneously gone downhill *and* taken off....

The film, a ramshackle episodic affair designed to bring cartoonist Rube Goldberg's vision to the screen, had flopped; but Moe, Shemp and Larry had shone. Soon Shemp had his own movie contract, playing Knobby Walsh in the "Joe Palooka" shorts, and brother Jerry had come aboard as one of the Three Stooges—sans Healy—

appearing in occasional features and a continuing series of popular shorts. (Jerry's family nickname, Babe, was replaced with "Curly" when Jerry shaved his head to bring yet one more distinctively wacky hairdo into the act.)

Yet Ted Healy remained a presence in their lives, warmly congratulatory when they ran into him, finding him sober; and bitterly resentful when he was in his cups.

And Healy—the man, who had done the Stooge slapping before Moe took over— was why Moses Howard sat in this booth on a lovely sunny day that he should have been spending with Helen and the kids, Joan and Jeff.

Instead, he waited for Henry Taylor, a screenwriter who had written several B westerns in the earlier '30s. The two were to have lunch to discuss the untimely death of Moe's mentor, friend, sometime adversary, and former boss...Ted Healy.

This year, 1937, had been a good one for the Three Stooges, three years out from under Healy's oppressive thumb. They had made another eight shorts for Columbia, headlined shows on the east coast, and were making far more money than they ever had with their abusive boss. Things were good, things were great; but Healy's death had cast a depressive pall over Moe. Their split from their mentor had been acrimonious, bitter, and many an insult, even a threat, had been traded; and yet down deep, Moe still counted Healy a friend. Had loved the lousy son of a bitch.

Catching movement out of the corner of his eye, Moe looked up to see a short man come in and stop at the hostess stand; the unprepossessing gent had thinning silver hair, and a doughy complexion, eyes made buggy behind thick-lensed glasses as he cast his gaze around the restaurant.

Henry Taylor finally saw Moe waving at him, smiled, waved back and shambled over. The screenwriter's slightly threadbare suit was gray, his shirt white and tie blue with red flecks, and although Moe was hardly a clotheshorse, Taylor's entire outfit probably cost about as much as Moe's small custom-made shoes.

Moe half-rose in the booth and extended a hand. "Henry, how have you been?"

Trembling slightly, Taylor shook hands with Moe. Despite his shaky condition, his grip remained firm. Shrugging, he said, "Up and down— you know how this town is."

Indeed, Moe did. Though he and his brothers had suffered the vagaries of show business, their careers seemed blessed compared to Henry Taylor's. Screenwriter on a series of westerns for John R. Frueler's struggling Big Four Film Corporation, Taylor seemed to have hitched his wagon to a slowly falling star.

Though Big Four had done all right in the early thirties, the film company was now on the verge of bankruptcy, and Moe had no idea how the scribe was making ends meet. Moe counted on picking up the check today, just as he had whenever he and Taylor had gotten together over the last couple of years.

Moe managed to maintain his patience through small talk and lunch, but once the waitress— a pretty blonde whose smile of recognition told Moe she was either a fan or an actress— cleared the dishes and refilled their coffee cups, he could wait no longer.

Grabbing the *LA Times* from December twenty-third, Moe pointed at the story about their mutual friend. "What the hell happened to Ted?"

"Papers say he died of 'acute toxic nephritis.'"

Shaking his head, Moe said, "That's what they said on the twenty-third. On the twenty-second, the day after he died? They were printing a different story—about Ted being in a brawl."

"That does sound like Ted."

"Doesn't it?"

"Early reports often get it wrong."

Moe frowned. "Early reports often predate the fix going in."

"What can you do?" Taylor said noncommittally. He obviously meant this generally not specifically.

"C'mon, Henry," Moe said, his voice rising slightly. "Ted was your friend, too...."

Taylor shrugged again. "Yes he was. And he was also a fourteen-karat son of a bitch."

"When he drank."

"When he drank," Taylor admitted. "And we both know he drank a lot."

Moe could hardly deny that. "Was he drunk the night he died?"

"Moe...you knew Ted. You surely know the answer to *that* question."

Ted was drunk most nights.

Taylor shifted in his seat. "Look, Moe, the coroner's already ruled, Ted's already in the ground. You need to let this go."

For the first time, Moe thought he saw apprehension in Taylor's eyes, perhaps exaggerated by the thick lenses; but it was there. "What is it, Henry? What's really going on?"

Shaking his head vigorously, Taylor said, "Nothing. Nothing! If you want to swap war stories about our rambunctious, loveable, hateable old pal, I'm your man. But if you want to stir up trouble, well....You just need to let Ted rest in peace, Moe."

"I can't," Moe said quietly. "He was my friend. He gave me and my brothers and Larry Fine our careers....And now something's out of kilter where his death's concerned. And I want to know what!"

Quickly Taylor rose, a wad of bills appearing from his pocket. "Gotta get going, Moe. Let me grab this, for a change."

Staring at the roll of bills, as his friend peeled off a five and dropped it on the table, Moe had a sinking feeling. "Where'd you get the moolah, Henry?"

Taylor seemed to not hear the question, already heading for the door.

Picking up his paper, Moe trailed after the writer, finally catching the older man outside, at the intersection of Hollywood and Vine.

"Come on, buddy!" Moe said. "What's going on?"

"I just can't talk about it anymore," Taylor said, his eyes darting.

This was not a good corner for laying low.

"What aren't you *telling* me?" Moe pressed.

Taylor shrugged. "Look, Moe— there's no good that can come from you digging into this sad situation. Ted's gone and maybe he's, well...finally out of his misery."

"Henry...you can do better. Ted deserves better."

Henry drew in a deep breath, most of it bus fumes; then he let it out and said, "Well...if you must, check out the list of pallbearers. *That* will tell you everything you need to know..."

Before Moe could speak again, Taylor slipped between two cars, crossed the street and sped along pretty well for a man of his age as he disappeared into the group of pedestrians strolling Vine Street during the lunch hour.

Standing on that legendary corner, Moe wondered what Taylor had meant by his "pallbearer" remark. After a shake of the head, he walked quickly in the opposite direction, climbed into his parked Ford roadster and opened the newspaper on the steering wheel.

He skimmed the article down to the last break headlined

"Services Today." The funeral had been at ten a.m. on the morning of the twenty-third, at St. Augustine's Catholic Church across the street from the MGM studio. Father John O'Donnell had presided, burial had been at Cavalry Cemetery where Ted had been laid to rest beside his mother. Then, finally, the list of pallbearers....

Ray Mayer was another comic, a friend of both Ted and Moe. Dick Powell, the actor, had recently appeared in a movie with Ted. Directors Busby Berkeley and Charles Reisner had both worked with Ted over the years. His manager, Jack Marcus, had been there too. Did Taylor think Ted's manager was up to something?

Moe considered that. He knew Marcus, a former actor himself, was devoted to Ted and had done his best to take care of Ted, both personally and professionally. Moe found it impossible to believe Marcus was in any way connected to Ted's death.

The final two pallbearers were MGM execs Harry Rapf and E.J. Mannix. Rapf, generally considered a good guy throughout the industry, had produced over forty films, worked as an executive at Metro-Goldwyn-Mayer and was credited with having discovered a Texas beauty named Lucille LeSeuer, a little lady now working as Joan Crawford. Known as "The Anteater" by anyone who had ever seen his face, Rapf had been making money off MGM employee Healy, who been working regularly in comedy support roles.

E.J. "Eddie" Mannix, on the other hand—a bespectacled, balding guy who looked more like a high school science teacher than a movie exec— was known throughout the industry as one of MGM's chief "fixers." A fixer's job was simple: if a star stepped in shit, the fixer cleaned the shoe and sprinkled on perfume...sometimes very expensive perfume. More than once, Ted's drinking had forced MGM to call out one of their top fixers, either Howard Strickling or Eddie Mannix.

When Moe read the name Mannix, there was no doubt in his mind where Taylor had been pointing.

The question was, how did the notorious fixer figure into whatever was going on with Healy's death? Mannix's presence screamed cover up—but covering up what?

Folding the paper, Moe saw only one way to find out.

Spotting a phone booth across the street, he decided to let someone know just what was going on, and where he was headed. Eddie Mannix had a reputation for making problems disappear and Moe knew the rep to be well-earned. Digging all his spare change from his pocket, he called Larry, who was still on the east coast, and explained what he had learned and where he was going.

Larry's voice reverted to its familiar whine. "What happen, Babe hit you too hard with that pipe wrench last shoot?"

"No," Moe said, his patience wearing thin.

"You know this guy Mannix's rep. He knows people."

By "people" Larry meant gangsters.

"I know his rep," Moe said. "Do I sound scared?"

"No. You sound terrified. This Mannix, there's talk he divorced his wife the hard way. Or maybe that's the easy way."

Larry was referring to the death of Mannix's wife, Beatrice, a few months ago, who died in a car accident that whispers said might not have been all that accidental.

"Yeah, I heard the talk. Talk is cheap in this town."

"This could be expensive, this time. And you're still going?"

"Of course I am. Ted and me, we were friends for a long time."

"Are we talking about the same prick?"

"Larry, I owe him. You owe him."

"Yeah, well, he still owes us thousands for what we did for him, and do you think we was in the will?...You want me to go with you?"

"No," Moe said, "but I, uh...appreciate it, pal, your concern."

"You need somethin', pucker up and ask."

"Well, uh...how 'bout this. If you haven't heard from me by midnight, call somebody."

There was a long silence.

Finally, Larry said, "By midnight, you could be...what time is it where you are?"

"A little before noon."

"Okay. By midnight, you could be dead for twelve hours. So I'll call an undertaker."

"Thanks for the vote of confidence, Porcupine," Moe said.

"Oh, do I have a vote? I vote you don't go."

"I have to."

"You'll go when you're good and ready...and you're ready. Well, what should I tell Babe when you don't come back?"

"Tell him," Moe said dryly, "I'm a victim of circumstance."

"...Why can't you be like Shemp? Scared of your own shadow?"

"Just not my style, Chowderhead. See you in the funnies."

He hung up.

Back in the roadster, Moe drove the seven or so miles to Culver City to the Metro-Goldwyn-Mayer studios. Funny, Moe thought, that Hollywood's biggest studio wasn't even in Hollywood....

A pole gate barred the entrance and when Moe pulled up and stopped, a cement block of a guard lumbered out of his small shack. The midday sun was behind the guard and Moe couldn't make out anything about the man other than his formidable build.

"Moe Howard!" the guard said. "How've you been?"

Putting a hand to his brow to block the sun, Moe recognized the guard. Tommy Flatley had occasionally been used by the studio as a babysitter for Ted Healy, and Moe had met him through Ted. Short, wide, with a flat face and perpetual grin, Flatley had a sunny disposition, for a strongarm, and Moe had hit it off with the guy, though he hadn't seen the guard in nearly a year.

"Tommy, life is good. Me and the boys are kings of Poverty Row. How about you?"

The Stooges' studio, Columbia, was the biggest of the smaller studios who had been collectively dubbed Poverty Row.

Flatley shrugged. "Can't complain. Or if I did, it wouldn't get me a raise, is for sure."

"...Terrible news about Ted," Moe said.

Nervously, the guard glanced toward the offices on the lot to his left. "Yeah. Terrible. Goddamn shame."

"He could be a monster, Ted, but a talented man. Say, I'm here to see Eddie Mannix—is he in?"

"Appointment?"

"Naw. But I think he'll see me. We're friendly."

This was not quite a lie.

"Let me find out." Flatley disappeared into his shack, made a phone call, then came back out. "Mr. Mannix can spare you a few minutes. He's in building twenty-three... they're working on the new Gable picture. You know where twenty-three is?"

Moe nodded. "Think I'm a dope? Right after twenty-two!"

"Smart ass," Flatley said good-naturedly, then he raised the gate for Moe to drive through.

Building twenty-three, a large soundstage, loomed on the backlot of the MGM grounds. Parking next to the massive structure, Moe noticed that the big thirty-foot doors were closed, as were the few windows and the small door just to the left of the large ones. The whole building seemed to be saying, Stay away.

He strode to the small door.

A sign on it read:

IF RED LIGHT IS ON, DO NOT ENTER.

"TEST PILOT" SET—DO NOT ENTER!

Moe had heard about the production through the grapevine, and knew it to be a drama starring Clark Gable, Spencer Tracy and Myrna Loy. He glanced above the door at a small red light bulb, which was glowing. But even as he looked at it, the light winked off.

He opened the door quietly, stepped inside and closed it after him. For a few moments, he stood motionless while his eyes adjusted to the interior darkness. Perhaps fifty feet away across the huge floor, from around and above, lights and cameras were trained on a set decorated as an office. A large crew was gathered around and only when he got closer did Moe begin to recognize some of the people.

Laughing as they stood around a desk on set, Gable, Tracy, and acting legend Lionel Barrymore all waved when they caught a glimpse of Moe. He returned the gesture and saw a heavy-set fellow, his back to Moe, turn to follow the actors' eyes.

Eddie Mannix.

When he saw Moe, Mannix grinned and walked over to

greet the head Stooge. Bald with close-cropped dark hair , Mannix had dark, bird-like eyes behind black dark-rimmed glasses. He wore a tan shirt under a darker tan jacket with a chocolate brown tie. Five or six inches taller than Moe, and maybe thirty pounds heavier, he nonetheless moved with an easy grace. If anything made him seem less like a science teacher and more like the cutthroat Hollywood exec he was, the gait was it: he walked with a swagger that said he was King Kong in this particular jungle, and damn well knew it.

Extending a hand, he said, "Moe Howard! What can I do for you? Ready to come back and work at MGM again? Our shorts department could use some funny fellas like you boys...."

"You're too kind, Mr. Mannix," Moe said, still shaking the man's hand as Mannix steered him on a course that led back to the door.

By the time the handshake ended, they were outside and the door was closed again.

"I thought Wallace Beery was up for that part," Moe said, jerking a thumb toward the building. "Not that Barrymore's exactly a piker."

Mannix shrugged. "Things change...and it's not like Lionel isn't a major player."

"The best," Moe said.

"Besides...Beery went to Europe for the holidays."

Moe nodded. "Lucky guy."

Mannix grinned but his eyes were growing suspicious. "I don't remember you being Beery's agent, Moe. What can I do for you?"

"Mr. Mannix, I—

"Please. Eddie. The name's Eddie. We're all street kids, here."

"Eddie. Thanks. I...I want to talk about Ted."

"A fucking tragedy," Mannix said instantly, his voice ice-cold. "I was a pallbearer, you know. God-awful thing. Tragic loss of talent. You were out of town, weren't you?"

"Yeah," Moe said. "We were in Grand Central Terminal, waiting for a train to Boston, when I heard the news. It was all I could do to get through those last few days of our engagement, and get back here."

Mannix patted Moe's shoulder. "Well, Ted was a dear friend to many of us."

"Uh...evidently not." Moe's voice was now as cold as the fixer's.

Behind the eyeglasses, the dark bird eyes grew smaller, harder. "What do you mean?"

"No offense meant, Mr. Mannix. We both know what you do around here, around town. I want to know if you covered up Ted's murder."

Mannix took a step back like he had been punched, his mouth dropping open, a hand going to his chest. "Murder?...Now that's not funny, Moe."

"Not meant to be, Eddie. Ted gettin' in a fight was in the paper, one edition...next edition, it's dropped. That smells of your invisible byline, Eddie."

"Careful, Moe...."

"The doctor who treated Ted the night he got beat up refused to sign the death certificate, but suddenly the coroner does— writing off the beating as superficial. You couldn't get to the *Times* before they printed it, but everybody else fell in line, didn't they?"

"First of all," Mannix said, his voice thin and brittle, a hand raised as if in benediction, "I have no idea what you're talking about. Second of all, you are way the hell out of line, little man."

"Am I? This whole thing reeks of studio cover-up. You know it, I know it."

"That's strong accusation."

"Which I notice you're not denying."

Mannix shook his head. "All right, if that's what you want, I'll deny. I deny it. Now, do you mind if I get back to work?"

Moe stepped between the bigger man and the door. "I have an idea you do your best work after hours, and off the lot."

The fixer's eyes were as hard now as they were dark; a very small tic twitched at the corner of Mannix's left eye. "Moe, you do not want to do this. Ted is dead and buried. You know what a brawler he was, and what a drunken troublemaker he could be. If anything, you and I are both surprised he didn't stumble into the grave he dug himself years ago. You've confronted me and got this off your chest—fine. Now. Let it go."

"You're the second person to tell me that today...in so many words."

"However it's phrased? Good advice."

Moe drew in a deep breath and let it slowly out, watching Mannix's twitch work. Then he said, "Just tell me the truth, Eddie, and I will let it go. I'll go back to being a dumb little bastard who doesn't know up from down....I promise."

Mannix took a long appraising look at Moe. He too took in a deep breath, let it out slow; and then the eyes softened, the man's entire manner shifted.

"All right," Mannix said. "I know he was like another brother to you...but if I give you the straight dope, will it end here?"

"I just want to know, Eddie. Mr. Mannix."

The exec gave the lot a quick furtive glance, making sure no one was within earshot. "It happened at the Trocadero on Sunset. Ted was in there, drunk as a skunk, but...happy. He had already been to Clara Bow's and the Brown Derby. He was really tying one on to celebrate the birth of his son."

Moe sighed. "Yeah, I know he just had a kid. Makes this thing even sadder....Then what?"

"Ted started up an argument with these three college kids."

"College kids?"

Mannix nodded. "Ted offered to meet them outside and take them apart, one at a time. But when they got into the parking lot, the three kids jumped him and beat the ever-loving shit out of the poor soused-up bastard."

Moe frowned. "And that's why you covered it up? To protect some college kids?"

"One of them has a father who's a good friend of Mr. Mayer."

"That doesn't—"

"Moe, Ted started the thing, and an inquiry would only blacken his memory....Anyway, Mr. Mayer says keep a lid on it, that's what I do."

"And I thought I was a stooge," Moe said.

Shrugging, wincing, Mannix said, "Think what you will of me, Mr. Howard—but I get slapped around a lot more than you and your pals....Okay? We done here?"

Getting into his car, Moe felt unsatisfied. Something still didn't sit right to him. Why would a major movie studio give two shits about three college kids when they'd beaten to death a personality who was an asset to MGM?

The more Moe mulled it, the thinner Mannix's explanation seemed....

When he got back to the gate, Tommy Flatley came out

of the shack and waved him down.

"Find out what you wanted?" the guard asked.

Moe shook his head. "I don't think so."

"Hmmm hmmm. The college kid story?"

"Yeah, Tommy, why? Don't you believe in fairy tales, either?"

"Doesn't matter what I believe, Mr. Howard..." He leaned close, like a car hop taking an order; he was almost whispering. "...but if you stop by the Hollywood Plaza Hotel, you might talk to someone who has a different story."

"Really."

Tommy nodded. "Ever hear of a fella called Man Mountain Dean?"

Moe had indeed.

Driving back to Hollywood and Vine, Moe pulled up in front of the Hollywood Plaza Hotel at 1637 N. Vine Street and parked.

Inside, he went straight to the desk clerk, a tall reed of a man with slicked back blond hair and a crisp dark suit.

"Man Mountain Dean, please," Moe said.

The clerk nodded and without looking at the register said, "Room 1624....Aren't you the Three Stooges, sir?"

"Just a third," Moe said, and slipped the guy a buck and headed over to the elevator.

A gray-haired attendant in a faded uniform asked, "What floor?"

"Sixteen."

The ride was quiet and fast. When they got to the floor, the old guy opened the door and said, "Thank you."

Moe, wondering what he'd be doing at the fellow's age, slipped the "boy" two bits and strode down the hall until he got to room 1624.

He knocked and waited.

Nothing.

He knocked again and waited some more. He was just about to walk away when the knob rattled. Then, a moment later, he heard the chain slide back and the door opened. Moe found himself looking up into the face of a bleary-eyed giant with a mane of wild dark hair and an equally untamed beard, clad in bib overalls, t-shirt and barefoot.

"Frank Simmons Leavitt," Moe said with a sly smile, "how the hell are you?"

The man ran a hand over his face, then looked down, grinned and picked up Moe, off the floor, in a bone-popping bear hug. "Moses Horovitz! You little bastard!"

The big man was playing, but Moe had the sudden feeling his chest might explode at any second. "Puu...puuuu... put m...me doow...down!"

Man Mountain Dean did as directed but gave Moe an extra squeeze as he did, completing the impromptu chiropractic adjustment. "It's goddamn good to see you, Moe! How long has it been?"

Moe shrugged, partly in answer, partly to see if his body still functioned. "Couple of years anyway. Where did we run into you last?"

"Kansas City, I think." The big man was leaning against the door jamb. "You boys was there the night before we went in to wrestle. You, your brother Shemp and Larry was leaving, while the other wrestlers and me were coming in."

"Kansas City," Moe echoed. "A long way from home for us New York kids."

Dean nodded, shaggily. "You ever get back to the city? The old neighborhood?"

"Yeah, we were just there last week! You?"

"Naw. I'm pretty much a California kid when I'm not on the road. I've been gettin' some movie work." He smiled. "Not like you guys, though. The Three Stooges! Big stars, you little fellas became."

Moe grinned back. "We're eating regular."

The wrestler's face turned somber. "Sorry about that horse's ass Ted. I know you was good friends."

"Thanks, Frank. Actually, that's why I'm here."

"Thought it might be." His eyes lost their spark. "You want to know what I know, right?"

"If it's not too much to ask."

Dean nodded. Shrugged. "Come on in."

Moe did, Dean shut the door and waved for Moe to take a seat. The room was home to a single metal-frame unmade bed, a small radio on a nightstand with lamp, a bureau with no mirror, and a table with two chairs. Not a shabby room exactly, but no suite at the Waldorf-Astoria.

Moe took a chair facing the bed, figuring Dean couldn't have fit in one of those chairs on a bet. And indeed the wrestler sat rather gingerly on the edge of the bed.

"I suppose," Dean said, "you heard about the college boys."

"Yeah," Moe said.

"Well, it's bullshit. That fixer Mannix, more of his bullshit."

"So I figured."

Dean took a deep breath and let it out. "I don't know what good it'll do, telling you..."

"Neither do I. But I need to hear it."

Dean shrugged again and bedsprings squeaked. "Okay. I'll tell you what I know, but nothing else."

Moe was still trying to make sense of that when his old friend launched into his story.

"It wasn't no fucking college kids. At least that's not what Ted said, when he come around."

"He came here?" Moe asked, sitting forward.

"Yeah. He got the shit kicked out of him at the Trocadero by three guys—not college kids. He said he offered to fight them one at a time, outside; but when they got to the parking lot, they jumped his ass and wailed on him pretty damn good."

"Why would he come here, then?"

"He stumbled in wanting me and Joe Frisco to go with him and go back and make it a fair fight. He wanted us to pick up Doc Stone, too, then go back to the Trocadero so he could get 'even and a half.'"

"...You didn't go?"

"Hell no! You know I'm not afraid of a fight, Moe, but Ted was beat up worse than a redheaded stepchild. I got the hotel sawbones to patch his up his broken ass."

"How did Ted get here?"

"Joe brought him."

Joe Frisco, another Los Angeles comedian, was a good friend of Healy's. The other guy Dean had mentioned, Doc Stone, was a small-time actor and part-time boxer.

"So...what happened?"

"Ted told me while the doctor patched him up. He was at the Trocadero celebratin' his kid bein' born when he got into an argument with this guy."

"What guy?"

Dean shrugged. "Ted didn't know the guy's name, but the guy isn't alone—turns out he's a cousin of Pat DiCicco, who was also present."

Moe felt the words like a blow to the gut. "DiCicco the hoodlum?"

"Is there another? Anyway, they're not the only ones. DiCicco and this other guy are there with Wallace Beery."

Everyone in Hollywood knew that Beery hated Ted for stealing scenes in a movie the pair had done earlier in the year— *The Good Old Soak*, which had not exactly taken Hollywood by storm, but word around town was Beery still had it in for Healy.

And Beery could be a brawling brute, with or without liquor, not nearly as lovable as his screen image.

Nodding, Moe said, "So that's why Beery 'spent the holidays' in Europe—he's lying low. What about DiCicco?"

"I heard he took a run-out powder to Mexico. But nobody seems to know why."

"And we don't know who the third guy is," Moe said quietly.

"Doc might," Dean said.

"Doc Stone?"

"No! No, sorry. Too many docs. I mean, Doctor Wyannt LaMont, hotel doctor here. I'll take you down to his office, and you can talk to him."

After Dean took time to put on a pair of clodhoppers, the big man and the little man took the elevator to the first floor and by the front desk cut down a short hallway. The door had the doctor's name painted on it in black block letters.

Dean knocked but opened the door without waiting for a response, and led the way in.

The room was an examining room with a central metal table and wall-hugging cabinets of medicine and a counter with bandages and more. At a small desk off to one side, reading a medical journal, sat a squat, heavy-set man of fifty or so with graying hair and pink chipmunk cheeks. He wore a white doctor's smock over a white shirt and what Moe could barely make out as the knot of a blue tie.

The doctor put down the journal as they entered, obviously unoffended by the intrusion.

Man Mountain Dean said, "Dr. Wyannt LaMont, I'd like you to meet Moe Howard."

Rising, beaming, the doctor extended a hand. "Mr. Howard, it's truly a pleasure. I enjoy your work immensely. Splendid absurdity."

"Well, it's silly, all right. Nice to meet you, too, Doctor."

Dean filled the doctor in.

The doctor said, "Once I saw how badly beaten Mr. Healy was, I sent Frank here to call the police and an ambulance. Then I was alone for several minutes with my patient. And he told me that this other man was DiCicco's cousin, a New Jersey kid named Albert Broccoli, who just moved out here to try to get into the movie business."

"Did he tell you what happened?"

"Oh yes. Ted even freely admitted to starting the fight. He said there was something he didn't like about Broccoli's face, so he just hauled off and clocked the guy. That was how the altercation began."

"What about the ambulance?" Moe asked. "The papers said nothing about an ambulance—"

"By the time it got here, Ted and Joe Frisco had left. Ted said his friend...Joe, was it? Was just going to take him home."

"Thanks, Doc," Moe said.

In the lobby, he said his goodbyes to Man Mountain Dean, then used the phone booth there to make some calls. Finding Broccoli took a bit of doing, but an agent friend prompted Moe to try a bar Broccoli frequented on West Sunset.

A short drive later and he was inside the club, his eyes adjusting to the dim lights, one of those chrome and mirror cabarets, but a junior job. On the stage some underclad overly cute female dancers were rehearsing for the night's show and around the bar maybe four patrons otherwise had the place to themselves.

A fellow matching Albert Broccoli's description sat at the

bar, an empty stool on either side, his back mostly to Moe.

Settling in next to him, Moe said, "Buy you a drink, friend?"

A rugged-looking guy with dark, wavy hair and piercing brown eyes turned toward him. The eyes widened, a finger pointed. "Hey, you're..."

"Yeah, I am. Let's not advertise it."

"Sure, sure. Well, hell, you can buy me a drink any time, Moe. The laughs you boys have given me...."

He waved the bartender over and got another bottle of beer for Broccoli and a cup of coffee for himself. "You Albert Broccoli?"

"Yeah, I'm Al Broccoli. How did you know? And, uh, no offense, but...what's it to you, Moe? Or should I say, 'Mr. Howard'...?"

"Moe is fine. We have mutual friends."

"Call me Cubby, then. Most everybody does. Mutual friends, huh? Like who?"

He seemed just a big gregarious, likable kid—more like one of those imaginary college students than the brutal Beery—and Moe wondered what Ted had said to piss off the young man; or maybe Ted had pissed off DiCicco and the kid had just jumped in on his cousin's side.

"Mutual friends like Ted Healy," Moe said. "For one."

Broccoli's face sagged. "I...uh. I don't know....didn't know Healy. I hear he passed away. You used to work with him, right?"

Moe leaned in a little. "Cubby, don't play stupid with me. I'm an expert at playing dumb and you don't make the grade. We both know you know exactly what I'm talking about."

Broccoli put up his hands as if surrendering. "Okay. But I wasn't in on it."

"In on what?"

"The fight."

"I heard you were. I heard Ted popped you."

"Well, yeah, he did pop me, but that's not a fight. That's one-sided, hell, that's assault. All I did was, I tried to congratulate him on the birth of his son and got socked in the snoot for my trouble."

"Then what?"

"Then nothing. I knew the guy was drunk. Celebration got away from him—we all know guys who booze makes nasty. So I let it go."

"Somebody didn't let it go."

Broccoli shrugged. "Well...my cousin Pat saw me with a handkerchief to my bloody nose and wanted to know what happened. After I told him, him and Beery started giving Healy a bunch of lip. That's when Ted said he'd meet us outside. We were a bunch of cowardly bums and bastards if we didn't. So, anyway, when we got out there, Beery and Pat, they...hell. They just beat the hell out of him. It was...it was horrible. Way out of line. Jesus."

"And you did...nothing?"

The young man sighed and swigged some beer. "I did at the start...I kicked him once, just to get even for what he did to my nose, you know? But when those two got carried away, I just kinda froze...backed up and froze." He shrugged. Sighed somberly. "That's it, Mr. Howard. Moe."

"So, then— the three of you beat him to death."

Broccoli held up his hands again. "No, we didn't! I swear. He got up. On his own steam. He was tough in his way, Healy. Him and that friend of his Frisco, who come along at the end there, they left. He was beat to shit, but I swear he was walking. He seemed...okay. Just another guy got the wrong end of a barroom brawl."

"What did you guys do next?"

"Ah, hell. That asshole Beery panicked. He called the studio. Pat and me, we had another drink inside the Troc, then Pat drove me home."

"And where did Pat go?"

Shrugging elaborately, Broccoli said, "Home, I suppose. How would I know?"

Moe shook his head. "I hear you want to get into the movie business."

Broccoli nodded glumly.

"Well, kid, it better not be as an actor, because a good actor is a good lair, and you're not that good. Where did Pat go that night?"

The kid called Cubby tried to hold it together, tried to look tough, but eventually, the roof caved in. He was trembling and his eyes had teared up. "Pat was still pissed and thought Healy might rat us out to the police. I think maybe...I don't know for sure and I ain't about to ask....I think maybe Pat went over there and had another little... 'talk' with Ted."

A second beating on top of the first was probably enough to kill Healy. For twenty-four hours Healy fought the effects of the beating or beatings before his heart finally gave out.

But Moe knew that there was no way anyone would be doing jail time for Ted's death, not in this one-industry town with a star like Beery involved; but at least he thought he had gotten most of the truth.

He could go to the cops with his circumstantial case, but where would it end up going? Most likely into the porcelain filing cabinet where a flush from the fixer would take the careers of himself and the other Stooges with it. Still, Ted had been a friend and mentor since they were kids back in Brooklyn. Moe felt like he had to try something.

"Cubby," Moe said, at last. "I want you to tell this story to the cops."

"No way. I shouldn't have told you. Three beers ago, I wouldn't have."

"Somebody's going to have to tell the truth, kid. You can do it, and paint yourself in a good light...or I can do it. Take your pick."

Moe watched Broccoli carefully to see if the bluff was working.

"...All right, I'll come forward. I'll tell the cops what happened."

Moe drew a breath and let it out. "Good. And you better."

"Or what? You going to come back here and slap me around?"

Rising to leave, Moe managed a weak smile. "Me? Why, Cubby—haven't you heard?"

Broccoli frowned.

"That," Moe Howard said, "is just not my style."

NOTE FROM THE AUTHORS

Numerous books on the Three Stooges were consulted, in particular *The Three Stooges: An Illustrated History* (1999) by Michael Fleming, as well as newspaper files of the day. Though essentially sticking to the facts, this story should be viewed as fictionalized.

A PEBBLE FOR PAPA

The winter of '28 had refused to release its frigid grip on the city's throat, so the crowd dining at Papa's Ristorante was sparse. From the outside Papa's looked no different than a dozen other hole-in-the-wall restaurants in Little Italy.

Couples were scattered here and there, some huddled over their table gazing into each other's eyes, others ate spaghetti and drank wine. None of the patrons were paying attention to each other; no one noticed the big man in the brown fedora and cashmere overcoat enter.

The diners had no idea that this was the head of the Irish mob, though one look into Lou O'Hara's dead black eyes would have told them that something about this guy was not quite... right. Without even a glance toward Papa's other customers, O'Hara stomped through the restaurant and flung open a door at the far end of the dining room.

His hat and coat were taken from him by an attendant, and he was shown to a chair at the long oak table that dominated the center of the room. Around him were most of the other crime bosses of the city. O'Hara ignored them except to nod toward Raven Malone, who occupied the chair on his left. The leggy brunette beauty had a crimson-nailed finger in everything from blackmail and prostitution to murder.

She was O'Hara's kind of woman.

The door to the private banquet room opened and Giacomo Ghilini, "Papa" to most everyone in the city, took his rightful place at the head of the table. A powerfully built, thick-chested man, Papa was angry but he didn't let it show. Not even when his hooded brown eyes fell on the reason this dinner hadn't yet been served -- Lou O'Hara.

Papa saw it as a lack of respect to start the meal before all his guests were seated. O'Hara, head of the biggest independent outfit in the city, was really nothing more than a two-bit strongarm who had made it to the top through cruelty, callousness, and an uncanny ability to remain standing when those in line ahead of him had fallen. Though O'Hara's late arrival showed flagrant disregard for his host, Papa was not going to allow himself to be dragged down to this thug's level.

He bestowed O'Hara a smile, almost a grin. "We didn't want to start without you, Lou."

O'Hara nodded noncommittally, mumbling something about having some business to take care of, but made no attempt to apologize for his tardiness.

"Vito," Papa said motioning to his son and chief lieutenant who sat on his right, "pour Lou a glass of wine."

Vito nodded and did as he was told. Papa noted the contempt in his son's eyes as Vito handed the glass across the table to O'Hara. A good boy, Papa thought, but he must learn to mask his feelings better. He still thought of his third son as a boy, his student, his protégé, though Vito was pushing forty and already graying at the temples.

O'Hara accepted the wine without thanks and gulped down nearly half before he set the glass on the table in front of him. Uncouth, Papa thought. A pig.

Papa studied the faces around the table. O'Hara was on his left, the Irish mobster's white shark's teeth drawn into a grin for Raven Malone. Beyond them were Deng Chou Lo, leader of the Chinese Tongs, coldly impressive in his traditional silk, dragoned garb; and the ragu-nosed Lawrence Rafferty, city councilman bought and paid for with Ghilini money. Next was another Papa purchase, police Lieutenant Adam Maynerd, in a gray suit that matched his complexion, and finally past him sat Wa Tse Wang, head of the Triads, in a natty three-piece suit whose only Chinatown touch was a many-blossomed tie.

Papa trusted none of them.

Rafferty and Maynerd were allies, but once a man had been bought, Papa believed that sooner or later he'd be bought again. Both Wa and Deng had met privately with Papa recently and he had been forced to work out new accords with each to keep them from going to the mattresses. Raven Malone seemed far too ambitious to settle for the arrangement she had with the Ghilini family, and O'Hara? Well, O'Hara was just plain nuts.

On the right side of the table were the attendees that Papa considered his allies. Vito of course, Josef Freid, aging head of the Jewish gang, Papa's secret grandson Toshiro, Rabbi Seidelman, a close friend for many years, Papa's adopted daughter Beatrice, and Leonard Ford editor of The City Times. At the opposite end of the table was Monsignor John Rossi, priest to the Ghilini family, and most of the rest of the mob as well.

Silent waiters in white jackets and black bow ties served the group their dinner. Though Papa claimed to be nothing more than an honest restauranteur, those seated at this table, unlike the diners in the other room, knew that wasn't true. He was, instead, the man who held the city in his palm.

Papa received his plate last. As the waiters made their exit, Papa looked down the table to Monsignor Rossi. "Father, would you like to lead us in grace?"

The priest nodded and rose. The Confessor, as he was known within the mob, was a compact man of moderate build whose shoulders seemed to sag a little from the heavy weight they bore. His longish silver hair was combed straight back away from a face that seemed far more ancient than his sixty-one years. He clasped his hands, bowed his head.

"Oh, Heavenly Father, we thank you for your blessed bounty we are about to receive and for the kind hospitality of our host, Papa Ghilini. We are grateful to you for all good things. Amen."

Papa broke off a piece of bread and offered it to O'Hara who accepted it without thanks and wolfed it down along with his salad.

"I want to express my gratitude to all of you for coming," Papa said as they ate. "It is good to see that we can all get along again, even after -- ."

"So why the hell d'you call us all here?" O'Hara interrupted.

Papa glared at O'Hara and just as quickly smiled. "As I was saying, even after this recent...unpleasantness, it's good to see that we can still get along. It is my hope that this dinner can serve as the glue that binds the peace we have negotiated."

"Peace serves the best interests of us all," Councilman Rafferty piped in. "The pie's plenty big for everybody to get a piece."

O'Hara shot Rafferty a withering look. "How the hell would you know? You don't dip into shit. You take exactly what Ghilini hands you and leave it at that."

Rafferty looked down, suddenly very interested in his plate.

"Lou, Lou," Papa said mildly, patting the air. "Mr. Rafferty is merely..."

"Full of shit," O'Hara finished for him. "Deng," he went on, "how big a percentage are you paying to the Ghilinis?"

The leader of the Tongs glanced quickly at Papa, then turned his eyes to O'Hara. "Our relationship with Mr. Ghilini has proven to be quite profitable for both of us."

"Has Papa supported you in the sale of opium?"

Deng leapt to his feet. "We do not sell drugs."

Grinning, O'Hara said, "Why is that, Deng? Is it 'cause you don't wanna make money...or 'cause Ghilini here told you he'd put you out of business if you did?"

Deng said nothing as he slowly resumed his seat.

"Lou," Papa said, his voice rising only slightly. "I've told you before, we will not sell drugs in this city. There we draw the line."

Papa hated narcotics and the trouble they brought. He had seen what that vile poison could do, and it was a thing he was loathe to see again. Sure, he made his living from people's weaknesses, but drugs were different. Where gambling and prostitution were activities men partook of their own volition, narcotics were like a whirlpool. They swept you up, then they swept you under and you drowned before you even knew you were in trouble.

O'Hara was glaring at him.

"The issue is closed," Papa said, fighting to keep his voice even.

"Like hell it is," O'Hara exploded. "I'm tired of you tryin' to tell me where and how I can make my money, old man. If I want to sell drugs or whores or fucking red-white-and-blue iceboxes, it's none of your goddamn business and you and your combo of Chinks and petty grafters ain't gonna stop me."

The others were eyeing Papa as he carefully wiped his mouth with his napkin. This was not how this meeting was supposed to go. Papa had sent out the invitations for this meet the previous Sunday, to assure that the heads of all the gangs would be here when he announced his retirement. It was to be a celebration of his stepping down and Vito's ascension to his throne.

And here was O'Hara throwing a fit like a child, challenging his authority in front of the others. Papa felt he could count on most of the others to fall in line with whatever he ordered. After all, they always had before. The course of action he was considering was dangerous, but Papa felt it was the only way to amicably stave off O'Hara's challenge.

He tried to read the faces of the others before he spoke. They were guarded, waiting to see what action he would take. Only Papa felt suddenly weary. He wondered if his decision was coming a year, even six months too late. He drew in a deep breath and let it out slowly.

"Lou," he finally said, reasonably, amicably showing the bastard far more respect than he warranted, "this is not a dictatorship as you would have the others believe. We have made business decisions together. And we have prospered because we have stood by those decisions."

O'Hara was twisting his napkin between his fingers. His knuckles were white, but he said nothing as he continued to glower at his host.

Papa continued: "To prove to you that we are all involved in the decision-making of this organization, we'll put this drug issue to a vote of the board. The decision will be final. And I'm confident, after this vote is taken, we'll have no more talk of drugs in this city."

O'Hara swiveled on the rest. Their eyes fell away from the Irishman's dark stare and Papa was sure he had O'Hara right where he wanted him.

Papa said, "Vito, you will cast the ballot of the Ghilini family."

Vito cleared his throat. When he spoke his voice sounded shaky. "You...you all know that the Ghilini family has been against drugs since the beginning. We will not change now."

Beatrice, unable to wait her turn, jumped in. "I'm with Papa too. As I'm sure Toshiro is as well."

All eyes turned to Toshiro who shifted nervously in his chair. "I'm here representing the Yakuza," he said. "You all know that. You also know that when the Yakuza first came to this city, it was Papa Ghilini who found a place for us. Back then, he was the one who helped us thrive when he could just as easily have squashed us like a bug. We are forever in his debt and we vote to follow the current policy."

Papa's eyes darted to O'Hara who seemed about ready to tear his napkin in half. It was all Papa could do to keep his smile to himself. "Josef?"

Freid cleaned his gold-rimmed glasses with his napkin. Papa noticed that the man's hand was shaking ever so slightly.

"Papa, you put me in a difficult position. You know that my partners and I are basically law-abiding businessmen these days. Over ninety percent of our holdings are now completely legal. I feel as if I am being asked to vote on an issue that does not concern me. I'm afraid I must abstain from this ballot."

Papa's eyes met Freid's and the old Jew looked away quickly. A quiver ran through Papa's gut.

Deng spoke up. "Papa, though it grieves me to agree with Mr. O'Hara about anything...I'm afraid on this issue, he is correct. Though Councilman Rafferty rightly points out that the pie is large, there are so many pieces being meted out that the Tongs are getting barely a sliver. It is possible that opening the drug market could give us the larger piece we feel we deserve."

Wa echoed the opinion of his countryman.

Due to Freid's abstention, the count would now be close. Even if it had come down to a tie, Papa would have the deciding vote. But with only Raven and O'Hara himself left, Papa was suddenly feeling sick to his stomach. If Raven Malone didn't side with him, it would be a stalemate, and the one thing he had fought to keep out of the city might well become a reality. With each passing thought, another jet of acid shot into Papa's stomach.

He did not feel at all well.

*****

O'Hara rises, his maniacal grin a malignancy spreading over his face. From nowhere, a machine gun appears in his hands. Papa watches in mute horror as fire leaps from the barrel. The stream of bullets rips through Vito even as he rises. Papa feels his mouth drop open as he sees only a red mist hanging in the air where Vito had been standing. O'Hara turns the weapon on Freid, the hot steel rain decapitating the Jew. Papa struggles to rise from his chair, but he is somehow glued to it, frozen in anguish as he watches O'Hara mow down Toshiro and Beatrice. He cannot scream, or move, or even whimper, though he feels hot tears rolling down his cheeks. Finally he breaks the spell and heaves himself up. He dives for O'Hara...

Papa, bathed in sweat, awoke to find himself sitting up in bed. Mama was sleeping peacefully next to him, blissfully ignorant of the thrashing that had been going on next to her.

"Jesus," he whispered, crossing himself in the darkness. This had not been the first nightmare of the night. He had gotten blessed little sleep since last night's meeting and the few times he had dozed off had been punctuated by these turbulent, violent dreams. Slipping his feet over the side of the bed, Papa bowed his head, and for the hundredth time went through the events of the meeting.

He had known that he was taking a chance calling for the vote on selling drugs, but he had figured the odds were on his side. His whole career had been built on playing the odds and this time, this one time, he had been woefully mistaken in his calculations.

Now instead of handing over the reins of the biggest operation in the city to his son, Papa was left in charge of a family that was considered, for the first time, as vulnerable. What had taken him a lifetime to build had been put at great risk, if not destroyed, over dinner. A voice inside him wanted to blame Raven Malone and the others who had sided with O'Hara, but he shook his head and drove it away.

It was his fault, his own ego that had caused his error. He pounded a hammy fist into his thigh and swore under his breath. Regaining control, he peeked over at Mama to make sure she was still asleep. He then looked at the clock on the nightstand next to him.

Five o'clock.

Two more hours and The Confessor would be at the church. Papa accepted counsel from very few people, but Monsignor Rossi was a man on whom he could depend for sound advice, perhaps the one man who could help him avoid the war that now seemed inevitable.

Pushing himself to his feet, Papa padded to the bathroom. He cleaned up and dressed in a brown suit, his favorite. His white shirt felt a little snug at the collar, but Papa ignored it. Being careful not to wake his wife, he crept through the bedroom and downstairs to the kitchen. After he brewed the coffee, he sat alone at the table, contemplating the steam that rose from the mug.

The Tongs and the Triads would probably stay in line as long as they were sure that he remained in charge. And though Raven Malone had secured her position at the table by being an independent thinker, it was clear to Papa that O'Hara was the wild card in the deck. He hoped that between Rossi and himself they could come up with a plan that would allow this to truly be a Good Friday.

He sipped from the mug and worked to clear his mind. Over the course of his reign, Papa's ability to dispassionately view a situation had been the key to his survival. No matter what the circumstances or the people involved, Papa never let his emotions get in the way of making the right business decision.

His son, Paulo, had been proof of that.

O'Hara, though, was making that a difficult proposition. Papa's gut was telling him to have the crazy Irishman whacked, the consequences be damned, but his head told him that there had to be another way.

Papa took a deeper swallow of coffee. The heat felt good as it trailed down his throat, taking away the chill of the kitchen. He needed to get through today, just today, then he could rest over the weekend. Even O'Hara wasn't crazy enough to start anything on Easter weekend. Papa would talk to Father Rossi, get some rest, then make his decision with a cool head and a clean soul. Unencumbered by his anger at O'Hara, Papa knew he could come up with a plan that would keep his business in order and maintain the peace.

Rising, Papa shuffled to the front door. The morning newspaper was on the porch. Papa picked it up, took a moment to stretch his stiff back, then returned to the kitchen to read the paper over his second cup of coffee.

He barely glanced at the front page before turning to the editorial section. After O'Hara had stormed out of the meeting last night, Papa cornered Leonard Ford and called in a favor owed him by the newspaper editor.

"I think," Papa had told the jittery little man, "that The City Times is due for an editorial on the growing drug problem, don't you?"

"I was thinking that myself," Ford said with a grin. "I was even thinking that it might be a good time for the paper to take a stand against organized crime. Maybe do an expose on O'Hara? You know, the city's biggest racketeer sort of thing?"

Papa shook his head, no.

Ford nodded. "Might cloud the issue. Later on, perhaps..."

Papa had nodded back. It had been that simple. He grinned slyly as he read Ford's editorial. First Ford praised the police for keeping drug use to a minimum in the city, then in the next breath railed against them to not allow junkies and drug sellers to proliferate the streets.

Swigging his coffee, Papa re-read the final paragraph.

"And let us not forget the warning of the noted Irish judge John Philpot Curran who said, 'The condition upon which God has given liberty to man is eternal vigilance.' Words for our intrepid police department to live by."

Papa wondered if O'Hara was reading the editorial even as he was. Though O'Hara would know that Papa was behind Ford's rantings, there was nothing the Irishman could do about it. And Ford had outdone himself. His editorial would have people talking all weekend. Papa made a mental note to speak with his friends within the clergy. Easter weekend might be the perfect time for a scathing rebuke of drug use from the various pulpits of the city.

His plan was simple. Turn the city against drug use before O'Hara and the others could get the product to the streets. Simple economics might well succeed where Papa had been unable to. The size of O'Hara's supply would be inconsequential if there was no demand.

Noting the time on the kitchen clock, Papa finished his coffee, laid the newspaper on the table, and reached for his overcoat. Monsignor Rossi would be at the church by now. It was time for Papa to make his confession and confer with the family priest.

His driver, Sonny, had not yet arrived so Papa decided to walk the half-mile to Sacred Heart Cathedral. The late March wind whistled in from the north, whipping Papa's overcoat around his legs. Heavy dark clouds announced Old Man Winter's intention to lay one more load of snow on the city before abandoning it to spring.

Despite the temperature, Papa did not hurry. Winter, which signified a state of hibernation to so many others, invigorated Papa Ghilini. His body didn't adjust to the cold as easily as it had when he had been a young man, but he still enjoyed a winter walk as much as he ever had.

He passed few people as he made his way toward the cathedral. It wasn't just because of the weather. Papa knew, through his friendship with Monsignor Rossi, that although the city had a rich, storied Catholic history, many of the younger people considered it the tired religion of their grandparents.

Perhaps that was part of the reason that His Eminence

Cardinal Vincenzo Micelli would be presiding over tonight's Celebration of the Lord's Passion service. Nothing like having a Cardinal in the church to drag the parishioners out of the woodwork.

The frosty air nipped at Papa's ears and nose. He looked up and could see the cathedral looming two blocks ahead. It was a stately brick building rising three stories, dwarfing the houses and duplexes of the old residential neighborhood. Papa was approaching from the east. On his right was the former rectory, a two-story brick house, that now served as offices for the parochial school. A concrete portico connected that building to the side of the cathedral. Two black streetlamps flanked the sidewalk that led to the front doors. Each was draped in purple ribbons that signified the season of Advent.

Papa's shoulders hunched inside the overcoat; he looked like a turtle drawing its head inside its shell as he trudged up the walk. The wind had turned even more biting. The large doors were at least twice Papa's six-foot height, but they moved easily as he tugged on the handle. He stepped into the vestibule and shook off the chill. Maybe, he thought, it was time to reconsider his feelings about winter. Though the walk had done him good, the cold seemed to have penetrated to the bone.

The church was quiet as a mausoleum as Papa stepped to the door of the sanctuary. On either side of the door were sculpted angels. Each angel's face reminded Papa of the Madonna. They were beautiful women in blue and white robes. Each was kneeling and holding a punch bowl-sized ceramic clam shell that normally contained the holy water; however during this week they stood empty, representing a world without Christ. Papa made the sign of the cross.

He entered the sanctuary and glanced toward Rossi's

confessional. The door was closed; someone was with the priest. The vaulted ceiling of the cathedral rose thirty feet over Papa's head. Gilded conical shaped lights hung from the open rafters; stained glass windows depicting the apostles lined the sides of the church. Between the windows, engraved in marble, were scenes portraying the stations of the cross. The pews were divided into four sections separated by three aisles that led to the altar. Papa looked toward the fifteen-foot wooden cross that hung behind the altar. Shrouded in purple satin, it would remain so until Easter Sunday.

Just behind the last row of pews, on a small table, sat a bowl filled with pebbles. Each had a black cross painted on it. The bowl of stones replaced the holy water during Lent. Papa picked up one from the bowl and kneaded it between his fingers as he took a seat in the last row.

He noticed a few parishioners praying silently in the pews nearer the altar. An old woman was in the front corner of the sanctuary lighting a votive candle. Papa watched as the crone blew out the match and made the sign of the cross. She folded her hands, prayed silently for a moment, then genuflected toward the altar before she started up the aisle in Papa's direction. As she approached, Papa hoped that she wasn't coming back to take confession. He needed to speak to Rossi as soon as possible, but he knew that if the old woman sat down in one of the pews he would allow her to go first. Manners and respect, he told himself, these were still important things, whether Lou O'Hara and his mob thought so or not.

As she finally neared Papa, she smiled and nodded. He didn't recognize her, but he returned the greeting. She paused for a moment next to his pew, caught her breath, then left the sanctuary.

Papa's attention had just returned to the large cross on the wall at the far end of the church when he heard the confessional door open behind him. Papa turned his head slightly and from the corner of his eye saw his neighbor Tomasino LaPaglia come out. When Tomasino, bent and aged, saw Papa, a grin formed on Tomasino's wrinkled face and a twinkle appeared in his rheumy eyes. The men shook hands and exchanged brief greetings. Tomasino complained about the cold weather and how it angered his lombago, then exited as Papa entered the confessional.

Papa closed the door and sat down, still worrying the pebble between his thumb and middle finger. "Bless me, Father, for I have sinned. It's been..." his voice trailed off. Papa ran a hand over his face, and was startled by the looseness of his withered flesh. "It has been...a long time since my last confession."

"That's all right, my son."

Having his old friend on the other side of the screen made Papa feel more at ease.

"Go ahead, my son."

"I come..." Papa hesitated, feeling a catch in his voice. He swallowed and took a deep breath before continuing. "I come to you today, Father, with a heavy heart."

Monsignor Rossi remained silent.

"Over the years I have confided many things to you, my friend. But there are many more things that I have kept to myself." Papa strained to see the priest through the screen separating their cubicles. All he could make out, though, was Rossi's shadow. "Last night's meeting, for instance. I intended to announce my retirement."

Papa waited for a response. There was no movement in the far cubicle.

"I thought if I stepped down, and Vito took over, that

things would...even out. I know that O'Hara and some of the others think I am getting weak. I don't believe that to be true, but I thought that perhaps they still had enough respect for Vito's strength that he could ascend and maintain the position of the Ghilini family. I see now that I misjudged."

The priest said nothing for a moment, then finally, "We are not young men anymore, old friend. Those running things today, they don't understand respect. All O'Hara and his kind understand is greed."

"There is more to life than money, Father. This much I have learned from the church."

Papa could see the priest nodding.

"Of course," Rossi said. "But it isn't just the money. O'Hara is greedy for power. And who has the power?"

The question hung heavy in the confined space. There was no need for Papa to speak -- they both knew the answer.

Monsignor Rossi continued, "Maybe it is time for your way of doing business to change." He paused, giving Papa a chance to digest this before he went on. "Look at our friend Freid."

"Freid," Papa blurted, louder than he would have liked, the pebble tight in his fist. He regained control, and said, "It was Freid who helped put me in this position. If he had supported me last night everything would be right in my world. Vito would be running the Ghilini family and there would still be peace."

"Do you not see why Josef made the decision he did?"

"Yes. He is losing his nerve."

Behind the screen, the priest was shaking his head. "I don't think the answer is that simple, Giacomo. Josef is an honest businessman now. And like all honest businessmen, he is worried what will happen if things with O'Hara get out of hand."

Papa rubbed the pebble between his hands. "And by not supporting me last night he has all but assured a war between O'Hara and my family."

"That is one possibility," the priest said patiently. "Another is that O'Hara will bring narcotics into the city and the authorities will stop him."

Papa shook his head violently. "O'Hara will attack me then, thinking that the police are acting on my orders."

There was a long silence before Rossi said, "Not if you step down first."

"Surrender?" Papa exploded. "Walk away from all I have worked for over the years? And what do I receive in return?"

And in the gesturing palm Papa stretched out, toward the shadowy shape beyond the screen, lay the pebble.

The priest's voice was quiet but assured. "What I am saying, old friend, is that if you are not seen as being in charge, there is no reason for Lou O'Hara and the others to come after you."

Papa's stomach constricted. He felt bile rising in his throat. He thought last night had been the ultimate betrayal, but now here he sat in the one place he thought he would receive solace, understanding, and the one person he thought capable of giving him those things sat on the other side of this flimsy screen trying to convince him that the betrayal of others was the best thing that could happen to him. Forgetting he held the pebble, Papa's touched his heated brow, against which the tiny stone felt cold indeed. Beads of sweat slithered down his face and he struggled to shrug out of his overcoat in the tiny space.

When he spoke again, his words were measured. "Father, do you remember the last time someone tried to bring drugs into the city?"

"Yes."

"What happened?"

"Your son, Paulo, was killed trying to stop them."

Papa's voice became very quiet. "Yes, Paulo was killed."

"Do you want that to happen again? That is why I am counseling you to get out now, old friend. You have lost one son to drug runners. Do you want to risk another?"

"You know," Papa said wistfully, "you were never privy to the whole truth about that event."

"They killed Paulo, and I assume that he was avenged."

Tears mixed with the perspiration on Papa's face. "That is not quite the truth, Confessor."

"No?"

"It was Paulo who tried to bring the narcotics into the city, against my wishes. He knew that I wouldn't tolerate that poison coming in, so he did his best to hide what he was doing from me. He didn't hide it well enough. Do you know what I am telling you?"

He could see the priest shake his head, whether a gesture of ignorance or incredulity, Papa did not know.

"What I am saying is that I had my son, my own flesh and blood, killed for disobeying me."

Papa heard the sharp intake of breath beyond the screen. Papa was shaking now. He clutched the tiny counter in front of him trying to regain control of his emotions, the pebble tumbling from his fingers to make a tiny clatter on the floor of the booth.

"I have shed the blood of my own son in order to keep this sin from entering the city, and now you tell me to allow this demon to do that very thing?"

"I...I did...didn't know..."

"Nor does anyone else....I pulled some strings out of

town."

"H...how could you?"

Papa's voice was a whimper now. "I tried. Don't you think I tried? I did everything I could to get Paulo to stop, but he wouldn't listen. He thought he knew more than his father. He thought he was stronger than the family. I couldn't allow him to spread that poison into the city. I've seen it in other places. It starts with the weak, but eventually it also swallows the strong and the children. How someone, anyone, could sell bottled death to the young was more than I could comprehend. I wouldn't have stood for it if it had been one of the other gangs. There was no way I could stand by and let someone in my own family contaminate the future. Now I must take a stand with O'Hara as well."

"That was years ago, Giacomo. The times are different. O'Hara is a powerful enemy with many allies."

"I have allies of my own," Papa said.

"O'Hara has Raven Malone as well as both the Tongs and the Triads."

"I have the Yakuza."

"Do you think that you can trust Toshiro and the Yakuza?"

Papa's voice was cold steel. "Yes."

"How can you be so sure?"

"Do you remember Giuseppe?"

"The son you disowned?"

"Yes. Have I ever told you why Giuseppe was sent away?"

"No."

"In the war, Giuseppe took up with a Japanese woman." Papa paused. "The fruit of this illicit affair was a child."

"Yes?"

"If Giuseppe hadn't abandoned both mother and child, he

would still be part of my family. That child was Toshiro."

"Toshiro is your grandson?"

Papa nodded. "When Toshiro came to this country it was I who arranged it. I paid for his education. He earned a degree in business and it was my hope that he would be the first of the Ghilini family to go legitimate...A fitting, if ironic, fate for my bastard grandson. That was not to be. I found out that he was fencing stolen art, using his business as a front. I decided that if he was going to enter the business anyway it would be best if he did it in such a way that I could keep an eye on him. It was under those conditions that he was sent to join the Yakuza. Though they are heavily into narcotics in Japan, the Yakuza has been restricting its activities in the city to extortion and prostitution. And now with Toshiro entrenched as one of their leaders, they will be a formidable ally. One, I'm sure, that O'Hara thinks will move to his side. That mistake may well be his last."

"I thought I knew you, Giacomo...."

"Even with what I have told you today, Confessor, there is still much more you do not know. But I thank you for your time. Whether you know it or not, you have been of great assistance to me today. I now know what I must do."

"I have done nothing but listen."

"That," said Papa, pulling his overcoat on, "is an important quality to find, Father. It is hard these days to find a good listener."

Rossi started to say something, but Papa didn't hear him as he stepped from the confessional, without having taken time to receive forgiveness for the worst sin he'd ever brought to The Confessor, not noticing the pebble he crushed under his heel.

*****

The bell in the steeple was ringing, calling the parishioners to worship. The Good Friday service, The Celebration of the Lord's Passion, was one of Papa Ghilini's favorites. As Papa and his family made his way into the sanctuary, he crossed himself. He looked at the shrouded cross above the altar, then glanced around the congregation as he moved toward the front of the church. Toshiro was sitting with Beatrice in the back row. Papa gave his grandson a curt nod and continued down the aisle. He smiled to himself. They were a handsome couple. A few rows in front of Toshiro sat Police Chief Harry Hammons and his family. The chief glared at Papa who nodded back, forgiving the copper his sins, if only for tonight.

Papa, Mama, and the rest of the Ghilini family made their way to the front of the sanctuary. Papa and Mama sat in the front row while the others took up most of the next four rows.

Papa felt the warmth of Mama's hand as her fingers entwined in his.

Monsignor Rossi stepped forward to deliver the Liturgy of the Word. As the priest read the words, Papa's mind turned back to his meeting with Vito earlier in the day. Papa and Vito lunched together nearly every day. Today had been no different except they hadn't eaten. Both men were fasting in commemoration of Good Friday, so they had sat down over coffee in the back room of Papa's Ristorante.

"You look pale, Papa. Are you still worried about O'Hara?"

Papa shook his head. "Just tired, my son. O'Hara concerns me, but I am not worried."

Vito's brow furrowed. "I don't understand."

Papa's smile was sad, exhausted. There was still so much for Vito to learn. "Women worry, Vito. Men may be concerned about a problem, but it is our job to solve it. Worrying is wasted energy."

His son nodded.

"We are correct to be concerned about O'Hara and his cronies. They are dangerous people."

Again, Vito nodded.

"With the plan I am about to outline for you, you will defeat them. After that, the Ghilini family's position will be assured."

Papa had outlined his strategy for Vito who grasped the subtlety of it even faster than Papa thought he would.

Glancing down the pew, Papa studied his son for a moment and permitted himself a private smile. Vito was going to be just fine. Papa could step down now, knowing that the empire he had spent his whole life shaping would live on for years after he was gone, in good Ghilini hands.

Cardinal Vincenzo Micelli stepped forward to lead the Veneration of the Cross. Though Papa usually paid close attention to the sacraments of his faith, again he found his mind wandering.

Vito had been astonished to find out that Toshiro was his nephew. Losing both his brothers had been difficult for Vito to endure. To find out now that he had family he was unaware of invigorated his son like nothing Papa had witnessed before. But it also seemed to knock him off balance.

"And you never told anyone he was your grandson?" Vito had asked.

"To tell anyone that Toshiro was family would have put him in danger. Don't you see that?"

Vito shook his head. "I'm your son. If you can't trust me, who can you trust?"

"It's not a matter of trust, Vito. If I had told you about Toshiro before this moment, your behavior, no matter how minutely, would have changed toward him. Someone might have been able to figure out why, and that would have placed Toshiro in mortal danger."

"I would have protected him."

Papa did not argue. "And now you will. Until today it has been my job to protect Toshiro, and the rest of our family as well. Now, my son, that job will fall to you. I'm stepping aside. You will oversee everything from now on."

Vito had been as shocked by that pronouncement as he had of learning of his new nephew. Papa had only smiled at his son's surprise.

"Don't be concerned, Vito. You are ready."

The words still rang in Papa's ears. He believed what he had said to his son this afternoon. Vito was ready to take over the family.

Cardinal Micelli stepped to the altar. His voice carried to the far reaches of the church, even though it seemed, to Papa at least, that His Eminence was speaking in a conversational tone. "We are gathered here today to give thanks to our Holy Father for his gift to man. The Lord so loved his creation that he gave his only begotten son to sacrifice himself for our sins."

Papa glanced at Monsignor Rossi who stood to the Cardinal's left. The priest was listening patiently. That talent was, Papa decided, Monsignor Rossi's greatest gift.

"It was on this holy day," the Cardinal continued, "that Pilate washed his hands, leaving the mob to decide the fate of Jesus."

Papa bowed his head.

"The soldiers stripped Jesus, put upon him the scarlet robe, then placed upon his head the crown of thorns."

Unconsciously, Papa ran a hand through his hair.

"They placed a reed in his right hand, bowed before him, and mocked him, saying, 'Hail, the King of the Jews.' Then they tore the reed from him, spit upon him and beat him."

Papa felt a single tear slide down his cheek.

"Then they tore off the robe and led Jesus into the streets. They bade him to bear his own cross, then marched him through the streets to the jeers of the mob. Then, along with the thieves, he was crucified. The soldiers cast lots for his garments. Above his head hung a sign that read, 'This is Jesus, King of the Jews.' Even the thieves tormented him, saying, 'If thou be the Son of God, come down from the cross.' But he did not."

As the Cardinal went on, Papa could feel himself shaking. No matter how many times he heard the story, it never failed to touch him. Papa turned to look at Vito again. His son's eyes bore into him as Papa heard the Cardinal say, "My God, my God, why hath thou forsaken me?"

Then Vito smiled at him and Papa felt a warm glow that had not coursed through him for a long time. Not since before Paulo died. Papa's plan was in place, and the threat of O'Hara seemed about to be neutralized. As Papa made his way to the steps of the altar to accept his communion, he realized that the radiance he felt was, of all things, happiness.

As the choir sang the hymn, Papa moved to the communion rail, eased himself to his knees, and clasped his hands in front of him. Father Rossi stood just across the rail. An altar boy placed the paten under Papa's chin and he accepted the host when the priest laid it upon his tongue. Praying silently as he heaved himself back to his feet, Papa made his way to the outside aisle and back to his seat.

He noticed the Cardinal was sitting in a straight back chair near the altar. The man appeared to be weary from the performance of the service. Papa turned his attention to the line of worshipers creeping up the aisle to the rail. As one group rose and moved away, others took their places and knelt. Papa noticed a thin, balding man in a dark suit. As the man rose and moved to Papa's left, Papa thought he saw the bulge of a gun under the man's jacket.

Papa watched the man make his way to the outside aisle on Papa's left. He was sure now that the man was wearing a shoulder holster. Papa studied the man's deep-set eyes, framed by high cheek bones; beak of a nose, what little hair he had left slicked down at the back of his skull. Papa watched from the corner of his eye as the man took an aisle seat in the smaller outside pew two rows behind Papa's.

Vito looked toward his father and Papa tilted his head toward the gunman. He watched as Vito turned to eyeball the guy, then glanced back at Papa and shrugged. His son had not seen what Papa had.

The bald man packing a gun was not one of their soldiers, nor was he anyone that Papa recognized from O'Hara's bunch.

As the Cardinal rose and moved to the front of the altar, Papa continued to watch the gunman from the corner of his eye. His stomach churned as he tried to decide what to do.

The Cardinal, hands folded across his stomach, said, "Lord, send down your abundant blessing upon your people who have devoutly recalled the death of your son in the sure hope of the resurrection."

Alarm bells clanged in Papa's head as he saw the bald man's hand easing under his jacket.

"Grant them pardon; bring them comfort."

The man was slowly rising now, and Papa wanted to yell but no sound would come out of his throat. His mind was screaming at him. It's a hit! It's a hit! But as Papa looked at the man's eyes, he realized he was not the target. The assassin's eyes were locked on the altar. Papa couldn't believe what he was seeing. Someone was going to whack the Cardinal!

"May their faith grow stronger and their eternal salvation be assured."

Papa was on his feet now as well. He felt Mama's hand on his arm, but he didn't look down at her. His eyes saw only the assassin and the gun coming out the hitman's jacket in what seemed to be slow motion. There was no way Papa could get to the assassin before the man could get off a shot. There was only one other course of action possible.

Hurdling the rail with an agility even he found surprising, Papa leapt toward the altar.

"We ask this through Christ our Lord..." The Cardinal's words trailed off as he saw Papa sprinting toward him.

"Amen," the congregation said as one.

"What are you..." the Cardinal bellowed, his eyes wide with fear.

Monsignor Rossi was moving to intercept Papa. The look on the priest's face told Papa that the man thought he had gone insane. The Cardinal took a step backward toward the cross as Papa shoved Rossi to the ground, a gunshot exploding from behind Papa as he knocked the Cardinal to the floor, echoing through the vast chamber.

Papa felt a tremendous jolt in his back. He'd been shot before and instantly knew that the assassin's bullet had found him instead of His Eminence. The impact drove him past the Cardinal and face first into the cross. He grabbed the shroud of the crucifix as he started to topple and the cross wobbled precariously. Realizing what was happening, Papa let go of the shroud but it was too late.

He heard the chorus of screams erupt as he fell backwards. Looking up, he saw the cross coming toward him and knew there was no way to avoid it. As the huge wooden crucifix tumbled, Papa turned his head and saw the Cardinal cowering on the floor, a look of utter disbelief etched on his face.

When the cross finally struck him, a whole world of color bloomed in Papa's eyes. There was a burst of pain, then suddenly no pain at all. His head lolled to one side and the blossom of color disintegrated as he watched the assassin retreating toward the door of the church. Papa's eyes fell shut. He was surprised at how much effort it took for him to open them again. As he did, he made out Police Chief Harry Hammons running toward the doors at the far end of the cathedral with his gun drawn.

"Help him," Papa heard someone whimper.

Forcing his eyes to stay open, he saw Monsignor Rossi bending over him. The priest was holding someone's hand, and though it looked a great deal like his own thick hand, Papa couldn't feel the cleric's touch.

Someone yelled, "Get the damn cross off him!"

Papa could see that several men, Vito among them, were lifting the cross off his chest. He was unable to understand why there was no difference in feeling when the weight was removed from his body.

"Is it bad, old friend?" Rossi asked.

Papa shook his head. The warm, sweet taste of blood filled his mouth and he coughed it up.

Rossi didn't leave his side, but turned to the altar boy. "Get my sacraments," he commanded.

"No time," Papa said, his voice a hoarse whisper.

Tears were running down the priest's face. "You should have the Last Rites," he said.

Papa tried to squeeze his friend's hand but could not. "It's all right, John. I'm at peace with myself -- and with my God."

Mama squeezed in on the other side and hugged him. Her cheek was wet and warm, but he felt no other part of her against him. That was all right, he told himself. He'd had the pleasure of her in his arms so many times before and that would be enough to carry him to whatever eternal judgment awaited him.

From outside the church came a sound that might have been a car backfiring, but wasn't.

His mouth was close to Mama's ear now. "I will always love you," he said.

Vito appeared above him. His son's face was clouded with anger and hate. "I'll get O'Hara for this, Papa. Don't worry."

"No. I was not the target. Don't forget your promise to me. That is what is important." Papa's body was wracked by another spasmodic cough and he felt more blood dribble onto his chin. When he could finally speak again, he said, "Only your promise. Remember, that is all that matters."

The edges of his vision were growing dark. From that blackness, Papa thought he saw Paulo moving toward him. His eyes fell closed and behind his lids Papa could clearly see Paulo coming toward him with his arms outstretched.

From that other place Papa heard Rossi say, "You saved the Cardinal, old friend. He is all right. You saved..."

Paulo embraced him.

"I'm sorry, my son."

"It is I who am sorry, Papa."

Papa kissed his son. "I love you, Paulo. I always loved you."

"I know," Paulo answered.

Then there was silence.

Thus did a man of violence die in peace, unaware of the masquerade his son Vito had arranged, involving a hitman who now lay dead in the street, shot by a Ghilini soldier...a son (a brother seeking vengeance for a slain brother) who would bask in the posthumous glory of his martyred father who had, so predictably, thrown himself between God and a bullet. A terrible gang war would simply not have to happen, because this great out-of-date figure had given his life for the Cardinal.

And in the great cathedral, toward the back, a mother was gathering her two children, to remove them from this scene of horror. She tugged hard at the hand of her youngest, a boy who had lagged to pick up a small stone.

THE DEVIL'S FACE

"Nothing personal, just business."

The first time I hear this statement, it comes from the lips of a pudgy accountant named Otto Berman. A balding man with a pearl onion for a snoot, Otto loves playing the ponies so much he is the inspiration for a character named Regret the horse player in short stories that I sometimes write.

He is also called "Abba Dabba," a nickname hung upon him by his boss, a sleepy-eyed gangster named Arthur Flegenheimer, who like most of the people I write about has a stage name of his own—Dutch Schultz.

Otto is also the man who masters the numbers racket and makes huge stacks of cash for Dutch and his cronies. On top of everything else, Otto is my best friend. Well, until two days ago, anyway.

Otto and the Dutchman, they are having a late dinner at the Palace Chop House, over in Newark, along with a Schultz henchman named Abe Landau and Dutch's bodyguard, Bernard "Lulu" Rosenkrantz, when two goons blow in, guns blazing.

My buddy Otto and the others end up completely dead.

Well, the Dutchman is mostly dead but is on his way.

This is why I am wearing the long face and sitting in that staple of Times Square, Lindy's. Usually, this joint, with its familiar white tablecloths, wooden chairs, and colorful banquettes is a happier place for me. If the mere fact that I am sitting in a place that feels like home does not cheer me, the cheesecake certainly will. Today though, I fear that even this concoction from heaven will not help.

I am at a corner table, the place maybe half full, the lunch rush well over. Guys are back at work and dolls are back to shopping. Outside, the day is October crisp, the sun high. When the door opens, the cacophony of trolley cars, autos, and the bustle of the city is like somebody switched on a radio.

For squares it is halfway through the day, but I am just beginning mine. When you are a sportswriter, especially one who covers boxing, there are not many early nights, and certainly no early mornings.

I am waiting for John Long, the police stenographer who sits at Schultz's bedside and scribbles the gangster's last words. Built like a jockey, the sandy-haired Long strolls in, spots me, and hurries over, scurrying head down, like he is escorting a customer to the clink.

He has a spade-shaped kisser, lively brown eyes, and a gray fedora that is now being driven like a steering wheel between bony fingers as he pulls up to the table.

"Damon," he says, eyes darting around the restaurant.

No response seems necessary, as I am clearly Damon. I nod for him to take the chair opposite.

He is as nervous as one of the stoolies whose singing voices he records note for note.

"I should not be here," says he.

"Relax," I say.

He gives me the pie eyes, like I just made a crack about his wife or his mother.

The waitress sweeps over like she is making an entrance from stage right. She is a cute little blonde number named Adelaide.

"Hi there, Mr. Runyon. Coffee for you and your friend?" Her voice is Helen Kane's. But then so is Betty Boop's, so no lawsuit is likely.

Long and I both nod.

"John, you are going to have a slice of cheesecake too, right?"

Something that might be the genesis of a smile tickles the corners of Long's mouth. "If you are."

I hold up two fingers and Adelaide favors us with a big smile as she scribbles the order on a pad. We sit in silence until she takes the hint and winks at me before sashaying away to fill our order. She would like to be in show business and I have connections.

"So, what happened?" I ask.

"You read the papers."

I feel my temper rising and I pull off my glasses and give them a quick wipe with the cloth napkin. Patrice, the wife, says it is something I do when I do not want people to see that I am excited or angry. I practically rub the lenses out of their wire frames. Maybe she has a point.

I say, "The papers inform me Otto Berman is a henchman of Dutch's. You and I both know this is not the case."

"I am sorry about that," Long says. "You know how these damned reporters make things up."

I throw him a look.

"Not you, Damon. Those other reporters."

"Uh huh," I say. "But that still does not tell me what happened."

"Not much to tell," Long says.

"Four men are dead, at least two murderers on the loose, and you say there is not much to tell?"

Long shrugs a little, but says nothing.

Adelaide arrives with our order. When she and her smile are gone and we are cutting into our cheesecake, I ask, "You truly do not know anything?"

"Just what the detectives tell me," Long says. He chews a bite. "Good cheesecake."

"Do not change the subject. What do the dicks say?"

"Two guys with guns burst in," Long says, "and shoot the hell out of everybody and everything."

"No idea who they are?"

Long runs a hand over his face. "I could get in trouble tellin' you..."

I stop him cold. "Have I ever done you wrong, John?"

He lets out a breath, eats another bite of cheesecake, chewing, tasting, thinking. Finally, he says, "You know Ernie Edwards?"

"Elephant Ernie?" I ask.

"Yeah. He hates that nickname."

I shrug.

John says, "Ernie's a good detective, you know."

That does not mean he is any straighter than your average copper, which means at least somewhat bent. Elephant Ernie is not even that fat, mostly the nickname has to do with the fact that he never forgets anything—ever.

John is saying, "Ernie tells me that witnesses tell him that the two doing the shooting are Bug Workman and Mendy Weiss."

A broad-faced Lower East Side Heeb, Charles Workman, "The Bug," is a favorite shooter of Louis "Lepke" Buchalter and a certain enterprise of Lepke's called Murder, Incorporated. Common knowledge has it that Bug has previously killed for Schultz on orders from Lepke. Killing Dutch himself is no skin off Bug's long, crooked nose. The Bug will kill his own mother, if the price is right.

Emmanuel "Mendy" Weiss is Lepke's right hand man. More compact than Bug, Mendy is no slouch where lacking scruples is concerned.

I ask, "Are Bug and Mendy about to be pinched?"

Long shakes his head. "No evidence."

I cannot help but smile. There is seldom evidence when certain gangsters are gunned down or certain other gangsters are doing the gunning.

"Who is buying the contract?" I ask.

"Rumor has it, it is Lucky."

"Why would Luciano do that?"

Leaning in like he is passing along a tip on the seventh race at Hialeah, Long says, "Schultz wanted to bump off Dewey."

I say nothing, removing my glasses and giving them a quick swipe with the napkin as I consider this. Thomas E. Dewey, the U.S. attorney, has a hobby of making life hard for the gangsters. As a target, he is not small potatoes. Some guys think he may even run for president someday. Killing him would bring the heat of a thousand suns down on the Commission, the ruling body of organized crime in the city.

Long says, "Word has it the Commission refuses to give Schultz permission to kill Dewey. Well, old Dutch tells them to go do something to themselves that is physically unlikely. Dutch says, in fact, that he will kill whoever the hell he wants, thank you."

Putting my glasses back on, I pick up Long's train of thought. "So the Commission decides to show Dutch that when they say, 'no,' they mean no."

"Yes," Long says.

"And Otto?"

Long shrugs. "Sometimes a guy is just sitting across from a guy who is getting gunned down. Happenstance."

"You spent the night with Schultz while he was dying, right?"

"Yeah, it was not pretty."

"Did he say anything?"

"What did he not say?"

"Let us return to what did he say."

"It was the ravings of a loon. The delirious rantings of a guy busy dying."

"Nothing about the gunmen?"

Long shakes his head once. "Not while I am with him, but I do not catch up to Dutch until after his surgery. There is the time he spends at the restaurant, the ambulance ride, the trip to the operating room. There are lots of people he could talk to before I sit next to him as he is spouting poetry."

"Elephant Ernie tell you anything else?"

"Ernie laid out what they think happened."

"Finally," I say. "Something interesting. Spill."

Long takes a quick look around to make sure no one is within earshot. "The four of them, Dutch, Abba Dabba and the rest show up, have a nice dinner. Then they are interrupted."

I say nothing, letting Long tell the tale at his own rate.

"A waiter at the Palace," Long says, "one Benny Shapiro, tells Edwards what happened."

"And Shapiro says?"

"Shapiro says that after the meal, Dutch excuses himself to take a leak. Almost as soon as he is inside the john, Bug and Mendy come through the front door. Schultz's guys all rise, but Otto, who is unarmed, catches a blast from Mendy's shotgun and goes down."

I shake my head.

"Then Shapiro, the waiter, he hits the deck, but he sees Bug push past the other two and disappear into the Men's Room. Mendy turns the shotgun on Lulu Rosenkrantz and shoots him point blank."

"Killing him?" I ask.

Long shakes his head. "Shapiro hears two shots from the Men's and then Bug comes out just as Mendy pulls a pistol and shoots Abe Landau in the neck. Musta hit the carotid artery, because Shapiro says blood is spurting everywhere."

"Jesus," I mutter.

"Then, despite the fact that they are both shot to hell, Lulu and Landau start shooting back. Bug and Mendy hotfoot it outside with Landau chasing them. He is shooting and also bleeding like a stuck pig. Mendy gets into a waiting car and tells the driver to go, leaving Bug behind. Bug hops away and Landau finally collapses over a trash can."

"What about Schultz?"

"This I am getting to," Long says. "Inside the Palace, Rosenkrantz has gotten change from the barman and calls for an ambulance before he passes out in the phone booth."

"And Schultz?" I pester.

"This is the best part," Long says. "Shapiro says Schultz comes out of the Men's and drops into a chair, collapsing on the table. He's got one in his gut, but manages to say, get this, 'I am not dyin' in no fucking terlet.' This quote may require a rewrite for your paper. Anyway, the Dutchman is out cold by the time the ambulance gets there."

"So then?"

"Then the ambulance gets there. Dutch has only been shot once and Otto is dead already. So, thinking that Landau and Lulu are the most serious cases of lead poisoning, the ambulance takes them first, and another is called for Dutch and Otto."

"If Dutch is only shot once, what goes so wrong?"

Long, his cheesecake gone, despite how much he is talking, sits back, wipes his face with his napkin, and lights a cigarette.

Not being one to miss a chance to smoke, I light up too.

"What nobody knows is the bullet from Bug's .38 has fragmented like a rack of billiard balls, pieces tearing into Dutch's spleen, colon, lungs, and God knows where all."

"But they do get around to getting him to the hospital."

"Yeah, but he is shot to hell and back before he gets there and nobody knows till he is in surgery that the bullets are rust-coated. Bug figures if he doesn't kill him by shooting him, he'll kill of Dutch with infection."

"Nasty."

"Nasty and smart."

"What does Dutch talk about when you are with him?"

Long shakes his head, then snubs his butt, and takes a drink from his coffee. "As I say, gibberish, mostly. A load of crap."

"Such as?"

"Okay. In his room, after his surgery, I think Dutch is coming around, but all I get is some nonsense. This is, I kid you not, the first words he says as he is coming out of it, 'Mama, mama, mama, I am a pretty good pretzler.'"

I give Long a look. "And this means what the hell?"

The stenographer gives me an elaborate shrug.

"Does he say anything even on the outskirts of making sense?"

"Oh God, he goes on a merry streak. He asks me to take off his shoes, which, by the way, he is not wearing any. Asks that we crackdown on the Chinaman's friends and Hitler's commanders."

"Does he now?"

"Yeah, then he says something about Phoenicia. That's in Greece, right?"

"Was," I say. "But not Greece, Africa. The Phoenicians were an ancient civilization. But did he mean *that* one, or the little town upstate?"

"There's a Phoenicia in New York?"

I nod. "Tiny burg, the Catskills."

"What the hell would Dutch be doing in the Catskills?" Long asks.

"I have no idea," I say, but I'm thinking that Otto Berman has a fishing cabin up there where he and I have gone a few times. It would not be a big stretch of the imagination to think that Abba Dabba has taken Dutch up there, too. I do not mention this to Long.

Instead, I ask, "What else does Dutch say?"

"He goes off on a rant about the devil."

"The devil?"

"Yeah. First it is the devil's face, then the devil's tombstone. Getting shot must have scared the hell out of him."

"Or scared hell into him," I say.

Possibly this is a coincidence, but for the last few years, Otto has a habit of saying, "The Devil's face, you say." I never know where the hell this expression comes from, and do not ask. Now, this mention of the devil's face gives me the creeps.

"Anyway," Long says, "then he mumbles, 'John, please did you buy me the hotel for a million?'"

"He is talking to you?"

Long shakes his head. "Some other 'John,' probably. Coincidence."

"What hotel?"

"It doesn't matter. It is not the hotel that's important."

"What is?"

"Who knows? But what Schultz says next is, 'I will get you the money out of the box...there is enough in it to buy four or five more.'"

Enough money to buy four or five hotels?

"You figure Dutch has a cash box hidden?" I ask. "In his business, this is not exactly unheard of."

Shrugging, Long says, "He babbles that there are Liberty bonds that somebody named Danny buys, and Dutch thinks it is a mistake because the bonds can be traced and the bonds should be taken out of the box."

I consider this for several seconds. Then I say, "There has been talk that since Dewey is coming after him, Dutch has stashed a secret treasure."

Long makes a face like his coffee has turned to vinegar. "Every bad guy since Cain slew Abel has had a 'secret treasure.' Every story of that kind I have heard has been hooey. My guess is Dutch Schultz's is too."

"You are probably right. He is a gangster, not Captain Kidd."

Not much later, Long leaves me, but the idea of Schultz's secret treasure does not. Neither does the bill. The stenographer sticks me with the check and the nagging idea that there is something in the Catskills I may want to have a look at.

Even now, I cannot tell you whether this story holds me because I am a reporter, or like my late friend Otto, I bet the occasional longshot.

Wheels McCracken is a getaway driver. I do not think

you are allowed to be a getaway driver unless your moniker is Wheels. He is a redheaded son of Scotland who, like me, does not own a car of his own. Wheels does, however, possess a knack for laying his hands on an auto when he needs one. Or, if you know him, he will help you "rent" a car.

This is the favor he has done for me. Now, early on a Saturday evening, I find myself in the sleepy burg of Phoenicia, New York. Among about only twenty people more than live on my block, I feel like a fish out of water. There is a small grocery, a few houses, and not much else.

The guy I am looking for does not live in Phoenicia, if you call that living. Clyde has a cabin on Esopus Creek outside of town. Clyde also has a last name, but I do not know it. When Otto brings me up this way fishing, Clyde is our guide. Otto introduces him as Clyde and that is as far as we ever get.

The road stops a quarter mile from Clyde's cabin and I work myself up a sweat trudging up the hill toward the place. Before I get within twenty yards, Clyde is standing on the front porch.

He is a little taller than me, even thinner, and has the complexion of a worn saddle. In his seventies, he moves like a man half his age. A life outdoors as a fishing and hunting guide has left him in better shape than most.

As I near, a grin spreads. "I know you," says he. "You're Otto's friend."

I nod.

"Good to see you," Clyde says. "Where's Otto?"

There is no easy way to say it, so I do not spend a lot of time looking for one. "Shot to death, two days ago."

The old man's smile disappears. "Hell."

"Yeah," I agree. "Not all of Otto's friends were salt of

the earth, Clyde, like you."

Clyde nods. "He's introduced me to a few of them."

"Is that right?"

"Yeah. He comes up here a few months ago with a couple of guys in suits that look expensive. Alphabet soup boys."

"Alphabet soup?"

"Long names," Clyde says. "Lots of vowels."

"Ah," I say.

"Both of them, names this long." He holds up his hands about a foot apart like he is showing me the size of the one that got away.

"Flagenheimer?"

"That's one of them."

"Rosenkrantz?"

Clyde shrugs, less sure. "You want to come in?"

"Please."

From the outside, the cabin is not much. It is allegedly white, but the last time this building is white, I was in short pants. The front porch gives it a friendliness that the rest of the property does not share. High on a hill, probably to make it easy to defend, the land is clean but unwelcoming. There are no flowers nor anything that suggests that visitors are appreciated. Even the mailbox sits down at the bottom of the hill, out of view of the house, just another unwanted caller.

Inside, I am surprised to find the place very cozy. Waiting are a large leather chair, reading lamp nearby, a made bed, a dining table with a lamp on it, a fireplace, and in one corner, a radio. The place smells of hot coffee. My sniff at the air conveys this.

"You want a cup?" he asks.

"Sure," I say as he gestures for me to sit at the table.

"Gotta drink it black. I do not have milk or sugar."

"Black will do nicely," I say. "Otto's friends come up to go fishing?"

Clyde puts the cups on the table and sits down opposite me. "The alphabet soup boys? Naw. In those suits, they are not looking for fish."

"What *are* they looking for?"

Clyde shrugs. "Not sure. They ask a lot of questions about places around here."

"Places?" I ask. I sip the coffee. It is good and I tell him so.

"Thanks," Clyde says. "Places like Esopus Creek and where it runs, the Devil's Face, the Devil's Tombstone."

Trying to play it easy, I say, "I have heard of these places, but do not know where they are."

"The creek is the creek, but the other two are rock formations not far from town."

Good places to hide treasure, maybe?

"So," I say, "do they go to these places?"

"Not with me. They just talk to me, then the alphabet boys and Otto take off."

My mind is racing. "Do they ask more about one place than the other?"

"Not really," Clyde says. "Devil's Tombstone is closer to town, but a hundred fifty feet up. The Devil's Face is farther from town, but not far from highway 214. Maybe eight, ten miles out."

"Do you show them how to get there?"

"I make them maps."

"You can do this for me, too?"

"Sure. You're a friend of Otto's, too. Are you trying to solve his murder?"

"I know who killed him. So do the police."

"Who?"

"Alphabet soup boys. *Other* alphabet soup boys...."

He nods with the attitude of a man who has seen bigger animals eat smaller ones.

I watch Clyde sketching out the maps, it occurs to me that I will never find these places in the dark. I have not always been a city boy, but bumping around in the woods of the Catskill Mountains on a chilly October night might not be the course of action most wise.

I ask, "Is there a hotel in Phoenicia?"

Clyde nods, hands still busy. "Those other guys, they have lunch there, but they do not book rooms. Hell, they do not even stay overnight."

"I mean for me."

He looks up from his work. "Oh. Well, that is different. You know I am caretaker for Otto's place, right? I do not think he will mind if you use it one more night. For old time's sake. Soon as I finish these maps, I will get you the key."

"Thank you," I say.

Clyde waves me off. "Otto sure as hell will not be using it anytime soon and besides, it is just up the road and you will not have to go all the way back into town."

When his task is complete, Clyde gives me two maps drawn on plain white paper. I inspect them and make sure I know which line is which road.

Satisfied I will not drive off the edge of the world, I ask for the key and Clyde digs out a key and hands it over. "You remember where the cabin is?"

"I do," I say.

"Well, if you need anything else while you are in my neck of the woods, feel free to stop by. If I can help you with whatever you are trying to do for Otto, I will be happy to help. He was a good man."

It is a short drive and a less strenuous climb up a less steep hill to Otto's cabin. Compared to Clyde's more Spartan accommodations, Otto's cabin is downright luxurious. Still only one floor, but unlike Clyde's, Otto has a separate bedroom and indoor plumbing. The furniture is leather and barely used. There are several oil lamps, and even art on the walls in the form of several old advertising posters.

It is just short of midnight now and the one thing Otto's cabin is missing is heat. I would not turn down a change of clothes or something to eat, but I have arrived at the cabin short on supplies. Naturally, the cupboards are bare, too.

Dropping onto a chair at the dining room table, I realize that the last I have eaten is at a lunch counter back in Newburgh, some hours ago. As I light a cigarette, I am considering my chances against the "Cinderella Man," heavyweight champion of the world James J. Braddock. I am the one that dropped the nickname on him, and he is easily almost a foot taller and fifty or more pounds heavier than me. But tonight, if the prize is a slice of Lindy's cheesecake, I might well have a shot at taking the big man down.

I try to study the maps, but the light is dim and it is fast becoming a very long day. I find myself not really tired, but distracted. I fold them up and put them in my inside suit coat pocket. I could turn on Otto's radio, but that seems like too much trouble.

Instead, I stare at the framed poster on the wall across from me. A pretty, buxom brunette pin-up girl wears a devil's costume and smiles. She also wears a hood with horns and a red bathing suit with a bifurcated tail. She is advertising Red Devil Chewing Tobacco. Though I smoke heavily, I find chewing a detestable habit. The brunette devil across the room is making me reconsider.

As I am studying this impish Judy, I hear Otto's voice say, "The Devil's face, you say."

Could it possibly be that easy? The doll in the poster seems to have a glint in her eye now. Am I as delirious as Dutch, or does she wink at me like Adelaide?

Before I can even rise from my chair, the cabin door bursts open and I find myself gazing down the barrels of a shotgun and a .38 pistol. Behind the guns are two mean-looking mugs, Bug Workman and Mendy Weiss.

I see both of them around town with Otto and the Dutchman, but in this bucolic setting, their arrival is jarring. Almost as jarring as being on the wrong end of the tools of their grisly trade.

"Runyon," Bug says. This greeting is more an accusation. It sounds like the growl of a cornered animal, even though I am the one who is trapped.

I rise from the chair and turn my back to the devil. Get thee behind me, Satan.

"What the hell are you doin' here?" Mendy asks. Though it is less of a growl than the Bug's, this does not make Mendy's voice music to my ears.

I move slowly, taking off my glasses and cleaning the lenses on my tie. "I might ask you gents the same thing."

Mendy grins. The smile on this devil is far more sinister than the one at my back. "We asked you first."

I slip my glasses back on. If this is a bump-off, I would already be standing before Saint Peter, preparing to plead my case.

I say, "I am here to commune with nature as I pay my respects to my dear dead friend."

Bug takes one step toward me, jabbing the pistol in my direction. Something between a laugh and a grunt escapes him. "You expect us to buy that bull? You are here for

Dutch's loot!"

I give them the innocent look, the same one I hand Patrice when she asks me if I have been to the track. These monkeys do not buy it any more than she does.

"You are a reporter," Mendy says, "and you have a nose."

"Everyone has a nose," I say.

"We have been following you all day, newshound. We know what you are up to."

"Boys, boys," I say, "leave us not do anything rash."

Mendy says, "Look, Runyon, you are known to keep your distance and your mouth shut, when it is smart to do so. Play *this* smart and you may wake up in the morning not dead. You was in that old coot's cabin for almost an hour. What did he tell you?"

Bug says, "If we have to go visit the codger, he might not be as smart as you and he could end up dead. Would you want that on your conscience?"

"I would not."

Mendy says, "We do not want to hurt you. There is going to be enough heat after the Palace. If a famous type such as, for example, yourself was to show up additionally dead, well...you can see why we are reluctant to do you harm, besides not disliking you in particular."

I do not believe a damned word he says, but he tells me I am smart, so I prove it by keeping my mouth shut.

"Me and Bug, we could use an insurance policy."

I stand mute, as I am not in the insurance racket.

"Lepke has all the leverage. If the heat gets too hot on him, then me and the Bug here will take the fall for bumping the Dutchman and his boys. Lepke knows we will not say boo, 'cause if we do...well...alive in prison is better than dead, I suppose."

"I suppose," I say.

"If we got Dutch's loot, me and Bug, we disappear like Claude Rains and even Lepke does not find us."

Then I say something that means I am not as smart as Mendy says I was.

I say, "And I would never tell Lepke what you boys are up to."

Something flares in Bug's eyes and he steps even closer with that damned pistol and I wish to kick myself but am not that limber. This crazy bastard's knuckles go white around the trigger and I think I have just uttered my last words. I had been hoping for something better than, "And I would never tell Lepke what you boys are up to."

Mendy puts a hand on the Bug's shoulder and for the moment, I am allowed to keep drawing breath.

"Runyon, if you tell Lepke? Before he gets us, we will get you, that Mexican wife of yours, your son, and everybody else who you ever goddamn knew. Get me?"

I nod. I also tremble.

"Hell with this," Bug says, stepping forward, pressing the gun to my temple. "I say we drop him right here and go back and talk to grandpa in that cabin. Then we will not have to concern ourselves about keeping the ink slinger quiet."

The barrel is cold against my skin and despite having guns pointed at me before, never this close, mind you, I try hard not to piss myself.

"The coot made maps for me," I say, noticing a quaver in my voice. "I will give them to you."

Bug eases the barrel back a quarter of an inch, then a half, then he pulls back enough for me to stand upright again.

"The maps are here," I say, gesturing to my suit coat. "I am not going for a gun. I do not own a gun."

Mendy says, "Go on then."

I reach in my inside coat pocket and withdraw the maps.

The tension is hard on all of us.

Mendy reaches out and takes the papers. "What the hell is this?"

"The treasure may be at one of these two locations," I say. "Either Devil's Face or Devil's Tombstone."

"Why do you think this?"

I tell them of Dutch's death bed ramblings.

"You do not know which place it is?" Bug asks, waving the pistol again.

"How the hell would I?" I ask, getting sore now. "It is not like Dutch and I are bosom buddies. Maybe you should ask before you shoot him."

Bug's eyes go very big and his finger curls tight around the trigger.

I say, "This is why Clyde gives me a map to both locations. If it is not one, it may be the other. If it is neither, then Dutch was just raving because persons unknown shot him."

"I do not like this," Bug says. "He is pulling a fast one."

Mendy stuffs the maps in the pocket of his suit jacket and leans into me so the barrel of the shotgun is right in my gut. "Would you be pulling a fast one, Runyon?"

"I would not. You boys have the maps and the guns. What do I have other than an ambition to continue breathing?"

Mendy considers this. Then he says, "We know where to find you in the city."

"And I know you know. So where can I get a one-up on two guys like you?"

Silence separates us. A small animal cries outside, having met a bigger one.

"He is telling it straight," Mendy finally pronounces. "He knows we can bury him in the city as well as we can bury him in the woods."

"This is unfortunately true," I say.

Bug backs off a little. "If the loot is not at one of these spots, we are coming for you, Runyon."

I throw up my hands. "If there *is* a treasure, Dutch buried it, not me. If you cannot find it, blame his death-bed ramblings!" I resist adding, *Or the guys who shot him.*

The boys threaten me a few more times, then they leave, off to pick up the secret stash of Dutch Schultz's hidden loot.

I give them a few minutes before I go take down the poster. Behind the devil poster is a safe. I look at the dial and shake my head. I am not now, nor have I ever been, a safecracker. As I silently curse Otto, something else he tells me from time to time rolls through my brain.

"Damon," Otto's voice whispers from the past, "sometime during the day, every day, I bet the combo of seven, fourteen, nine."

"Why do you do this?"

"My birthday, pal! July 14, 1889."

It is weird that he uses the word "combo" when he mentions these numbers to me. I try the dial: 7-14-9. Damn if it does not open right up for me. Abba Dabba has been planning for this day all along. He has been dropping clues just in case his hanging out with Dutch proves to give him a fatal case of lead poisoning, a prediction that has come true. He wants me to be the one to find the loot.

Inside are two canvas bank pouches. The first one is full to the brim with cash, denominations fifty or above, more than I am willing to stand around and count since I do not know that Bug and Mendy are gone for good. I set that down and pull out the other one.

Inside, I find that Dutch is telling the truth to John Long. Liberty bonds—a pile of them. And, like Dutch, I feel that these may well be traceable. I decide that there is no good to come from being greedy. I shove that bag back in, spin the dial on the safe, and kiss the devil lady on the lips when I have hung her back on the wall.

If Mendy and Bug return and are smart enough to spot the devil doll on the wall, they will find treasure waiting for them behind her face, never knowing of the cash that has departed with Runyon.

It is now time for me to get myself back to Times Square, where I belong. I have roughed it enough.

The possibility that Bug and Weiss will come after me is real, but I have two things on my side. Number one, I now have a rainy day nest egg that I can buy them off with, if necessary. And number two, I am a celebrity, and not in a Dutch Schultz way. It is difficult for a killer to avoid the Sing Sing death house croaking such a famous face. Or anyway byline. I may rub elbows with gangsters, but that does not make me one.

Besides, if I see my friend's killers on the street, I can always tell them, "Nothing personal, boys, just business."

*****

In 1938, three years after the events of this story, Damon Runyon was diagnosed with throat cancer. A 1944 surgery for the condition left him unable to speak. His only communication from then on was through written notes. When he passed on December 10, 1946, his old pal Walter Winchell pleaded with "Mr. and Mrs. America" for donations to battle cancer.

With those contributions, Winchell established the Damon Runyon Memorial Cancer Fund, which still seeks a cure for this deadly disease.

One donation, never publicized, was a canvas bank bag, stuffed with big bills, that showed up on the doorstep of Winchell's home.

THE TWO BILLYS

He was no damn coward. Had he been, the dark-haired, muscular mucker named Billy Byrne could not have survived a West Side of Chicago upbringing. He had grown up hard and fast in the neighborhood that ran from Halsted to Robey, and from Grand Avenue to Lake Street, where being a coward was the greatest of all sins.

Not only was Billy not a coward, he had felt fear but twice in his young life.

The first had been as a lad barely into his teens. He was afraid neither of his opponent Coke Sheehan nor the outcome of their knuckle duster. But during the brawl—a dispute over Sheehan welching on paying him money owed for a robbery the two had pulled together—Billy had hit the other boy in the head with a brick, rendering Sheehan unconscious and possibly croaking him.

The possible croaking of Sheehan itself had not scared the mucker, not really; but the idea that the coppers and a judge might make him swing at the end of a rope for it, well, that was damned unsettling, and had sent him briefly into hiding. The brick-bashed Sheehan had survived—too tough and dumb to die, most likely—and eventually Billy had returned to the streets.

The second occasion that had brought Billy that blue funk called fear was right before and during round one of his first prize fight against a top-notch brawler talked about as the next heavyweight champion. So the fight drew a big crowd that hooted and hawed through the introductions of what they figured to be a sorry mismatch, and the jeering went on for the first three minutes as the would-be future champ battered Billy.

Yes, Billy was afraid. Not of losing, nor of his opponent—it was that damned crowd. This brand of fear was simple stage fright, and soon Billy overcame that emotional fog to mop the floor with the "future champion."

The mucker sent the palooka back to the farm in the fifth round.

And yet this mucker unafraid of even the Maylay headhunters of Daimyo Oda Yorimoto, stood there in his sweats on the floor of Professor Cassidy's gym with trembling fingers—fingers unfolding a note just handed him by a messenger boy about as threatening as a new-born pup.

He did not need to read a word to know it was from her—Barbara Harding, the woman he loved, the woman he had left to another man, one befitting her station, not twenty-four hours ago.

The note announced her by way of its fragrance—sweet lilac, like that first hint of Spring. She always smelled that way to Billy, even when they had been marooned on a Pacific island and were on the lam from Yorimoto's headhunters. Even when they were living in hiding on an island in the middle of a raging river on Yoka, and especially when she had safely returned to her father's Riverside Drive mansion...always and ever, she wore the fragrance of lilacs and Spring.

A pang of something else other than fear—regret, joy, *something* he could not quite identify—shot through him as he recognized her flowing, smooth handwriting.

Billy,

I need you, something horrible has happened.

Come at once.

Barbara

*****

Nearby in the gym, the stout, Cro-Magnon-browed Cassidy watched two lightweights spar in the main ring. The aroma of sweat, not lilacs, hung in the air, and Billy heard the manager yell at one of the boxers, "Keep your left up for Chrissakes! He'll take your bleedin' head off."

Next to Billy, the messenger boy stood silently, waiting for a response and maybe a tip.

Carefully, the mucker folded the note and palmed it.

"Any answer?" the boy asked.

The mucker shook his head, and found a dime for the boy, who left, but not in a rush, mesmerized as he was by being this close to real live fighters.

Standing there, watching but not seeing the lightweights spar, Billy felt his insides roiling like dark storm clouds as he tried to figure out a way to ignore Barbara's summons. It had taken every ounce of strength he had to walk out the door yesterday. To return a day later, into that world where he knew he did not belong, that would be harder than any bout Cassidy could wrangle for him. He knew he had no place in the Hardings' mansion, and he knew Barbara was better off with someone of her own station, like William Mallory...but God how he loved her. If he walked back in, could he find the strength to walk out again?

Billy changed into his suit and tie—not fancy enough for a visit to a millionaire, but they would have to do—and, coming out of the locker room, he almost ran into Professor Cassidy.

"You gonna be gone long?" the manager asked.

"Who said I was leaving?"

"If I couldn't read that mug of yours like a map, I'd be a poor damn manager indeed. How long, son?"

"I don't know."

"Is it the skirt?"

Billy nodded.

"We'll be here when you get back," Cassidy said, and strolled away toward the sparring ring.

Turning, Billy went out and grabbed a spot on one of the trolley cars. Cassidy's gym was not far from the Battery, and the ride gave Billy time to think as the trolley clanked and rattled northward.

She was there, as she always was, in his mind's eye—her auburn hair pinned up, leaving her high-cheekboned face and large green eyes uncovered. This look allowed people to meet her as she met the world - head on. Barbara was impetuous, strong, brave, and she had saved Billy's life. Maybe she hadn't taken a bullet or a blade for him; but she had saved him, nonetheless.

Teaching Billy that the straight life was not a cowardly road to travel, she had won him over; and along the way she had shown him how to speak and act and carry himself like a gentleman, as well. Billy found himself wanting to be a better man just to please her. Even his mucker's mind could perceive that this was a transformation little short of miraculous, though for him that transformation had turned out to be far easier than he might ever have imagined.

A man might act a right sissy for the love of a good woman, and Barbara was a good woman, all right. But Billy knew in his mind, if not his heart, that she was not for him. Wealthy, from a good family, a genteel woman, Barbara Harding deserved better than a hard-scrabble slum tough, no matter how much he may have changed.

Riding that trolley back to the mansion of her father—the wealthy, well-born Anthony Harding—Billy did his best not to read disaster into that tucked-away note. But how could he not?

"Something horrible has happened."

What could that be? What could be so bad that she would summon him so soon after he had thrust her into the arms of another man?

Billy hopped off the trolley car and briskly walked the last few blocks. Even from a distance, in this incredibly swank neighborhood, the Harding manse stood out as a monument to wealth and breeding. A multi-millionaire who was no doubt overjoyed that the mucker was finally out of his daughter's life, Harding would not likely be pleased to see who was about to come calling....

On this beautiful Saturday afternoon, the swells who lived in these posh digs were out taking the air as Billy passed. Some looked down their noses at the mucker, whose clothes, though nicer than anything he had ever owned, were a far cry from the day coats of the gentlemen strolling the avenue next to ladies in fine frocks. A few nasty glances, with the rest ignoring him, only emphasized how out of place Billy was in these airy environs.

As he strolled the last block, Billy saw something across the street that put a prickle on the back of his neck. Ducking behind the ornate stairway two doors down from the Hardings', Billy was free to gaze, and having done so was glad he had followed his instincts.

On the opposite side of the avenue, hidden in the shadows of a stairway himself, a man could be made out, well, not a man—a boy really, dressed not that different from himself. The boy's eyes were glued to the Hardings' front door. Whatever problem had prompted Barbara to send for Billy, he felt certain that the lookout across the street was part of it.

Billy doubled back to the corner and came around to the mansion's rear, keeping his eyes peeled for compatriots of the lookout; but he saw no one. Coming up to the servants' door in the back, reversing the very route he had used to quit the Harding house yesterday, Billy wondered if maybe he should just kick the door in and go in, fists up.

Picking the lock and going in quietly was not in Billy's bag of tricks, after all. But considering there was a lookout across the street, and that Barbara had been able to get a note out, he figured the danger inside the house itself was probably minimal, at least for now. He chose to knock—politely.

Smith, Mr. Harding's gentleman's gentleman, opened the door a sliver. A thin, severe man with mutton chops and a seemingly perpetual scowl, Smith stepped aside and let Billy in, saying with a sniff, "Miss Harding and her father are expecting you...in the drawing room, *sir*."

Why did those who attended the rich have even more snobbish an attitude than the rich themselves? This a boy of the slums would never understand.

The back entryway, a mere vestibule, led into the kitchen near the servants' quarters and the rear stairwell the help used. The shadowy little space held the afterglow aroma of a hearty breakfast. Billy felt, and heard, his stomach growl.

"Through here," Smith said, leading the way into the

kitchen.

One maid, a blonde, sat at the table, polishing silver. Another, a brunette, stood over a sink plucking feathers from a chicken. The walls hid behind massive wooden cabinets, their doors made of glass, revealing opulent plates, cups, and silver.

Smith marched him through the ornate dining room with its fancy chandeliers, oaken table and chairs with padded brocade-upholstered seats. Huge landscape paintings lined the oak-paneled walls. While a dining room, this seemed a man's chamber, the colors deep and dark, the wood of the highest quality. Cigar smell hung in the air. This room, this house, belonged to a very successful, important man, and Anthony Harding was certainly that.

Finally, after a walk that rivaled the jaunt from the trolley stop, Billy found himself at the front entrance way. Here the servant led him across the marble-floored foyer, passing the wide carpeted staircase, finally stopping at the doorway to the parlor.

At the edge of that doorway, Smith announced, "Mr. Byrne," with all the joy of a judge handing down a verdict.

As the butler stepped aside, Billy entered the room to find Mr. Harding standing across the room near the fireplace, his face a mask of dismay. Seated in a velvet-covered chair, her eyes red from crying, a hanky clinched in her fist, Barbara looked up as Billy entered the room. She looked pale and her countenance had not worn such alarm since they were being chased by headhunters.

Rising, she rushed into Billy's arms, pressing hard against him, the scent of her filling his nostrils and for a second, he thought he might come completely apart, like a china figurine flung on a hardwood floor.

Then, remembering where he was, Billy glanced over

to see that Mr. Harding had discreetly turned to poke at the burnt-out ashes of last night's fire rather than see the impropriety of their embrace. Though a quite proper man, Harding knew how his daughter felt about the mucker, and as long as this was as far as things went, he would indulge her. She was, however, engaged to another, and that must never be forgotten.

Pulling away from the woman he loved, Billy saw tears running anew down her cheeks. "Here, here—what's all this, then?"

Barbara dabbed at moist eyes. "It's the *other* Billy—he's been kidnapped."

Sharing a first name with one William Mallory wasn't the only way the two were joined. They were also in love with the same woman. Mallory, however, was of her station, Billy decidedly not.

His hands found her shoulders supportively. "What happened?"

Looking to her father, who said nothing, Barbara explained. "After you left me yesterday, after you called Billy to come back, and told him that I loved him, wanted to marry him..."

The more she went over these painful recent memories, the more he realized how deeply he had hurt her. He was not much for reading people, especially the wealthy, but Barbara he knew. She loved him, she had said so, and meant it; still, he felt she needed to be with someone who held a position in society—the "other Billy," William Mallory, fit the bill.

"...he came over. We discussed it. We even set a date."

Despite his having been the one who quit her, Billy felt hurt that she had fallen back in with Mallory so quickly. They had set a date *already?*

Obviously anxious to move this along, silver-haired Anthony Harding stepped forward. His words were matter of fact and clipped, but his eyes punctuated them with fear and concern.

"After he left here," Harding said, "Mallory was taken. Abducted."

"You *saw* it?" Billy asked.

Harding shook his head as he withdrew a piece of paper from his pocket—a note not that different from the one from Barbara.

Billy accepted the paper from Harding and read: *We have Mallory. You will pay us $500,000. If you involve the law, Mallory dies.*

The young lookout across the street became immediately clear to Billy. If just one copper stopped at the Harding house, the lookout's gang would sure as sin croak "Billy" Mallory.

"Why you?" Billy asked.

"Pardon?"

"Not why not abduct you instead, sir, but...why are you the person to whom that note was given?"

"I would suppose that it's because we have far more money, even more than Mallory's own family. Also, I'm sure given the impending nuptials, that makes us easy, tempting prey."

"Sir, who even knew about Barbara and Mallory getting back together? It's only been one day."

Harding harumphed. "I suppose I had something to do with that. As soon as the decision was made, I sent telegrams to all the newspapers in the city. I wanted to make sure the announcement was in the next edition."

Billy understood, and in a way did not blame the man. Anything that broke Barbara from a mucker like him had to be cause for celebration for her father.

"So," Billy went on, "one of the messenger boys, or somebody at one of the papers, decided to grab Mallory and hold him for ransom."

"Yes, or let the information slip to an underworld associate," Harding said.

Leaning close again, Barbara said, with a terrible tentativeness, "I was hoping you could do something."

Billy's eyes met hers. "Something like...get him back?"

Hanging her head, Barbara nodded.

"My instinct is to refuse," Billy said.

The girl looked up at him wide-eyed.

"This isn't my city, and I don't know enough guys on that side of the law to find Mallory before whoever has him does away with him. If it was Chicago, I might have a shot, and even then, only maybe."

Dabbing at her eyes with the hanky again, Barbara said, "So, then...you *won't* help us?"

Billy gave her a small grin, just a little ghost of what had been between them. "You taught me not to always follow my instincts. Anyway, this is different. Whoever took him provided us with a potential stool pigeon. So we may have a chance."

"A stool pigeon?" Harding asked, frowning.

"Someone to spill the beans."

"What?"

"To tell us exactly where Mallory is."

Baffled, Harding asked, "And who would that be?"

Billy said, "The lookout they posted across the street to keep an eye on your house."

Harding's eyes widened and he took a step toward the lace curtains that covered the window.

Billy's voice had a sharp edge. "Don't do that, sir! Not if you want us to maintain an advantage."

Stopping in mid-step, Harding nodded that he understood.

Looking at Barbara, Billy said, "Now, here's what we're going to do. I'll leave by the same back door I came in. Give me two minutes to get in place, then telephone the police."

"But they said not to involve the law," Barbara said, her voice desperate. "They'll *kill* Billy."

"No," the mucker said.

"How can you know that?" the girl asked.

But it was Harding who answered: "Because when the police arrive, and the lookout takes off, Mr. Byrne here will follow him."

Hysteria lurked in her eyes as she said to Billy, "What if you lose him, or the lookout gets there too far ahead of you?"

Again Billy took her by the shoulders. "Steady, girl. Have I ever let you down before?"

Numbly, the young woman shook her head.

"And I won't start now."

Stepping forward, Harding removed a revolver from his coat pocket. "I know you can handle yourself, young man... but you had best take this."

"I'm better with my fists," Billy said.

Harding's smile seemed genuine. "That might be true... but I've seen you fight with firearms. Take it."

Accepting the pistol and slipping it into a pocket, Billy nodded his thanks.

Clearing his throat, Mr. Harding said, "I had better go coordinate with Smith to make sure everyone knows his role."

With that, Barbara's father left the room. As soon as they were alone, she melted into Billy's arms. In spite of his best intentions, he drew her closer.

"You know I'll never be able to repay you for this, Billy."

Holding her away from him, he grinned down at her. "Well, you could. But we can't let that happen, can we?"

That brought a wan smile to her lips. "Before you go, let me ask you one small question...."

He wanted to say no, but this was Barbara, and he knew he could not refuse her.

"Ask it, then," he said, his voice thick with emotion.

"When you came yesterday...your call to William, getting the, the *other* Billy and me to get back together...how could it be so...so *easy* for you to give me up?"

His laugh had a roughness. "Easy?" he asked.

She just stared at him. Waiting.

"Leaving you for Mallory was the hardest thing I ever done," Billy said. "And the only thing close to as hard was comin' back here today."

She smiled her own small, ghostly smile.

"Then you *do* love me," she said, not a question.

He turned away.

"You *love* me! So why don't you want to *be* with me?" Swallowing, he said, "We ain't from the same world, sweetheart. It's a lot farther from Grand Avenue to Riverside Drive than either of us ever imagined."

She bowed her head. She knew, she had to know, there was truth in his words.

"Besides, Barbara, there's things you don't know about me."

"I know everything about you."

"No. You don't. I'm a wanted man."

That got her attention. "Wanted for what?"

He shook his head. "Maybe someday, when it's behind me, I'll tell you...but for now, trust me. You don't want to know. But this you *should* know: I ain't no good for you."

Mr. Harding reappeared in the doorway. "We're ready," he said.

With one last glance at the woman he loved—would he ever see her again?—Billy turned toward Mr. Harding. "I'll be on my way, sir. Luck to us all."

He retraced his steps through the house, Barbara trailing him, but his emotions were too full for him to speak, or even look at her. He went out through the servants' entrance, her voice echoing as he shut the door. "*Be careful, Billy. Be careful!*"

Once outside and away from the Harding mansion, Billy took three quick breaths, let them out, then walked quickly back to the corner of Riverside Drive. Before ducking back behind the brick pillar holding up a wrought-iron fence, Billy caught a glimpse of the lookout still holding down his spot, smoking a cigarette now—he really was just a teenaged kid. A boy headed down the wrong path, just as he had once been....

Waiting, Billy wondered which way the lookout would break. This would be easier if Billy knew the city better. In Chicago, he could follow a gnat across the city and never lose the damn thing. Here, Billy was a lot less confident, but Barbara was depending on him and that made all the difference. His belly had the same glowing heat a good shot of whisky used to give him in the old days.

Even if they were never together, just knowing that a perfect creature like Barbara Harding could love a mucker like him, well...it gave him hope. He would not fail her.

Before long, the neighborhood beat cop came along and Billy slipped back around the corner. Once the copper was past and headed for the Hardings', Billy went back to waiting.

The lookout, to his credit, was a cool customer. He

did not rabbit when the officer went up the stairs and rang the bell. The kid somehow managed to stay put even when Smith opened the door and spoke to the officer. It was only when the copper went inside and was behind a closed door before the young lookout skedaddled. To Billy's good fortune, the kid came in his direction, though across the way.

Billy followed the lookout south on Riverside Drive, keeping the street between them, until the kid cut east on 72nd. Billy crossed Riverside and followed the boy, lagging back enough to not arouse suspicion. When the kid hopped a trolley south at Broadway, Billy jumped on the step at the back.

The lookout appeared nervous as he found a seat, pulled off his cap, and mopped his brow. His eyes darted around the trolley and the passing neighborhood, but he did not take in anything to make him jumpier, especially with Billy appearing interested only in the passing architecture.

Billy figured that as long as the kid stayed on the trolley, his job would be easier. He kept his gaze off the lookout, who seemed to calm as the trolley clattered south; instead Billy just glanced over from time to time to make sure the kid was still in his seat.

At 23rd, the lookout jumped off and cut west. The afternoon sun was low in the sky and Billy knew he might have to stay closer than he'd like to make sure he didn't lose the lookout in the coming darkness.

They went west all the way to the Hudson and the Chelsea Piers. As the kid ducked in and out between crates that were in the process of getting loaded onto ships, Billy was stunned to look up at the liner he had heard of but never seen—the *Mauretania*—and stunned as well by the sheer size of the British passenger liner. A four-stacker, the *Mauretania* was larger than any vessel Billy had ever seen in his life, and for that matter most buildings. For a moment, the mucker allowed his attention to waver, and when he looked back, the lookout had been swallowed by darkness.

Cursing himself, Billy hurried ahead, trying not to make any noise or draw any attention as he scoured the dock area. Panicked, Billy looked back and forth as his speed increased. Evening was settling over the city, cool and indifferent to his plight, and the lookout was nowhere to be seen.

Then, coming to the end of the warehouse, Billy heard someone yell, "Hey, *you...kid!* You ain't supposed to be here!"

As Billy rounded the corner, he saw the lookout being held by a dock worker. Even though the boy was kicking and biting, he was making no progress in breaking the grip of the towering dock worker, a man even bigger than the mucker.

Slowing down, making like he was out of breath, Billy approached the struggling pair.

The kid was yelling now, "Let me go, you big lummox! If you don't let me go, I'll croak ya."

The dock worker chuckled until he saw the mucker coming, then his face turned serious. "This wharf rat your'n?"

Billy shook his head and smiled, blew out a couple of breaths like he had been running all night. "Naw, I been chasin' him for a good long while, though."

"You a cop?" the dockworker asked.

Palming Barbara's note, Billy flashed it like a badge and when the man looked in that direction, Billy cold-cocked him with an overhand left. The dockworker went down, taking the kid with him, the two of them hitting the ground, the man out cold, the kid rolling away.

Before the boy could regain his feet and run off, Billy grabbed him by the scruff of the neck and pulled him up to eye level. The kid reared to kick him in the groin, but this was not Billy's first alley fight. He turned and took the blow off his hip, then spun the kid face first into a crate.

Billy let go and the kid sagged to the ground, cut, bleeding, and covering a broken nose.

"Where they holdin' Mallory?" Billy asked.

The boy sat sullenly rubbing the various broken parts of his face.

Billy waited, and when he got tired of that, he grabbed the boy and picked him up to eye level again, then repeated his question.

"Geez, I can't tell ya. They'll kill me!"

Billy dropped the kid to the ground. When the boy tried to stand, he could only plop into a sitting position, where the mucker towered over him. Billy took out Mr. Harding's revolver and let the kid get a good look down the endless black beyond its snout. "Or you could *not* tell me, and *I'll* kill *you.*"

The kid said nothing. The tough little bastard reminded Billy of himself. Then the mucker drew back the revolver's hammer until it clicked, such a small sound, such a loud sound....

The kid went white and his eyes bugged. "You *can't,*" the young man pleaded. "I'm just a *kid!*"

"And you've seen how many kids die in your time, boyo?"

"Please...please...."

Changing tack and his tone slightly, Billy asked, "What's your name, son?"

"John. John Diamond."

"Do they call you 'Jack'?"

He shook his head. "They call me 'Legs.'"

"'Cause you can run."

"'Cause I can run."

"Just not fast enough. Legs, my lad, look into my eyes and tell me if you see anything there to convince you I won't shoot you when I count three...if'n you ain't told me where Mr. Mallory is."

The kid didn't cry, but tears brimmed at the edges of his eyes.

"*One.*"

Billy could see the kid was trembling now.

"*Two.*"

The boy hung his head.

Damn. Would this kid call his bluff?

"*Thr...*"

"At the far end of the warehouse!" the kid blurted. "The back end. Nobody goes in that way. Well, almost nobody."

Billy wondered if he really would have shot the kid at the count of three. He was glad he hadn't had to find out. "Who's holding him?"

"Jake Orgen's gang."

The mucker had heard of them. "The Little Augies?"

"Yeah."

"How many?"

"Four, maybe five."

"Orgen hisself in there?"

The kid shook his head. "He don't like bein' around the blood-and-thunder stuff. He's the brains."

Billy thought that over. Then he looked into a young face drawn with despair and said, "Don't go thinkin' you're a stoolie, Legs. Not unless they gave you so much dough you feel beholden."

"A whole buck. That's good money."

"Not dying-over money."

"No. Not that." The kid sniffed and hung his head.

Billy squatted next to the boy. "Look, it ain't my place to tell you whether to hang with these lowlifes or not."

The kid looked confused.

"But you done good. You held out when most others woulda long since caved."

"But...but I ratted."

"You didn't owe them nothing."

"But I *ratted.*"

Well, he'd tried. Rising, Billy said, "You get your ass home. I see you followin' me, I will drill you between the damn eyes."

The kid nodded, frowning, because the mucker's tone hadn't been as strong as his words.

"Those guys in there?" Billy nodded toward his goal. "They ain't never gonna know from me that it was you told me where to find them. Far as they know—in the unlikely event any of 'em live through me comin' to call—I just tracked 'em down my own self."

"Why you protectin' me, mister?"

"Let's just say once upon a time, I stood where you do now. I coulda been good, but I chose to be bad."

The kid didn't seem to understand.

"Look where it got me. I'm on the docks in the middle of a beautiful Saturday night pointin' a pistol at a kid and gettin' ready to go free a man who thinks the world would be a better place if your buddies were to fill me full of lead."

The kid seemed confused, and why shouldn't he? Young Legs Diamond had had his bell rung pretty good, including a broken damn nose, and Billy knew this little wise guy would eventually do whatever he felt like, anyway.

"So they call you 'Legs' 'case you're so damn fast?"

"I am good and damn fast, mister."

Billy let him see the gun again. "Show me."

The kid got off and ran like hell back toward the city.

Making his way down the long wall of the warehouse, night surrounding him now, water lapping at the pier, Billy actually felt at home. This river rat's paradise certainly was no place for Barbara Harding; but the mucker felt like he had just come home from some nameless war, ready to do combat again.

At last, he came to a dingy window. He had to stand on his toes to see in, and the dirty glass made it hard to see. But there in plain view, under one naked light bulb hanging like the condemned from a scaffold, sat William Mallory—still in his fifty-dollar suit, bound tightly to a straight-back wooden chair. Five feet away, four guys sat around a table playing cards. Even through the filth, Billy could see the guns on the table amid the money and cards.

As Billy headed to the back, he could hear shoes scraping just around the corner. Peeking, he saw a lookout lumbering toward him, a lookout who was no damn kid. The mucker waited and, when the big oaf got to the corner, doubled him over with a right, then knocked him cold with a rabbit punch left. The guy went down like a sack of wheat and, after a kick in the head, was just as motionless.

Billy stepped over him and stood before the door, gun in hand. If he could do just this one thing, and do it right, he could give Barbara a shot at happiness in that foreign world she was accustomed to....

He took a long, deep breath, blew it out, and kicked the door open. The guy on the far side of the table rose first and for that won the prize of a red-as-lipstick kiss-pucker bullet hole in the chest, falling over backward, fingers never finding the gun on the table. The goon to the fallen guy's left did manage to grab his gun, but that was all, a bullet tearing into his gut and sitting him down, on the floor not his chair; then he sprawled and twitched and bled and worked on dying. The kidnapper with his back to the door rolled out of his chair to the right, a bullet kicking up cement from the floor as he slipped behind a crate, gun in hand.

This all gave one other thug time to rise, seize his pistol, and fire a round that clipped Billy's shoulder, tearing more material than skin.

Billy swiveled and fired a round that gouged a hole in a wooden beam as the goon slipped behind it.

Two down, two to go...and only two bullets left.

Deuces were wild in this game, it seemed.

The one behind the crate was up now, grinning in a face dirty with a several day-old beard, his gun pressed to the temple of the trussed-up William Mallory.

"Drop yer gun, laddiebuck, or the swell gets it in his noodle!"

Billy had come so close. Now, he had one to his left and one to his right...and the latter had a gun to Mallory's head.

He was glad the wild-eyed, squirming Mallory was gagged—whatever the man had to say, Billy didn't want to hear it. Other than looking like an unmade bed, the gent appeared to be otherwise unharmed. Billy hoped to keep it that way, but was unsure about how. Just getting out alive his own damn self was looking dicey....

"I told you to *drop* it, boyo!"

Billy let his weight sag and let his aim drop from the man holding the gun to Mallory's head.

"All right," Billy said, sounding defeated. It wasn't hard to act that part. "All right...."

Billy started to squat as if to lay the gun carefully on the floor.

The thug at Mallory's left grinned wider.

As the weapon reached his waist, Billy brought the barrel up slightly, then fired. The bullet hit the goon in one eye, leaving surprise in the other, as the gunman slumped dead to cement and the bound Mallory just sat there.

Even before the smoke had cleared, Billy rolled left as the remaining goon fired a shot past him.

The one thing Billy hadn't counted on was that gut-shot goon finding the strength to rejoin the fight. Billy practically rolled right into him as the gut-shot man pulled the trigger. Something hot burned as it slipped past Billy's right side, carving flesh. The two men rolled together now, and Billy used his last shot to give the guy a second shot to the gut. This one killed the bastard, but the remaining goon got off two more shots, each just barely missing Billy.

Grabbing the dead man's pistol, Billy turned and fired twice, the first shot parting the man's hair, the second punching a hole damn-near dead center in his forehead. That was the shot that dropped him dead to the cement.

Rushing to Mallory, Billy pulled off the man's gag and started cutting the ropes with his jackknife.

"Byrne," Mallory gasped. "Where the hell did *you* come from?"

"Chicago originally," Billy said coolly. "Thought you knew that."

Mallory shook his head, dazed, shaken.

Billy asked, "Can you walk?"

"I'm fine," Mallory said, nodding. "I'm fine. A little roughed up, but shipshape."

Billy severed the last of the man's bindings. "Then we need to get out of here. Orgen may be coming to finish you off, once he realizes there's no being ransom paid. Or the coppers will show 'cause of the gunfight. Either way, it would be better if we weren't around."

"Agreed," Mallory said. "But you're bleeding, man! Your shoulder, your side...."

Billy shook his head. "These are nothin'. Now, move!"

Once they were well clear of the Chelsea Piers, the two men finally slowed to a walk.

On a darkened street, with no one else in sight, the night growing a little chilly, Mallory put his hand on Billy's sleeve and stopped him.

"Look," Mallory said. "Uh...what can I say but 'thank you?'"

Billy couldn't look at the man. "I didn't do it for you."

"I know. You did it for her."

They walked on, slowly now.

"Why?" Mallory said.

"You got it right the first time."

"No, I mean—why did you telephone me? And send me to her?"

Stopping, Billy made himself look into the man's eyes. "Same answer."

Mallory nodded slowly. "Okay. Just so you know—I won't let you down. By not letting *her* down. Understood?"

"Understood. 'Cause if you don't do right by her? What I gave those goons back there won't be nothin' compared to the medicine you take from me."

"That thought doesn't scare me as much as the thought of letting her down."

Billy smiled, just a little. "We have that much in common."

They walked in silence for almost a block.

Finally, Billy said, "Find the nearest police station. Tell

them what happened. Tell them some hardcase did all that back there at the piers, and you have no idea who the hell it was. Musta been some rival gang. Do you get me?"

"I get you. You were never there."

"I knew you were smarter than you look."

"Where will you go? What should I tell Barbara?"

"I have something to take care of back home," Billy said. He handed Harding's pistol over to Mallory. "Tell Barbara to tell her father thanks for use of the hog leg. I'm just sorry I couldn't clean it and reload it before returning it."

Mallory stared at Billy. "Byrne, you are an odd man. I don't think I will ever know what to make of you."

Billy shrugged. "Haven't you figured me yet? I'm just a mucker."

And they went their separate ways.

EAST SIDE, WEST SIDE

The tuxedo fit well, but Mickey Ashford still felt like he'd strapped himself into a strait jacket. A slender man, rather like a taller, unmustached William Powell, Ashford would have preferred something more casual. Dinner at Twenty-One meant dressing to the nines; but at least he'd have the soft muted sounds of a jazz combo in the background, and could savor a martini while he suffocated inside this penguin suit. Though two and a half years had passed since the repeal of the Volstead Act, Mickey still felt the urge to genuflect every time a martini glass touched his lips.

Across the table, her own drink still untouched, Mary-Anne Wallace, his fiancé of seven months -- blonde, twenty-nine, her slender, yet buxom, figure sheathed in a glittery white evening gown -- managed to maintain an almost schoolgirl giddiness that made Mickey grin.

"I can't believe that this time tomorrow night," she said, sotto voce, "we'll finally be married," as if speaking the words too loudly might jinx their wedding. Half of his native Chicago, and half of her native Iowa, and many of their mutual East Coast show business friends, were even now converging on Manhattan by train, bus, auto and even air, for fancy doings in a Waldorf-Astoria ballroom.

"And the day after that," MaryAnne was saying, "we'll be honeymooning aboard the Queen Mary, on our way to England."

The quiet conversations of the other well-dressed diners fluttered around them like cooing birds, but Mickey heard MaryAnne just fine. "What was that about 'finally' married?"

Her rouged lips paused in a brief kiss before they split into a wide smile. "I've wanted to be Mrs. Michael Ashford since the moment we met."

Mickey beamed at her. No matter how long they were together, no matter how many times he gazed at her, her beauty stole his breath away. Nor was he the only man to react in such a manner. Having seen perhaps one too many Ruby Keeler talkies, MaryAnne had left her parents' farm five years ago to find fame and fortune on the Great White Way, and though she hadn't yet landed a starring role, several producers had noticed her heart-shaped face, deep jade eyes, elegant nose, and full, ruby-rouged lips -- not to mention her trim, well-rounded figure -- and she'd already made a name for herself in secondary ingenue roles.

"You wanted to marry me how long?" he asked.

"Since the moment we met."

He stuck out his fine Irish chin and flashed what he'd been told were piercing blue eyes, hoping she'd ignore his thrice-broken nose. "Is it my dashing good looks?"

Her smile revealed straight white teeth, worthy of a tooth powder advert. MaryAnne shook her head, dark blond hair shimmering; she wore it longer than was fashionable, almost brushing her bare shoulders.

"It must have been my piano playing." Mickey had worked his way through college, playing with jazz combos, and had even made a few recordings with the Staccato Seven. The night they'd met, in a Rush Street joint, he'd been sitting in, for old times' sake.

"Well you are a wonderful piano player, but...no. I make it a point to stay away from show business romances."

"So that worked against me, if anything."

"That's right."

"So it was my dashing good looks, then."

"No, silly..." She arched an eyebrow. "Don't you know it's your money I'm after?"

"You didn't know I had money when we first met," Mickey said, and took a drag from his cigarette and pretended to pout a little, even as the giggle erupted across the table.

Patting his hand as it hovered over the edge of the ashtray, she said, "You really are quite a good detective, aren't you, dear?"

Mickey Ashford was indeed a "good" detective; more to the point, he was a successful businessman. The Ashford Detective Agency had grown from a one-man operation nine years ago into a fifty-operative affair headquartered in Chicago's Rookery. Pinkerton and Hargraves -- his major competitors -- had even been sniffing around, about wanting to buy Mickey out. So far he'd resisted their advances, but the amounts of money they discussed had definitely gotten his attention. He wondered if thirty-eight was too young to retire.

Knocking back the rest of his drink, Mickey glanced at the Rob Roy at MaryAnne's elbow. "Care for another, darling?"

"Before dinner?" she asked, mock shocked. "Are you trying to get me tight, Mr. Ashford? Can't you wait one more night?"

"Now look who's playing detective."

She smiled again, this time keeping her teeth to herself, a self-satisfied, wicked cat-that-ate-the-canary smirk.

"I can't believe that after you've known me this long," he said, as he discreetly signaled the waiter to bring another round, "you have so little trust."

"That's precisely why I don't trust you. I've known you long enough to learn how you think."

The waiter brought their drinks and MaryAnne managed to ignore both of hers as Mickey gulped most of his martini, the old glass not yet removed from the table. Before the waiter could exit, Mickey signaled for one more martini.

"You better watch that," MaryAnne said, "or you won't be any good to me later."

With some effort, he lifted an eyebrow. "Later?"

"In your room, of course."

"You're coming to my room?"

"If you're a good boy and don't drink yourself silly, I just might."

It was his turn to smirk. "Any other reason?"

"To make sure you're not trying to sow any wild oats before you march down the aisle. I've seen you turning your private eye on my maid of honor."

"Some maid of honor." Mickey affected a pained expression. "At least she won't be trying to get away with wearing a white dress."

She laughed, once. "Oh, so we're going to hit below the belt now, are we?"

"With any luck."

The teasing was a game they'd been playing for some time now. But the intimacy to which they both referred was recent. When they met, they'd both been around the block and back again; neither had been anxious to repeat past mistakes. They had decided not to fall into bed with each other, even though they both longed to do just that. Instead they took it slow, got to know each other, becoming friends before lovers; and they had stuck to their vow.

At least they had until that night a month ago in Mickey's Chicago apartment....

After dinner and a movie at the Biograph, the pair had retired to his flat for a nightcap before he escorted MaryAnne home. Mickey's place occupied half of the top floor of a six-story building at the corner of Addison and North Broadway, with a spectacular view of Lake Michigan, and scads of art moderne furnishings and knickknacks that Mickey never seemed to remember exactly how he had acquired. Behind the sofa, one tall silver lamp kept the room from being enveloped in darkness.

Two drinks into their nightcap, the couple found themselves on the couch in a clinch. His lips pressed hard against hers, his hands roaming over her evening gown, her arms wrapping around his neck, her fingers gliding through his thick hair, as they pressed against each other, their need growing.

Pulling away, her voice husky in the moment, she said, "We should slow down..."

His answer was to pull her closer and kiss her neck, his lips sliding down to her exposed shoulder.

Again she eased away from him, this time putting her hands against his shoulders, holding him off as she spoke. "Mickey, Mickey, we've got to stop."

He pulled back from her, brushed his hair back with a hand. "Do you really want to?"

MaryAnne's head drooped. "No, of course not...but we promised ourselves."

"That was before we knew how we really felt -- before

we decided to get married."

"I know," she said, her voice tiny now.

"Are you planning to have second thoughts about us?"

"No -- certainly not!"

"Then why..." He nuzzled the nape of her neck. "...why should we have any second thoughts, now...."

Mickey kissed her mouth, gently, then, as she yielded, more urgently. She returned the kiss and didn't fight when he gently eased the spaghetti straps of her gown over her ivory shoulders.

"My God," he whispered as he exposed her creamy breasts, nipples pink and perked, "you are so lovely."

MaryAnne pulled his face to her, but he needed no coaxing as he buried his face in her breasts, sucking first one hard nipple, then the other. She moaned and pulled gently at his hair as his tongue worked against the tiny bud.

Clothes went flying as they gave in to each other. Though she was nude in a matter of seconds, Mickey had more hoops to jump through to join her and she tried to assist him.

"My Lord, you've got more layers than an onion," she said, a wicked smile playing at the corner of her mouth.

"Just pull the damn socks off, will you?"

One at a time, laughing as she jerked on the toes of his black silk stockings, she got him free and they collapsed onto the couch in each other's arms.

She smiled at him, held his face in her hands. "Maybe you're right -- it is time."

"If we've come this far," he said, "it had better be."

Mickey eased her onto her back and slid to the floor as he kissed her breasts, stomach, thighs, and MaryAnne mounted him, moaning with pleasure as he filled her. The couple moved slowly at first, adjusting to each other as their passion swept them away. Mickey groaned as Mary-Anne's nails dug into his back; soon she let out a long, low gasp of pleasure as they each reached their climax....

Mickey, lost in his reverie in the midst of the busy nitery, snapped out of it when MaryAnne reached across the table and took his hand.

"Are you all right? You looked like you left me there, for a moment."

He grinned sheepishly. "Sorry, dear -- I assure you, I was with you...just remembering that night in Chicago."

She arched an eyebrow. "Which night would that be?"

Frowning at her fondly, he said, "I think you know what night."

"Aah, the night I seduced you."

"The night you seduced me?" he asked, surprise in his voice. "Don't you mean the night you finally succumbed to my charm?"

The waiter interrupted their repartee by bringing dinner. As they began to eat, MaryAnne looked into Mickey's eyes, and said, "It's a good thing they brought your food, dear. I think you must be a little tipsy."

"Me tipsy? I never get tipsy -- roaring drunk, possibly. Never tipsy."

"Roaring drunk, then -- which you'd have to be, if you think the likes of you could seduce me. Your memory, were it not pickled at this very moment, would be of me seducing you."

"Of course you're right, my dear. Can you possibly forgive me?" He held up his martini glass in toast to her.

"Now you're patronizing me."

"Oh, am I?"

She waggled her fork at him, a scolding schoolmarm, if an enticing one. "Finish your dinner, Mickey Ashford. I'm going to take you back to the hotel and show you exactly what happened in Chicago."

His eyes met hers, saw the intent, and raised his hand for the waiter. "Check, please."

Twenty minutes later, they found themselves on a couch even nicer than the one in Mickey's apartment. The Waldorf-Astoria prided itself on its appointments and management probably wouldn't have approved of what the sofa in room 1725 was being used for at this particular moment.

MaryAnne was astride him, full breasts swaying, as she rode him harder and faster, her beautiful face drunk not with alcohol but abandon. With each passing second their passion grew until they exploded together, and this time he cried out, in wonderful agony, then together they slumped in a heap on the sofa.

"Okay, okay," he managed between long gasps, "you seduced me. You were right, I was wrong."

"And don't you forget it," she said, tousling his hair, then bending in to kiss his cheek.

"Still...and I hate to be a, uh, stickler...."

"Do you, now?"

"But this was not precisely the way things went the first time."

"Are you saying I...we...need to try again?"

An eyebrow raised.

She slapped playfully at his chest. "Michael Ashford, you are incorrigible....Shouldn't we leave something for our honeymoon?"

"Is there something left?"

Pulling away, dodging the question, she said, "I have to go make sure Mae has checked into her room, and besides, it's supposed to be bad luck for you to see me before the wedding."

"Too late," he said, tapping her on the dimpled backside as she bent to pick up her clothes.

"If you'll look at the clock instead of me, you'd see it's still not quite midnight. Not the day of our wedding, at all."

"Have it your way. Call the desk and then I'll walk you to your room."

Ten minutes later they were both dressed and MaryAnne was hanging up the telephone, her expression confused. Mickey asked, "What's the matter?"

"It's Mae," MaryAnne said referring to her maid of honor, singer/actress Mae West. "She's checked in, but she's not answering her telephone."

Shrugging, Mickey asked, "So? You know Mae. Christ, she could be sleeping or bombed, or out on the town for all we know."

MaryAnne's forehead tightened. "It's not like her to not let me know. She's well-aware we'd want to know she arrived safely. I thought she'd at least leave a note."

"You want me to do something, don't you?"

MaryAnne brightened. "Would you?"

He shook his head, laughed a little. "Okay, I'll go to her room and knock on the door. You call the desk back and see if they have any messages for us. Now, what's her room number?"

She told him and Mickey slipped his shoes on and headed down the hall to the elevators. The hotel was quiet at this hour, and Mickey had the lift to himself as he rode up to the twenty-sixth floor where Mae's suite was located. Wandering down the hall, he couldn't tell if he smelled a hint of Mae's perfume or if that was just wishful thinking on his part.

He wouldn't have traded MaryAnne for Mae West, of course, nor would he betray his sweetheart, his bride-to-be...but he was human, and the petite yet voluptuous singer was one of the most sexually charged women he'd ever met. She radiated sex -- and trouble. After all, she'd been the girlfriend of top gangster Owney Madden, at least till New York's answer to Capone recently got sent up. Stopping in front of her door, Mickey tilted his head and listened. He noticed no light under the door and he knocked three times before giving up. The singer didn't seem to be in her room and Mickey had no idea where to look for her. The clock had edged past midnight when he returned to his room.

MaryAnne practically jerked the door out of his hand, the key he had just twisted in the lock slipping through his fingers.

"Any sign of her?"

He shook his head.

"I'm getting worried, Mickey. She should have been here by now."

"I take it there were no messages?"

"No."

"I'll walk you back to your room, then I'll go down and talk to the desk clerk myself."

"I should stay here. At least until you get back."

"I thought it was bad luck for me to see you on our wedding day."

She gave him a wan smile. "It already is our wedding day."

After putting on his suit coat and tie, and giving his hair a quick whip with his comb, Mickey led MaryAnne to her room across the hall.

"Maybe I should go down with you."

He took her in his arms and felt her tremble against him. "You really are worried, aren't you?"

MaryAnne nodded. "I'm afraid something's wrong.

You've done security for her before."

That brought a smile to his face. Though he'd asked MaryAnne to marry him seven months ago, they had actually met when Mickey had been hired by Owney Madden to keep an eye on his girlfriend, appearing in a Chicago at Colosimo's; MaryAnne had been in Mae's chorus, having met the star working on the film, "Belle of the Nineties" -- she'd been working a bit player on that shoot, and she and Miss West had become good pals.

Madden, who owned the famed Cotton Club, had been worried that his enemies might hurt Mae to get at him. He was about to go up the river for a spell and he hadn't trusted his own men to protect her, so in came Mickey.

"Stay in your room. I'll talk to the desk clerk and be right back."

MaryAnne shook her head, but handed over the key and Mickey unlocked her door.

"You promise to come right back?"

He nodded. "Ten minutes tops."

She said, "Okay," but he never heard. He'd already shut the door.

The lobby, as Mickey had expected, was vacant. He strode through the palatial hallways, passed the paintings on the wall in their ornate frames and heard his heels clacking like gunfire as he crossed the tile mosaic in the lobby floor. Ceiling fans whirred like aeroplane propellers, doing a decent job of cooling. He wished he'd worn the rubber soled shoes that he wore while working -- literal gum shoes. Though he saw no one behind the desk, his echoing footfalls must have roused someone because a tall thin man appeared there before Mickey could touch the bell.

"May I help you, sir?" the desk clerk asked, although

his voice was so condescending the question sounded like an insult. His hair was slicked back, parted in the middle. He wore a natty black suit, white shirt, and maroon tie with a maroon kerchief showing just enough out of the breast pocket. Mickey could tell the fellow was an officious ass and he doubted this would be much help.

"Yes. My name is Michael Ashford. I'm trying to locate one of your guests."

The clerk's nod was both bland and blank.

Mickey said, "Mae West -- the actress? She's in 2619."

"Yes, sir. The house phone is just around the corner to your left."

"She's not answering the telephone or her door."

"Perhaps, sir, she would prefer not to be disturbed."

"A possibility, I grant you," Mickey said, trying to control his growing frustration. "But not likely since she is scheduled to be the maid of honor in a wedding tomorrow. Mine. I think Miss West might want to speak with the bride-to-be before the event, however, so I doubt she's barricaded herself in her room."

Somehow the desk clerk's expression managed to turn even more vacant.

Mickey pulled out his wallet and eased out a five.

The desk clerk said nothing.

A second five joined the first and yet the man said nothing.

When the third Abe Lincoln joined his pals, a small smile nudged at the corner of the desk clerk's slack mouth.

"Perhaps," the clerk said, watching the bills creep out of the wallet and then across the marble counter, "I might have glimpsed the guest in question leaving the hotel shortly after nine-thirty."

"'Perhaps' isn't worth paying for, buddy." Mickey said, the bills still tucked under his palm.

"Ah -- I did indeed glimpse the guest in question."

Mickey raised his hand and the bills disappeared. So much of sleuthing was the judicious application of bribery.

The detective asked, "Which entrance?"

The clerk said nothing but his eyes flicked toward the Park Avenue side.

Out on the sidewalk, beyond the reach of the fans, the heat remained oppressive, even in the middle of the night. A doorman in red livery, his collar button unbuttoned, stopped fanning himself with his cap, put it back on, and stepped forward. He was around sixty, pot-bellied and sweating rivulets. "Get you a cab, sir?"

"Not just yet. Were you on duty when Mae West left the hotel?"

The man nodded. "You a cop?"

"Private."

The doorman nodded again, took off his hat and started fanning himself with it again, turning away. Mickey's admission of non-official capacity meant the doorman didn't have to bother with him.

Back to bribery. Mickey held up a five spot. "You know which cab she got in?"

The doorman snatched it out of the air like a frog's tongue clipping a fly. "Yeah, that'd be Bernie. Second cab in line over there -- he just got back."

"Thanks, buddy," Mickey said.

"Thank you, sir...but we're gonna have to have a little something for the first guy. He's been sittin' here for over an hour waitin' for a fare. If you take the other one...well... you get the picture."

Nodding, Mickey wondered if the whole damn town was on the pad; he longed for Chicago, where a cop gave you change on your fivespot. He took two steps toward the cab when MaryAnne swept up and entwined her hand in his elbow. She looked lovely in that sleeveless white dress with the red polka dots and the little red waistcoat that accompanied it at night.

"What are you doing here?" he asked.

She gave him the movie-star smile. "I tipped the desk clerk five dollars to tell me where you'd gone."

Mickey rolled his eyes.

She batted hers. "Was that too much?"

"No, but that bastard may be able to afford the cabin next to us on the Queen Mary, by now....I may have a line on Mae, and I need to follow it."

She shrugged. "Fine -- let's go."

"Let's go?" His hands went to his hips. "You think you're going with me?"

Her hands went to hers. "You think you're leaving here without me?"

He turned away from her. "I'll telephone as soon as I know something."

"You won't have to," she said, latching onto his elbow again. "I'll be right there next to you."

"MaryAnne -- "

"Mickey, did you ever imagine you were marrying a stay-at-home girl?"

He was still searching for a comeback when she said, "Good. Now tell me where we're going."

"To talk to Bernie," he said numbly.

"Who's Bernie?"

"Drives that cab over there." He pointed toward the two Checker cabs at the curb.

Mickey held the door while MaryAnne climbed in the back and slid across the seat. He got in next to her.

"Where to?" Bernie asked. He was in his forties, blond,

very pale, sweat pouring down his face, half a cigarette dangling from narrow lips.

Mickey asked, "You know who Mae West is?"

"Yeah." Bernie grunted. "I also know who Donald Duck is, and also Gary Cooper."

"Well, did you drive any of 'em, earlier?"

"I'm not sure."

Mickey pitched two bucks over the seat.

"Well, the duck and the cowboy I ain't seen tonight. But the dame with the shape, yeah, I took her downtown."

"Can you take us to the same place?"

The driver tripped the meter. "A man with money can go anywheres he wants to in this country."

Very little traffic moved through the city and it wasn't very long before the taxi pulled up to the corner of Twenty-First and Lexington.

"Gramercy Park Hotel," Bernie said, nodding toward it. "Left her off there couple of hours ago."

As they pulled around the corner to the front of the hotel, Mickey saw a black car parked across the street, two big guys in rumpled suits, sitting in it trying to look inconspicuous. He caught them eyeballing the cab as it rolled by.

"Around the corner," Mickey said. "Out of sight of that car."

The cabby didn't gun it. He just kept the same easy speed as they cruised past the black sedan, the front door of the hotel, then turned the corner.

Mickey passed the guy another two bucks as he and MaryAnne exited the cab; New York wasn't a city, it was a damn casino, and the people were walking slot machines. The couple crossed both streets so they were on the same side as the black sedan, coming up behind it arm-in-arm, just two lovers out for a late-night stroll.

"This hotel is where Bogart got married back in '26," Mickey explained as they neared the car.

"Oh really," MaryAnne said, her voice high, light. In a hoarse whisper she added, "What the hell are you doing?"

"Making it up as I go," he whispered back. "That's how detectives do it."

Then they stepped off the curb, as if about to pass behind the sedan. Mickey tugged lightly on MaryAnne's elbow, indicating for her to stay put while he moved to the driver's side window. The driver slouched, his hat pulled down over his eyes, and Mickey couldn't tell anything about the guy except he had at least one cauliflower ear and had to be pretty big -- even slouching the guy stuck up over the back of the seat. The passenger seemed only fractionally less imposing as he too tried to shrink further into the seat.

Pulling a cigarette from his silver case, palming his cylindrical lighter, Mickey said, "Plenty hot tonight, huh, pal?"

"Buzz off, buster, I ain't in no mood to talk."

Mickey leaned closer, the cigarette now in his mouth. "C'mon, pal, I just need a light. You've got a light, haven't you?"

"Ya ain't very bright are ya? I told ya to buzz off."

Mickey, moving quickly, jammed the round bottom of the lighter into the back of the guy's neck.

Feeling the cold metal and taking it for a gun barrel, the driver tensed but didn't move.

His partner did move, though, and fast. He threw open the passenger door and came barreling out. An icicle of fear cut through Mickey's gut as he looked over the car roof to see that MaryAnne had moved directly into the man's path. The guy had jerked a revolver out of his jacket and now had it leveled at MaryAnne.

To Mickey's surprise, MaryAnne pulled her skirt up over her thighs, revealing her long, glorious legs. The guy's eyes moved down to check MaryAnne's gams. As the clown gaped at her, she took a step forward to knee the guy in the nuts, but he stepped back, his gun still leveled at her, his eyes snapping up to meet hers.

She shook her head slowly, letting her skirt lower. "Well, it worked for Claudette Colbert...."

The driver used the diversion to slam the car door into Mickey, driving him backward and knocking the lighter out of his hand as the wheelman came piling out of the car and into the detective.

The passenger grinned at MaryAnne who took one quick step and smashed her spiked heel down on the man's toes. As he yelped in pain, she finally delivered her knee to his groin, dropping him to the sidewalk in a moaning heap.

Grabbing the guy's gun, MaryAnne stepped around the car to find the driver sitting on top of her fiancé, about to drive a ham-sized fist into Mickey's face. Pressing the revolver into the man's back, she said, "Please don't hit him -- I'm marrying him later today and I want to keep him adorable."

As the driver's head spun around, MaryAnne stepped back and let him see this was no fake, no cigarette, but a real pistol. Mickey scrambled to his feet and tapped the driver on the shoulder. When the man turned to face him, Mickey hit him with a solid right cross, knocking the guy cold.

They went around to the other side of the car where the passenger finally seemed to be catching his breath. When he saw MaryAnne coming toward him with the pistol, he cringed and held up his hands palms out. "Keep her away from me, mister. She's nuts."

"That's right," MaryAnne replied pleasantly. "Nutty as a Baby Ruth bar -- and don't you forget it."

Mickey squatted next to the man. "Who are you boys?"

The guy shook his head and MaryAnne took a half-step forward.

"Okay, okay! We work for Paramount."

Mickey frowned. "The movie studio?"

The guy nodded slowly. "Security."

"For Mae West?"

Confusion spread like a rash over the man's pock-marked puss. "Mae West? No. We're supposed to make sure no one bothers Mr. Raft."

Mickey and MaryAnne traded a look.

Motioning toward the street, Mickey said, "You better help your buddy back into the car."

As he started to rise, the guy asked, "What about my gat?"

MaryAnne shook her head. "You don't appreciate my legs, you don't deserve a...a 'gat."

A fiver got the room number from the bellboy and, with MaryAnne in tow, Mickey rode the elevator up to the seventh floor, using the time to add up all the money they'd spent on this little errand already. The total did not make him happy. They went down the hall and he found the correct room about halfway down. Still thinking about the money, he pounded on the door. He succeeded in getting two other occupants of the floor to open their doors, but the door he'd knocked on remained closed and behind it he could hear no sound. Either Raft slept sounder than the dead or he wasn't in there.

"Maybe they're...uh...busy," MaryAnne offered.

Mickey shook his head. "If they're that quiet, they're not doing it right," he said, giving her a wicked little smile.

"Well, if they're not in there and the goons are still outside," she said, her pretty features screwing up in confusion, "just where the hell are they?"

He considered that for a moment, before snapping his fingers and taking off back toward the elevator, MaryAnne now hustling along behind in his wake.

"Where are we going?" she panted as she finally caught up with him just as he pushed the button to call the lift back.

"The roof," Mickey said, as if that explained everything.

Before she could ask him anything else, the door opened and the little white-haired elevator operator smiled at them. "What floor?" he asked.

"The roof," Mickey said again as they entered and the little man closed the big door.

"The roof it is. You two going up for a nice romantic dance?"

"That and a cocktail or two."

"Ah, youth...."

Suddenly, MaryAnne understood why Mickey was taking them upstairs. The elevator opened into a glass enclosed room that resembled -- and felt like -- a hot house where all the plants had been replaced by men and women. The gents all wore tuxedos, though most of them looked like they would have preferred something much cooler. The ladies more closely resembled the colors one expected to find in a garden, long dresses like blossoms of red, blue, green, whites, and assorted pastels. At one end of the glass room, an orchestra played a Duke Ellington piece, not badly. Looking over the crowd, Mickey tried to spot Raft and Mae West; but if they were up here, they were swallowed in the throng that probably numbered nearly two hundred despite the heat of the evening.

"Let's split up," MaryAnne suggested. "We'll have better luck that way."

Before he could argue, she pointed toward the bandstand, and took off in the opposite direction. He moved to his left, the lights of the Chrysler Building twenty blocks to the north plainly visible through the glass ceiling of the room, a spectacular view -- but Mickey wondered how they kept snow from destroying the ceiling in the winter. The thought of winter did little to stave off the heat, however, so he kept moving, eyes on the crowd as he searched for two stars not in the heavens.

As he edged closer to the orchestra, he realized that this was Ronnie Staccato's big band, an expansion of the combo he'd appeared with in Chicago. As Staccato segued into another Ellington piece, the crowd barely had time to applaud before they were dancing again. Mickey was almost to the bandstand when he caught Ronnie's eye. Short, thin, his blond hair combed straight back, Staccato was the blue-eyed singer of the orchestra, as well as its leader, and the one that drove the women wild.

The bandleader winked at Mickey and signaled toward the stage. Mickey tried to shake his head, but it was already too late. Staccato's baton slowed the tempo of the band and he stepped forward to the microphone.

"Ladies and gentlemen, you're in for a rare treat tonight. We have a special guest in the audience tonight, all the way from Chicago, our former keyboard man -- who traded in the ivories for a magnifying glass and roscoe -- Mis-ter... Mickey Ashford."

The crowd applauded automatically and as Staccato held his hand out toward Mickey, there was nothing to do but climb the bandstand and take a bow. He did, falling in next to the blond bandleader, the spotlights at the back of the room blinding him, making it impossible for Mickey to see Raft, Mae West, MaryAnne or for that matter the Statue of Liberty, had it been beyond the first few feet in front of the stage.

He waved, took a step toward the stairs, then Staccato leaned into the mike again. "Folks, wouldn't you like to hear Mickey noodle a tune?"

The applause grew even louder and Mickey realized that he'd have no alternative. He hoped that while he was playing, MaryAnne was searching for her missing maid of honor. Acknowledging the applause, Mickey moved to the piano and sat down.

"Cole Porter?" Staccato asked.

Thinking about his current investigation, Mickey nodded. "Make it 'Anything Goes'."

Staccato counted it off and then they were going, the two men doing a duet on the vocal while the band followed along. When the vocal chorus ended, Mickey did a nice long easy ride, giving these Manhattanites a taste of some jazz, Chicago-style.

Lost in the music for a while, Mickey just played and played; then when he'd given it back to the band for their more straightforward dance band rendering, he gazed out at the crowd. Seated there, Mickey could see the audience only slightly better than before; and he couldn't see Raft or Mae West. As the song wound down, he finally spotted MaryAnne and she pointed toward the elevator doors. He could just see them closing in the distance and thought he caught a glimpse of a silver dress, but that was all.

As the song ended, he rose, but the applause of the audience kept him on the bandstand for "Night and Day," before he finally got off the stage and he and MaryAnne were able to snag the elevator to hot foot it back to Raft's room.

"Guess you haven't lost your touch," MaryAnne said.

"As you'll see tomorrow night...."

He knocked on the hotel room door and waited until it cracked open.

"Ashford!" The small, Valentino-handsome dancer was in a wine-color silk robe, his dark slicked-back hair immaculate; his expression was uncharacteristically alarmed, for so cool a customer. "What the hell are you doing here? I thought you were still playing with the band upstairs."

"So, you did see me."

"How did you get my room number?"

"You can buy anything from the desk clerks in this town. The fun part was getting past those studio goons."

"How did you even know I was here?"

"I'm a detective, remember?"

Mickey had met Raft while the latter was working for Owney Madden. The actor and the gangster were best friends; in fact, anybody who knew them both could tell that Raft's underworld personality on screen was a dead copy of Madden's style.

Anger flared in Raft's eyes. "What do you want at this hour?"

"I need to talk to Mae."

"Mae who?"

"George, not all dicks are thick....With Owney your best friend and all, makes you look kind of bad, doesn't it?"

After a short tense silence, Raft said, "Mae and Owney, they broke up."

"Yeah, he went to prison. That tends to slow romance. Boy-girl kind, anyway."

Raft's mouth flickered in his version of a grimace. A hand dipped into the pocket of the robe and emerged with a small automatic in it. "Look, Ashford, I'm not gonna be shaken down by the likes of you."

Despite the weapon, Mickey did not back up. "This isn't a shakedown, George -- I just wanna talk to Mae a minute."

"She ain't here, I tell ya."

"Fine. I'm going down to the lobby. If it comes to you, in a trance or something, how to get ahold of Mae....Have her call me on the house phone, in five minutes."

And approximately five minutes later, in the lobby, the detective answered the phone and the unmistakable voice came on the line: "Mickey, why don't you come up and see me?"

"I tried, sweetheart, but that dance partner of yours wouldn't let me in."

"You makin' a comeback? Tinklin' the ivories again, like that?"

"Not hardly."

"You're not working for Owney, are you, sweetheart?"

"No! Is that what Raft thinks? Here...."

Mickey handed the phone to MaryAnne. The two women seemed to talk forever. Long enough for Mickey to find a paper cup of coffee and go outside to enjoy the sunrise. Finally, MaryAnne joined him out on the sidewalk.

"You look tired."

He nodded. "Feel tired."

"Too tired to get married?"

"Nope. Ready to do it right now."

"It'll wait for the Waldorf. I'll make an honest man out of you yet." She hugged his arm. "This is the beginning of more than just a mere marriage, you know."

"Yeah?"

"We've solved our first mystery together."

"Darling, George Raft shacking up with Mae West is no mystery. It may be a crime, but -- "

Then he was hailing a cab, and soon they were both getting in the back, to bicker over where they should have breakfast, and whether it should be food or something else -- that sweet loving bickering that is music to the ears.

MYSTERY TRAIN
Somewhere in the Florida Everglades
1959

Howie and The Howlers had the small crowd at Waldrop's General Store jumpin' and jivin' as the band wailed. In the 'glades, there weren't a lot of places a man could get a beer, let alone a cold draft and a hot band. There was, in fact, only one, Waldrop's. On one side, the grocery carried essentials, bread, milk, and the like, but also had an aisle of packaged cookies, canned goods that included fruit and vegetables, even had some dry goods and hardware items. The store was a little of everything and not a lot of anything. Hell, big Stan Waldrop even had a gas pump out front.

The other side was a café, but on weekend nights tables got pushed to the walls, a band would play, and the swampers would mosey in to kick up their heels. Usually it was a few locals strumming guitars, playing a washboard with spoons, and singing songs everyone knew. Occasionally, a road band would get lost and play Waldrop's for gas money. Like tonight.

The band had taken a wrong turn and, running low on both gas and money, had struck a deal with big Stan to play for a couple of hours in exchange for a full gas tank and directions.

Howie and The Howlers, a rockabilly band from upstate, were young, wore leather jackets, and had greased back hair. Now they broke into a cover of Sid King's "Shake This Shack Tonight," and given their volume, were trying their best to do exactly that.

A friend would have described Stan Waldrop as portly, but there were damned few friends in the 'glades. Stan knew that most of the guys, especially the five that usually congregated beside the cracker barrel, just thought of him as fat.

A man of property, Stan Waldrop needed to convey his position. Clothes made the man. He wore an open-collared white shirt, black pants and vest, and a big white hat that made him feel like a plantation owner. He did, after all, own a damn sight more than the whole cracker barrel gang put together. So, he really didn't care what they thought about his size. It was the same outfit he had worn to woo and win the heart of his wife Liz. No reason to go changing up now.

As if on cue, his wife slithered into the café from their bedroom in the back and instantly commanded every eye in the room. A petite blonde wearing a skirt that showed a lot of leg, and a sheer white blouse that did nothing to cover her thin black bra, her breasts threatening to escape and leave the swamp behind, Liz oozed sexuality. She brushed against Stan, her skin not quite as hot as the surface of the sun.

She leaned in, her voice husky in his ear. "Get me a beer, willya?"

It wasn't a request. Dutifully, Stan went over, raised the lid on the cooler, pulling a Schlitz out of the icy water. He used the opener attached to the cooler and pried off the cap. When he turned, every man in the place, and even a couple women, were watching Liz dance by herself.

Stan liked that other men wanted what he had. He would have been happier if Liz didn't enjoy teasing them quite so much.

Thankfully, the song ended. He strolled over and handed her the cold bottle. She leaned her back against the wall, thrust her breasts out, really giving the café crowd a show as she took a long pull on the cold beer. She was already pretty well lit, Stan knew that. Since they got married, she split her time between pretty well-lit and completely shitfaced. Her party girl attitude had been a big plus to Stan when they were dating. Now that they were married, he had a different perspective. Still, as he watched her drink the beer, he knew there was nothing he could do to stop her, still, he said, "Jesus, Liz, give it a rest, willya?"

She gave him a smile, but her eyes flashed anger, then she ran her tongue around the neck of the bottle before taking another long pull.

Even as he watched the muscles of her throat work as she swallowed, Stan knew he would do anything to keep her. In the corner, the band broke into a cover of Don Woody's "Barking Up The Wrong Tree."

Howie, the lead singer, compact, sinewy, blue eyes shining, white teeth flashing as he sang, "You're barking up the wrong tree, that's what she said to me," had his eyes glued to Liz and her swaying hips. She moved toward the screen door to the railed porch that ran three sides of the building.

As the tall, skinny Howlers bass player did his last "woof woof," into the microphone, Howie was already announcing the band would be taking a ten-minute break.

Stan held a tray with bottles of cold Coke. Soda he would give away, but if the Howlers wanted beer they would pay like everybody else.

Howie grabbed a Coke and kept right on moving past Stan and out the same door Liz had just gone out. Stan wanted to follow the singer, but the other Howlers and the small crowd hemmed him in.

Outside, the air was hot and thick, it felt like breathing water to Liz. Damned humidity never let up, and tonight there was a cloud of green fog rolling toward the back of the store from the swamp.

Steamy or not, it was still better than being inside. That singer was cute, and, unless she missed her guess, he would be out here any second, sniffing around, just hoping to get a little piece of her. They all wanted a piece of her - Stan, the cracker barrel gang, the men who brought their girlfriends and wives to hear this half-assed rockabilly band, all of them, and all Liz wanted was out of this swamp and back to the city—any city.

No sooner was she looking at the screen door than it squeaked open, Howie strutting onto the porch like she had willed him to do it, like he thought he had something different to offer her than the rest of these yokels.

Swigging his Coke, he looked more like an excited boy than the man she was going to need to make her escape plan work. Instantly, she recognized he was just another wolf knocking at her door.

"Pretty hot," Howie said, a lascivious grin curling up the corners of his wide mouth.

"Yeah," Liz said, not giving him an inch.

"I bet you like it hot," he said, easing closer to her, grin growing as much as the bulge in his jeans.

She took a long pull on her beer. If she was going to

have to crack the bottle over this asshole's head to get his attention, she didn't intend to waste any more of the beer than she had to.

She watched as the weird green fog inched closer to the porch. She had seen fog in the Everglades before, but *green* fog, that was new.

"Come on, baby," Howie said. "I can show you a really good time."

She laughed in his face. "You sang my answer in your last song," she said.

"Huh?"

Giving him a glimpse of her most arctic smile, something she usually saved for Stan when he pissed her off the most, she sang, "You're barkin' up the wrong tree."

As the green mist enveloped them, Liz thought she heard Howie bark a harsh laugh, but then he was howling. And it wasn't like the howling he had been doing inside. Doubled over, barely visible in the damned fog, he writhed, the noises he was making sounding more like an animal than a man.

She backed away, terrified by whatever had taken possession of the greaser, but there was nowhere to go. The swamp nearly surrounded the store, the railed porch ended behind her, and Howie was between her and the door. If she went under the rail in the back, this time of night, she was as likely to run into a gator as not.

The howl turned into a shriek, Howie contorting, shrouded by the fog, and Liz shivered as she backed up to the rail of the porch.

"Stan!"

She had no idea if he or anyone else heard her scream. Fear froze her in place, eyes wide as Howie emerged from the mist. Except it wasn't Howie, it was some hideous animal, fur sprouting from its face like a wolf, fangs bared, but it still wore Howie's clothes.

"Stan!" she cried a second time, but again her fat husband and all the people in the joint failed to appear. The creature Howie had become took one menacing step toward her and for an instant, Liz wondered if her thinking of Howie as a wolf had turned him into one. Then, as the monster took another step, she realized it didn't matter.

Whether he was the kind of wolf she was used to or not, she would handle him the same way.

Growling, spittle flying from his gaping mouth, he moved toward her. When he was close enough for the stench of his breath to nearly overwhelm her, she brought the beer bottle down onto his skull with a satisfying crack.

The beast snarled in anger, bent slightly, and as he did, she kneed him hard in the balls. Falling back, the wolf howled in pain as Liz slipped under the rail of the porch and ran around behind the store, gators be damned. Hell, a gator might be preferable to the hideous bastard back on the porch.

Running as best she could in the dark, in heels, she tried to keep an eye peeled for stray reptiles and that fucking wolf that was, by the sound of it, now pursuing her. Where the hell was Stan, or anyone else for that matter?

Behind her, she heard the snarling of the beast and she ran even harder, kicking out of her shoes, then flying barefoot over the swampy ground, the back door with the single light bulb dangling over it seemed miles away though it was probably less than thirty yards.

The harder she ran, lungs burning, pain searing her bare feet, the growl of her pursuer growing louder with each step, she was certain she wasn't going to make it. She didn't dare even risk a look back.

The growling of the monster grew nearer, she didn't need to look. Only ten yards to go. She knew now she wasn't going to make it. Even if she did, given her luck, this would be the night Stan finally remembered to lock up the damned back door.

Liz flew, the distance to the door narrowing, the monster's footfalls heavy in her ears. She was so close, the glow of the dim bulb almost reaching her. Maybe she was going to make it.

Then the monster's hot breath touched her neck. She looked at the door and knew it was too far. Her step faltered, yet she pressed forward. The animal's claw grazed her shoulder, the pain like someone held a torch to her skin.

She stumbled, realized the beast was about to take her down. She was so close to the door but even if she got there, she would never get it open before the monster mauled her.

About to go down, give up, the back door swung open and light poured out, an answered prayer.

Only a few more feet.

Diving through it was an option, but how to get the door closed before the monster got inside with her?

As suddenly as the door had opened, the space went dark, filled with the shadow of big Stan Waldrop, rifle in his hands.

The first shot was into the air. Liz never stopped sprinting, the monster must have stopped in its tracks, its presence not so close to her.

"Down, Liz," Stan roared, the butt of the rifle jumping to his shoulder.

She dove, landing in the muck.

He fired.

The animal howled. When Liz looked up, it had disappeared into the fog and swamp.

"What the hell was that?" Stan asked.

"Howie," she managed.

"Howie...the singer? That was a fucking animal, a wolf. Jesus, Liz, how much did you have to drink tonight?"

"I'm telling you, Stan," she said, nearly hysterical. "That green fog rolled in and he turned into a wolf or whatever the hell he became. I can't explain it."

Stan knelt down to her. Her dress was ripped from her shoulders, blood trickled from where the wolf had scratched her, and her breasts were nearly exposed as she folded herself into her husband's arms and wept.

Looking out into the swamp, Stan said, "I don't what the hell that was, but I'm gonna find out, and I reckon I know a man can help me do just that."

*****

Riding through the Everglades in the backseat of a Jeep, sitting next to a blonde showing as much skin as she had covered, behind a fat driver who looked like a plantation boss stolen from the set of *Gone With The Wind*, her own new boss in the front passenger seat, Beverly Raith couldn't help but reflect on what had turned into the most surreal twenty-four hours of her life. Had it really only been one day since her desperation for a job had led her here?

True, she had been about out of options. Stranded in Salem, Massachusetts, she couldn't even raise the bus fare to get back to her family in the Midwest. A registered nurse, the petite blonde with the big blue eyes, had worked at Salem General. She had only made it through the winter there because the hospital didn't want the bad press that would come from laying off staff in the winter. On the first day of Spring, their fear of bad press melted faster than the snow that still covered the ground.

She was drawing unemployment benefits of not quite forty dollars a week, but that was not going to keep the wolf from the door. More importantly, it wasn't going to keep the bank from the door either. She was two months behind on the mortgage, but if she didn't find work quick, her owning the house would die, just like Jack her husband, just like their dreams of a life together.

That was what brought her to The Point neighborhood and the sidewalk in front of the ghostly mansion on the corner of Congress and Leavitt Streets. While most of the dwellings in the block were either apartments or row houses, the corner house stood alone amid the shadows of two big trees in the yard. A Victorian mansion, complete with widow's walk, the home looked like its best days had been a decade or so ago.

Behind lace curtains on the second floor, Beverly thought she saw movement, but a second check and she saw nothing. The place kind of gave her the creeps, but she needed the job and Myrtle in pediatrics had told her the Arcanes were weird, but their money was green, and right now, that was the only thing Beverly cared about. She needed a job and this Arcane position seemed the only thing she was likely to get.

She went up the walk past grass that still contained hints of snow, but probably hadn't seen the business end of a lawnmower since way before the snow fell last winter.

She knocked on the heavy wooden door and waited. She was beginning to wonder if anyone was home when the door finally swung open. Before her stood a slender woman who appeared to be only a few years older than Beverly's twenty-eight. Unlike Beverly's blonde pageboy, this woman had raven hair that hung nearly to her waist, and wore a black dress that made her porcelain skin practically glow.

"Mrs. Arcane?" Beverly asked.

The woman smiled, showing teeth even whiter than her pale skin, extended a frigid looking hand, and said, "I'm Alicia Arcane, you must be Mrs. Raith."

"Beverly, please," she said, shaking the woman's surprisingly warm hand.

Alicia waved her inside. "Come in, please. I've got tea set up for us in the dining room. Thank you for being punctual, it will still be hot."

The foyer of the house was almost as large as Beverly's living room. A wide central oak staircase led to the second floor. Above the center of the foyer hung a crystal chandelier. Beverly managed to keep her mouth from dropping open. On her right, next to the door leading into the living room stood a full suit of armor. She thought those only existed in movies about rich people, but this one, a black one with several dings and scratches actually looked like it had been used.

The double doors to the left were closed to what Beverly thought was probably a music room or library, at least that's what it would have been in the movie.

Alicia led her past the stairs and into a formal dining room. There were many windows along one wall, and even though it was a sunny morning, the room seemed dusky. The table was a long, ornate thing with one chair at each end and seven on either side. On a lazy-susan, the centerpiece appeared to be black roses in a black vase, two red roses extending just above them, a circle of shrunken skulls around the base of the vase. Beverly wondered what the hell she was getting into.

Alicia said, "Ah, the centerpiece. A little something Alexander picked up in his travels. He gets called to investigate some rather...unusual cases. The centerpiece was a gift from a tribe of pygmies in Madagascar."

"Pygmies?"

Alicia nodded, but did not further her explanation. "Tea?"

Still looking at the shrunken heads, Beverly managed a nod.

Pouring the tea, Alicia asked, "Sugar? Milk?"

"Sugar, please."

They each took a sip, Alicia offered lemon cookies that Beverly turned down, then they finally got down to business.

Alicia said, "I suppose we should discuss the duties of the job."

"Nursing," Beverly said, finally feeling on more familiar ground.

"That is the lion's share of the work," Alicia said, "but not all."

"Not all?"

"Alexander suffers from a rare mental disorder, Cotard's Delusion. Do you know it?"

Beverly shook her head. "I don't usually deal with mental patients," she said.

"Alexander believes he is dead."

That brought Beverly up short. "Pardon?"

"You heard me correctly."

Beverly gaped at the woman, considered simply fleeing, but there was something about Alicia's violet eyes that drew her in. Plus, she still needed the job if she didn't want to live on the street.

"He still moves around, walks, runs even when it's

necessary, and he still does investigations."

Beverly said, "But believes he's dead."

"Yes."

"How is that possible?"

"He believes he is a spirit that remains on this plane for the time being. He has seen the best doctors in the world, but no one has been able to make any progress with him."

Beverly found her concern turning to curiosity. "How long has he been this way?"

"Over twenty years," Alicia said, her face a mask of sadness. "Since his first case in Haiti."

"Haiti?"

"Yes. Alexander believes he was killed by zombies in Haiti, but since he wasn't killed by a living human, he thinks his spirit is doomed to walk the planet until the Rapture, only then will God free him, he thinks."

"How do you think I can possibly help him?" Beverly asked.

"The duties, as I said, are not normal nursing. In order to help Alexander cope with his...disability, you would be in charge of making sure he eats, sleeps, tries to keep a relatively normal pattern. When he does not, he lapses into something near psychosis."

"Psychosis?"

Alicia shrugged. "It doesn't happen often. I'll level with you, Beverly, this is not your typical nursing job. In fact, I would ask you to masquerade as Alexander's 'secretary' because medical personnel tend to upset him."

Beverly felt the home she and Jack had worked so hard for slipping away from her. As she rose, she said, "I'm sorry, Mrs. Arcane, I thought this was a nursing job and..."

Patting the air in front of her, Alicia said, "Please, hear me out. I'm desperate."

"I'm sorry..."

"And I know you are too, Beverly. We can help each other."

Beverly sat back down, stunned. "How did you..."

"When Myrtle paired us up, I did some checking on you."

Blowing out a breath, Beverly said, "What kind of checking?"

"I know you're a good nurse, and I know you're out of work and about to lose your house. I know your husband died in Korea and you have been holding on by your boot-laces ever since."

Beverly wanted to be outraged, but it was all true. "How did you..."

"The Arcane family has been in Salem for a very long time, Beverly, I have a lot of contacts."

Shaking her head, Beverly said, "I don't know if I can do what you ask."

Alicia reached out, put a hand on hers. "I think you can. I'm sure of it, in fact. But to be totally honest, there is one more thing."

"Yes?" As if this wasn't nuts enough already.

"Three other 'secretaries' have met with...untimely demises."

"Killed?"

Alicia nodded solemnly. "I'm sorry, but you should know. Sometimes Alexander's investigations can be dangerous."

"I can't do that," Beverly said, rising again. "I'm just a nurse, that's all."

"I understand your trepidation, but I believe you are much more than 'just a nurse.' You have been on your own for over five years and not given up or given in. You have moxie; you can be beneficial for Alexander."

"I'm sorry, I just..."

Interrupting her, Alicia said, "Stay one month and I will bring your mortgage up to date and pay you one hundred dollars a week."

Beverly's legs wobbled. "That's more than I made at Salem General and you'll get me out of debt."

"I'll do you one better, Beverly. Stay six months and I will pay your house off. You will own it free and clear, plus the hundred dollars a week."

Beverly had heard that every man had his price, and every woman too, she assumed, but she had always thought she couldn't be bought. Right up until now. The house was all that was left of Jack and she loved it. She loved it enough to take this crazy job with this lunatic she hadn't even met yet.

She wanted to walk out. She wanted to say no, but instead, she found herself nodding and saying, "All right."

Alicia clapped her hands together. "That's fantastic. Let me call Alexander down and you can meet him."

Wondering what she was getting into, Beverly watched as Alicia rose, went to a side table, wrote a note, the inserted the paper into a metal cylinder. She put that into a vacuum tube that carried the note up the wall and into the ceiling, presumably to the upstairs part of the house.

The hospital had used a similar communications system back in the old days, but it had been phased out for a fancy new intercom system. That they could afford, nurses, not so much.

Not waiting for a response, Alicia came back to the table, sat down again. "He should only be a minute, he was expecting to meet you today."

"Will he...how to put this...'see' me?" Beverly asked.

A small laugh burbled out of Alicia and she put a hand

over her mouth. "I'm sorry. Yes, he's aware that he can interact with living people. The biggest issue you will have is getting him to eat and sleep. He believes he does not require these things and I'm afraid you will have to outsmart him in order to get him to comply."

Beverly wasn't worried, she'd had plenty of fussy patients over the years. She smiled and nodded.

"Don't underestimate Alexander, Beverly. He's ill, but he is very smart, and very disturbed."

Abruptly, Alicia rose, Beverly following without thinking. Two seconds later, a tall, slender man wearing a black suit that might have been stylish half a century ago, descended the stairs. An Edwardian coat, frilly white shirt, and black looped bow tie took only some of the attention off the man's face. His dark hair was swept straight back, tiny wisps of gray at his ears. His Van Dyke beard was neatly trimmed but there was salt among the pepper there, too.

She had to admit, for an older gentleman, he was handsome, nearly as good looking as Jack. Although, one of the other side effects of Cotard's Delusion seemed to be a total inability to smile.

That was how she had met Alexander Arcane, but not how she had ended up, less than twenty-four hours later, getting the bejesus bounced out of her as the crazy man driving the Jeep careened down a cow path that the locals probably called a "road."

No, meeting Arcane had just been the beginning. She had, in fact, still had her hand extended to him as he said, "I'm sorry, I don't shake hands," when the phone rang.

Arcane excused himself to take the call, leaving Beverly standing there, hand out, feeling a little foolish.

Alicia said, "It's nothing personal. I should have warned

you, I'm sorry. Something else related to his first case, I'm afraid."

"It's okay," Beverly said, finally dropping her hand. "I understand."

"Thank you," Alicia said with a slight bow of her head.

Arcane came back into the room, steel gray eyes boring into Beverly. "How soon can you be packed and ready for a trip?"

"I beg your pardon?"

"We must depart as soon as possible; we're needed in Florida."

"Florida?" Beverly asked, stunned.

Alicia put a hand on Arcane's arm. "What is it, Alexander?"

"Do you remember Stanley Waldrop?"

"That man in the Everglades?"

"Yes," Arcane said. "He's just had an encounter with what he thinks is a werewolf."

First pygmies, now werewolves in Florida, it was all moving way too fast for Beverly. Involuntarily, she took a step back. "Maybe I should be going."

"No," Alicia said, the word a plea.

"I'm sorry?" Beverly said, wondering if she was suddenly a prisoner of these very odd people.

Arcane said, "I have to phone Perkins and have the plane fueled, then I must alert the I.N. If you'll excuse me, Mother will fill you in on the details."

Without so much as a look back, Arcane vanished back up the stairs.

When they were alone, Beverly shook her head. "I'm sorry, Mrs. Arcane, I'm afraid I can't..."

Alicia grabbed her arm with some strength, violet eyes imploring, as she said, "Mrs. Raith, Beverly, please, just this one time, this one case, accompany Alexander and

I will bring your mortgage up to date and pay you *two* hundred dollars a week, plus expenses. If, when you return, you want to walk away, I won't try to stop you, but this one time, please, help me, I beg you."

This was insane. Beverly's brain told her to run from this house this instant, get as far away from these crazy people as possible. But her heart, her damned heart, kept her feet rooted to the spot, to the house—not just house, home - she and Jack had built. Even as she tried to shake her head, she found herself nodding and saying, "This once."

Alicia threw her arms around Beverly. "Thank you, thank you."

The woman's embrace was surprisingly warm.

"After this though..."

Alicia didn't wait for Beverly to finish. Interrupting, she said, "Go home, pack a bag. The Everglades are humid and hot, bring bug spray, if you have any, and meet Alexander at the Arcane hangar at the airport. There are signs, you'll find it. Do you need money for cab fare?"

Beverly shook her head, but Alicia was already pushing two twenty-dollar bills into her hand. Where the hell had those come from?

"I can't..."

"Take it," Alicia ordered. "And hurry. A werewolf, oh my, Alexander will be in a rush to see this one."

She was practically pushed out the door then, and everything since had blurred together: rushing home, throwing clothes haphazardly into a cardboard suitcase, urging the cabby to rush as he careened across town to the airport, then hustling breathless up the stairs of the DC-3, an airplane bigger than any she had ever been on, the word ARCANE painted on its side.

Arcane had been waiting for her, not even bothering introducing her to the pilot and co-pilot, one of whom was possibly Perkins, the name Arcane had mentioned earlier, but whether Perkins was the tall, balding co-pilot or the attractive redheaded pixie of a pilot, Beverly had no idea.

The passenger compartment held eight seats, the back of the plane had been completely revamped. Behind the four rows of seats, the pilot's side of the DC-3 held a ham radio setup that reminded her of her dad's rig back in Indiana.

The starboard side of the plane was lined with bookshelves that had net covers to keep the volumes from flying around should there be trouble with the plane.

Arcane waved her to a seat. "Buckle up, we're ready to go. If you need anything, well, you'll have to find it yourself. They'll be flying the plane and I will be doing research with the I.N."

"The I.N.?" she asked, sitting down and tugging at the seatbelt.

He towered over her now, his shadow making his face hard to make out as he said, "The International Network. It is something of my own design. Experts from around the world who share information on their chosen fields through the use of..."

"Ham radios," she finished. "That's quite brilliant."

He bestowed a smile on her. "Thank you, I know."

So, he could smile. Normally his arrogance would annoy her, but there was something about him, whether it was the Edwardian suit or the wounded aura his illness gave him, but she found him almost charming.

He moved to the back and Beverly lost sight of him as the engines roared to life. She had never flown before, the train, sure, but she had not traveled by air. She was looking forward to it. Even though Jack had been a pilot, she had never gotten to soar with him - at least not in a plane. The bittersweet thought hung with her even as her stomach lurched when the DC-3 left the ground.

It wasn't long before they were soaring above Massachusetts, Salem behind them, the sunset turning the sky red outside her window as the plane rattled south.

"Red sky at night, sailor's delight," she whispered to herself.

She wondered if the author of that line had a potential werewolf encounter at the end of his journey. Doubtful.

In the rear of the plane, she could hear Arcane say, "So, Joaquin, you had a werewolf in Peru, how did the man get infected?"

The doctor listened, threw in an occasional, "Uh huh," and soon Beverly found herself drifting. As night closed in, the adrenaline of the day faded and Beverly found herself slipping into a restless sleep in her seat.

The fetid stench of the swamp nearly overwhelmed her as she stumbled through the knee-deep stagnant water, the werewolf somewhere nearby, but was she stalking it or was it stalking her?

She kept moving, something slithering past her ankle, and she stifled a scream. No good would come from giving away her position. She continued to slog forward, realized it wasn't the werewolf she was tracking but Arcane himself.

Then, as she broke through a thick growth of trees, she saw Arcane in front of her, sitting against a tree, seemingly passed out - or worse. She took one tentative step forward, then the water exploded as the werewolf rose in front of her, water cascading off it, teeth bared, its arm raised, razor-sharp claws ready to rip down through her.

Too terrified even to scream, she tried to run, but instead, her feet got caught and she plopped down on her ass, waist deep in swamp water as the werewolf's claws flashed mere inches from where she had stood. Her voice came now, the scream long and loud, then the werewolf bent over her, arms reaching out to strangle her, or worse, its mouth open, its breath foul, then it said, "Wake up, Mrs. Raith, wake up! You're having a bad dream."

She struggled against the wolf, finally managed to open her eyes, and saw Dr. Arcane in front of her, holding her by the shoulders.

"It's all right," he said, his voice surprisingly soothing. "Just a bad dream."

Looking around, she got her bearings. It had just been a bad dream, maybe a sign that she shouldn't have taken the job, but it was too late now, wasn't it?

"We'll be landing any second now," Arcane had said, and she had dismissed her misgivings, at least for the moment.

She watched as he packed a Gladstone bag. She was pretty certain he wasn't a medical doctor, but she decided that when she saw the long-barreled revolver go inside that maybe she didn't want to bring up the subject. Almost before she had finished her thought, the wheels had touched down.

Now, the airplane and her nightmare behind her, clattering over the dirt in the Jeep, the blonde floozy bouncing against her far too often, she just kept thinking about how much she loved her house, keeping it was all that made this misery worthwhile.

Up front, Arcane was talking to Waldrop. Beverly had to strain to hear their words over the racket of the Jeep.

"So," Arcane said, "this singer is the only one infected?"

The big man, Waldrop, shrugged. "Near as we can tell."

Turning to the blonde, Arcane asked, "And you were the only one of the porch with this singer when he turned?"

Liz nodded, the Jeep hitting a pothole and tossing the blonde practically onto Beverly's lap.

"Sorry," Liz said, sounding about as sincere as a door-to-door vacuum salesman confronting a disgruntled customer.

Arcane asked, "If he turned into a werewolf, why didn't you?"

It was clear from the look on Liz's face, her mouth an almost perfect red O of lipstick, that the thought had never once entered that pretty head. Finally, she shrugged.

"Did you two eat the same thing that day?"

Her husband spoke up for the first time. "We all had burgers I cooked on the grill. The difference was that green fog."

"Green fog?" Arcane asked.

"I didn't tell you that part on the phone?" Waldrop asked.

Arcane shook his head. "You failed to mention that." Waldrop started to make an excuse, but Arcane waved that off. "Tell me about the green fog."

Waldrop opened his mouth, but a glance from Arcane silenced him.

Turning to Liz, he said, "You tell me."

When the blonde was through with her story, Beverly wondered if maybe she had judged the woman a little too harshly.

Liz said, "If Stan hadn't been there..." her voice broke, and she leaned into Beverly, who hugged her close.

Arcane gave her a smile and a quick nod.

Tugging on his Van Dyke beard, he asked, "Can you give me more details?"

"Like what?" Liz sniffed.

Arcane considered that for a couple of bounces of the Jeep, then said, "You two were the only ones out on the porch, right?"

Liz nodded. "That's what I said."

"Why were you the only two out there?"

The question seemed to take Liz by surprise. She sat up a little straighter, shrugged. "How should I know?"

"Fine," Arcane said, raising his voice a little. "We'll do it the long way. Why were *you* outside?"

Liz looked angry enough to not answer, but finally she said, "It was a hot night. I took my beer and stepped out onto the porch hopin' to find a breeze."

"And this singer, what was his name?"

"Howie," she said.

"Howie followed you out?"

She nodded.

"And you have no idea why?"

Big Stan Waldrop spoke up. "Same as all men, he wanted a piece of my Liz."

Arcane raised an eyebrow at Liz and she nodded. Beverly watched as Arcane thought about that for a moment.

He asked, "Did Howie have a beer, too?"

Liz gave an indifferent shrug.

Waldrop said, "I didn't serve them boys anything but Coca Colas. They was all underage."

Nodding as if he had already known the answer, Arcane said, "That might just be our first clue."

Beverly wasn't sure how that was a clue. Arcane couldn't mean that Coca Cola would turn a man into a werewolf. She was a Coke drinker herself, and unconsciously, she examined her hands for excess hair.

She noticed that overhanging trees shaded the road

ahead, almost as if they were driving into a tunnel. Back in her girlish days in Indiana she had always enjoyed the outdoors, but this swamp was giving her the heebie-jeebies something fierce.

As they entered the corridor of shadows, the sun practically disappeared, and Beverly could barely make out the dirt road ahead of them.

They were maybe a hundred yards into the shadows when something swooped down next to Beverly. She lurched back, but Liz screamed and Beverly watched helplessly as the woman was lifted out of the Jeep by something Beverly couldn't quite discern. Waldrop hit the brakes, but it was too late. When Beverly turned, Liz was hanging from the arms of a werewolf who had been hanging upside down from a branch and grabbed her when the Jeep rolled beneath.

Beverly watched in mute horror as the werewolf dropped to the road with Liz, then took off across the swamp. Arcane was already jumping out of the front seat. He pulled the pistol and, of all things, a flask from the Gladstone and lit out after the wolf and its prisoner. Not knowing what else to do, Beverly got out and followed.

The wolf, still lugging Liz, veered off the road into the swamp, Arcane rushing to close the distance, Beverly sprinting just to try to keep them in sight.

She followed them off the road, the muck practically swallowing her feet, then she was falling even further behind Arcane.

The fetid stench of the swamp nearly overwhelmed her as she stumbled through the knee-deep stagnant water, the werewolf somewhere nearby, but was she stalking it or was it stalking her?

Beverly froze, her dream coming back to her. Exactly the same as her dream. How was that even possible?

She forced herself to keep moving, to put those thoughts out of her head. Just like surgery, don't think, just react to what was going on. She slogged forward. She could hear the wolf and Arcane still struggling through the muck ahead of her, but she had lost sight of them among the shadowy trees of the Everglades.

Struggling against the water, she kept forcing herself forward, then, like the dream, something slithered past her ankle, and she stifled a scream. No good would come from giving away her position. The swamp had gone silent up ahead, then she heard a scream, a gunshot, then a long, low moan.

She broke through a thick growth of trees, and just like the nightmare, she saw Arcane in front of her, sitting against a tree, seemingly passed out - or worse, Liz. Was that blood on his face or just a shadow? From here she couldn't tell, but now she trusted her vision from the plane. It wasn't a nightmare, it was a premonition. She had no idea how, but there was a power at work here. She was ready, she knew what to do.

She took one tentative step forward, then the water exploded as the werewolf rose in front of her, water cascading off it, teeth bared, its arm raised, razor-sharp claws ready to rip down through her.

Ducking, she felt the wind of the werewolf's blow, but the claws flashed past her without inflicting injury. She came up kicking, catching the beast in the stomach and knocked it off balance. That was enough for Arcane. Her boss must have been playing possum. He jumped on the wolf from behind, wrestled the animal to the soggy ground, Beverly jumping into the fray with him as the doctor shoved the flask into the wolf's open mouth and poured the contents down the animal's throat.

The wolf coughed, fought, kicked them off, then rose, peered down at Beverly like it was about to rip out her throat, then suddenly its eyes rolled back into its head and the wolf fell backwards out cold.

Looking to Arcane, she said, "Did you poison it?"

Rising, brushing the swamp off his coat as best he could, Arcane said, "Better, I got him dead drunk."

"What?" she asked, incredulous.

They watched as slowly, the wolf turned back into Howie, albeit, a naked Howie. Covering the passed-out man with his jacket, Arcane said, "The fog, I finally figured out, was from Cape Canaveral."

"That's so far away," Beverly said.

Arcane nodded. "But they send waste through the swamp on trains. One must have leaked and caused the fog that turned Howie here into a werewolf."

"But not Liz?"

"Because she had alcohol in her system. Somehow that counteracted the effects of the fog on her. I'll have to do more testing later, but in a nutshell, the alcohol turned him back."

"Amazing."

"How did you know he was going to ambush you like that?"

Beverly shrugged. She wasn't ready to talk to anybody about her premonition, especially her new boss that she barely knew. She gave him a Cheshire grin. "Woman's intuition, I guess."

Arcane grunted and returned the smile.

With the help of Waldrop, they got Howie loaded into the Jeep and got back to the store, Liz clinging to Waldrop like he might disappear if she let go. That night, the band wailed at the moon again.

Beverly found Arcane sulking in a corner as Howie and the Howlers rocked the house. "You cured him, Doctor, why aren't you smiling?"

He gave her a sour look.

"You want to dance?"

"To this noise?" he asked, pinching his face. "Honestly, Beverly, I liked him better as a werewolf."

A LITTLE FAITH

DEA agent Dan Malmon woke to find himself lashed to a wide wooden board, his feet maybe six inches higher than his head. The room was dimly lit, but without his glasses, everything beyond a foot or so remained a blur.

While most undercover DEA agents looked like a cross between Superman and somebody on *Sons of Anarchy*, Malmon came off more Clark Kent. With his almost skinny frame, that mop of curly dark hair, and the nerdy rimless glasses, he might have been an accountant or bank loan officer.

His cover played off that—he was supposed to be an unassuming money launderer for a Mexican drug cartel.

Bound to the board with piano wire that cut into his ankles and wrists, amplified every time he tried to move, Malmon didn't need to be told that his cover was blown. The leader of the cartel would not have given him up—Marco Robles had cooperated with the DEA to avoid Guantanamo Bay, and would hardly risk his country-club incarceration. From inside, Robles had vouched for Malmon—that is, for "Mark Ruebling."

Likewise, the cartel member who had introduced him to the Toledo-based gang of eastern Europeans he'd infiltrated would not have ratted him not—not Cliff Gonzalez, Malmon's DEA partner.

Straining, Malmon could see he had been stripped to his white T-shirt and the red boxers with the white hearts, a gift from Kate, his shiksa wife. Turning his head left, he confirmed the sense that his watch was gone—his wrist was bare, except for piano wire. Groggy, head throbbing, he had been uneasy when he first came around, uncomfortable obviously, frightened certainly; but now, seeing the watch gone, Malmon shuddered with genuine terror.

The watch, most certainly *not* a gift from his wife, had been courtesy of Uncle Sam. Kept decent enough time, but its best feature was the GPS chip inside that allowed his partner Gonzalez to track him should they be separated - as they were now.

To make matters worse, Malmon had no idea how long he had been out. He was supposed to check in with Gonzalez every twenty-four hours. He had missed at least one check-in, that much he knew. That meant Gonzalez would be searching for him, by now.

Only without the watch's GPS, how was his partner ever supposed to find him?

But he could hear his partner's voice repeating the old refrain, whenever Malmon got nervous: "Come on, man—have a little faith," as if he were in the room with him right now, whispering in his ear.

Only Gonzalez wasn't with him in the cold, damp room, and Malmon didn't think the chill he felt was entirely due to his surroundings.

The agent fought both his near-sightedness and the darkness to get better sense of the space. He hoped to recognize the place, but he couldn't see much—machinery, toolboxes, and a chain hoist attached to the ceiling—but he could make out little else.

Malmon knew the Turkish immigrant head of the gang, Ahmet Ergoyan, used an auto repair shop as a front for dealing drugs, running a chop shop on the side, though the DEA man had never seen the place. He couldn't be sure this room was part of that business, but it seemed a good guess. He thought he detected the smell of oil.

How the hell had he ended up here, trussed up like a Thanksgiving turkey waiting for the stuffing? The crazy thing was, he hadn't even been around the drug gang when things went south. He had just been sitting in the bar of the downtown hotel where "Mark Ruebling" was registered, waiting for Gonzalez. They would sit at opposite ends of the bar, and when Malmon headed for the john, his partner would follow, and there would be a quick report.

As he waited, Malmon ordered a gin and tonic from the pretty brunette barmaid. With his cocktail, she had also delivered a flirty smile and just a hint of cleavage thanks to her partly unbuttoned tux shirt.

Malmon had given her a ten and not complained when she sashayed off without even asking if he wanted change. She was very cute, though all it did was make him wish this assignment were over and he was spending time with Kate.

Where the hell was Gonzalez, anyway?

Malmon checked his watch and realized his partner wasn't late, *he* was a few minutes early.

Not far into the drink, the agent felt sweat dampening his shirt and suddenly his breath seemed short. Woozy, as if the drink had been his sixth not his first, he somehow eased off the bar stool and got to his feet, if unsteadily. Maybe better to meet Gonzalez outside, and get some air while he waited....

The barmaid smiled at him as he went, her eyes confused as he wobbled past her—she, too, knew he'd only had a single drink. As he went through the door, he heard her call out, but her words seemed foggy.

In the lobby, he felt his stomach doing somersaults, and the glass doors out to the street looked far away. The bartender, a burly guy in a tux shirt and black slacks, materialized at his side.

"You okay?" the man asked, his voice carrying the hint of an accent.

"Just need some air," Malmon managed, his legs feeling rubbery.

The bartender led him toward the doors to the street. "Let me give you a hand, friend."

Malmon sagged against the bartender, allowed himself to be steered, his eyes searching any passing person for Gonzalez. That was the moment when he suspected he'd been slipped a mickey—but surely not by that cute waitress, maybe...the bartender? *Or am I just sick?*

As they went out the door, Malmon felt his legs giving way, the bartender propping him up. A black vehicle pulled up to the curb, an SUV, even with his blurred vision he could see that much, and he was loaded into the back like a bag of grain, hitting the floor hard. For a moment he saw flashes of light, tiny star bursts, then a black hole swallowed the stars.

And him.

Now that he was awake, lashed to a board, head pounding, Malmon knew all too well that he'd been drugged, just as he realized this dank, indistinct space was where he might well spend the last minutes of his life.

Across the room, a heavy door squeaked open and a splash of light spilled in, whether from outside or just another room, Malmon could not tell. Three dark figures lumbered in. Between the bright backlighting and his near-sightedness, that much was all he could make out.

As they drew closer to him, and the single light bulb, he recognized the one in front—Ahmet Ergoyan, leader of the Toledo gang. Squat and swarthy with a curly mop of black hair and a matching full beard, Ergoyan gazed at his guest with dark eyes like cinders above a dark coal lump of a nose.

A Muslim Turk, Ergoyan had emigrated to the U.S. a decade ago. His file was a vast menu of possible crimes that he was suspected of committing, both here and back in Turkey; but not one conviction. The gang boss wore blandly casual attire—a white button-down shirt with an open collar and dark slacks.

Over the boss's left shoulder, Malmon could barely make out the burly bartender from the hotel. Although he resembled Ergoyan—a brother?—the bartender had hair cut so short his scalp was showing, no beard, and a beak of nose.

The third man was a medium-sized Hispanic new to Malmon, a man who might have seemed nondescript had he not been so sharply dressed—charcoal pinstripe suit, black Lacoste T-shirt, Italian loafers. Unless the agent missed his guess, this guy was a representative of the cartel. His hair was clipped almost as close as the bartender's, and his skin was the color of a football and about that smooth, pockmarks covering most of his hatchet face.

Leaning down over him, Ergoyan said, "Mr. Ruebling, welcome. I am about to call our meeting to order."

"Ahmet, what the hell—?"

"I will call you 'Mr. Ruebling,' if you don't mind, though I know that is not really your name. But before we are done here? I will know everything about you. This I promise you."

"Ahmet, what are you *talking* about?" Malmon asked, working at the right mix of confusion and outrage. "What are you doing to me?"

Lashed to a board in his undies and three thugs looming over him, confusion was easy, outrage a stretch.

Then Malmon's world exploded into a million pinpoints of light and his cheek burned. Ergoyan had slapped him hard and fast—so fast, the agent did not even see it coming.

"Do not insult me," Ergoyan said, his voice icy, "pretending you do not know I'm talking about." He sighed, as if summoning patience. "What I am I'm talking about is finding out who you *really* work for, and what you have told them of my work here."

"You *know* who I work for," Malmon said. "Marco *himself* vouched for—"

The Hispanic man held up a "stop" hand, then stepped forward, very close, and said, "The traitor Robles is dead. Died in prison, fell on something sharp in the shower."

Shit.

"It's amusing—he thought that being in a minimum security facility was a lucky break." Ergoyan's laugh was like a cough. "Yes, Mr. Ruebling, we know this man we once so loved and respected was feeding information to the DEA."

Shit shit.

"That doesn't make me dirty," Malmon said quickly. "I thought Marco was a stand-up guy! Hell, I did business with him for years, and—"

A hand raised as if to again slap, stopping Malmon.

Ergoyan waggled a finger before the agent's face. "Do not insult me. When you lie to me? You insult me. And I will not be insulted."

"I'm *not* lying."

And now the sharply dressed stranger leaned in; his breath smelled of tobacco. "But you *are*," the man said. "Do you know who I am?"

Malmon shook his head.

"Few do," the man admitted. "I am Alberto Cruz."

Malmon shrugged as best he could against his bonds. The name honestly meant nothing to him.

"I was Marco Robles's driver. Anyone Mr. Robles met, I met. As Marco's driver, I was invisible. No one ever noticed me. That made me a very effective undercover agent, a skill you might well appreciate. Anyway...I met all of Mr. Robles' associates, and none of them ever remembered meeting me."

Shit shit shit.

"And you, my friend? You I never met."

Ergoyan stepped in front of Cruz, as if the two were battling for a rebound and Malmon was the ball. Whoever got it first, got to kill it.

"We *will* find out what you know," Ergoyan said. He sighed with sarcastic regret. "I'm afraid you are in for a very long night."

The bartender stepped forward, a gallon bottle of water in one hand, a fat fold of thin towel in the other. Ice spiked up Malmon's spine—*waterboarding.*

Ergoyan, now on the sidelines, offered a tour guide's explanation: "Did you know this practice has been around since the Fourteenth Century? It has become much more well-known in the last ten years, thanks to your CIA. They claim it is an effective interrogation tool against suspected terrorists. Some claim otherwise. You will soon be able to form your own, informed opinion...Mr. Ruebling."

Malmon already knew plenty about the subject, having talked to people who had been on both sides of the torture. And he already had an opinion—he wanted no part of it.

"I never claimed I met Robles!" Malmon said. The fear in his voice required no acting. "He knew of my work through mutual business associates! Believe me!"

Ergoyan's smile was positively polar. "But I don't."

The bartender posed a wordless question to his boss and Ergoyan gave him a barely perceptible nod.

Stepping forward, the bartender gazed blankly down at him as Malmon pulled against his bonds until he thought the piano wire would sever his limbs. Whoever bound him had done one hell of a job. He felt the trickle of blood at his ankles and wrists, and still there was no loosening of his restraints.

Like the blood he was losing, hope seeped out of Malmon. Without that GPS signal, there was no way Gonzalez could find him, and Ergoyan would never release him after they were done torturing him, even if he did talk. His only hope was to somehow convince his captors that he wasn't a government man.

As the bartender neared him with the rag, Ergoyan put a hand on the bartender's arm and the man paused.

"Last chance," Ergoyan said. "Tell me everything. If I believe you, maybe I kill you quick."

"You're making a mistake. I'm just a damn accountant."

Ergoyan nodded at the bartender, who stepped forward, shaking out the thin towel. Malmon bucked hard against his restraints, but they didn't budge and the wire dug in and terror welled within him as if wanting to drown him before the water could.

The towel covered his face and, despite savagely shaking his head, he was unable to dislodge the thing. He had only seconds now. His heart pounded, as if trying to leap free of the body that could not escape its bindings.

He wanted to scream, but better to keep his mouth closed against the coming flood....

The first drop hit his forehead, like a signal of rain. Up until then, he had been fighting and kicking, but that first single drop of water touched him above the towel, on his forehead, and Malmon froze for a second, as if death itself had bestowed him a tiny chilled kiss.

For an endless agonizing second, he lay there unmoving, waiting, anticipating the next drop. Just a single second out of his entire life and yet it felt like forever. He wanted to talk, to tell Ergoyan anything and everything, share everyone he had met since birth, wanted to spit it all out, but it was too late.

The next drop was not a drop at all but a torrent. Water covered his nose, his mouth, soaking the rag. Instantly he was gagging, trying to cough up everything that had ever entered his body, fighting desperately to keep the water out. His lungs burned, his eyes were squeezed shut, and in his brain it sounded like he was screaming, though with the water coming in, he knew no sound escaped.

He writhed on the board, pulling desperately against the piano wire, blood flowing freely now as he yanked to no avail.

Then the flow of water stopped.

Malmon was left coughing and hacking, his lungs aching. He vomited but little came up. He gasped for breath, the wet towel cold against his face as the cascade continued.

His every muscle screamed, his pulse pounded, and his head ached, and he wished her were dead even as he thanked God he was alive, not that he could make a sound expressing either thought.

Waiting for Ergoyan's interrogation to begin, Malmon wondered what he would say. Could he even speak? The pain he felt now, the exhaustion, were like nothing he had ever endured. The elation at still being alive intermingled with the threat of further torture. He supposed he would tell Ergoyan just about anything not to endure that again.

Surprisingly, his breathing soon returned to near normal. Yet there were no questions. Just as he wondered when the interrogation would begin, the water returned.

Malmon gagged again, writhing against the wire, drowning under the thin cloth. There was no god here, no redemption. No devil either. Just water and more water and fighting to stay alive and wishing you were dead.

Finally, the downpour stopped and Malmon turned his head to one side and vomited, then struggled to draw in a few ragged breaths. He wondered if Ergoyan really intended to question him or had his captor simply decided to torture him to death....

The towel was removed. Someone wiped the puke away. So kind. So very kind. Malmon blinked against the light. Slowly, his breathing came closer to normal. Ergoyan loomed over him, the bartender and Cruz slightly behind him.

"The time has come for you to talk," Ergoyan said, his voice low, almost gentle, yet with a tinge of menace.

Malmon said nothing.

"What is your name?"

Considering his options, knowing that the water would come again no matter what he said, Malmon answered, "Mark Ruebling."

Ergoyan let out a long sigh. "You are not Mark Ruebling. But whoever you are, you are not a very smart man."

No, he was a dead man. That much Malmon knew.

Damned if he would go down helping this evil asshole. He thought of Dante...*all hope abandon, ye who enter here.* The sign on the gate to Hell.

The bartender stepped up to put the towel back on Malmon's face.

But he shouldn't, he *couldn't* abandon hope. Gonzalez would look for him, GPS or no GPS, he would go from haunt to haunt of the drug dealers, and if this was dank torture chamber was connected to Ergoyan's auto repair shop, Gonzalez would find him, he *would* find him....

"Never pray for yourself, Daniel," his mother had told him. "You only pray for God to help others."

Malmon took his mother's advice and prayed for Gonzalez to be successful in tracking him, bringing plenty of backup. For a split second, he smiled at his self-serving prayer. Still, it was within the letter of his mother's law, if not the spirit.

Then the water came again.

Kicking and jerking at his bonds, he felt the wire digging in, cutting him deeper even as his lungs burned and his stomach retched.

If this kept up, he would die tonight. He felt himself growing weaker and weaker, knowing he couldn't take much more. He saw the face of his father, long dead, and Rabbi Selkirk, also dead for years. The two men came to him now, arms outstretched, beckoning him to let go and come home. He desperately wanted to join them, to make this punishment stop. Death was no longer anything to fear, but the promise of welcome release. Yet even as he struggled, Malmon realized that if Ergoyan's man was good at this, he could be kept alive just long enough for him to lose mind before succumbing to the waterboarding....

Again, the water stopped, Malmon puking and battling

for each aching breath.

The rag was removed and the trio peered down at him.

"Anything to say?" Ergoyan asked.

He would not give up. He wanted to, more than anything, just make the pain stop, but some kernel of something...stubbornness?...faith?...wouldn't let him. He would keep hanging on, because his partner *would* come - he believed that. He had to believe that....

But there was a card left to play.

"I *am* DEA," Malmon blurted, spitting water.

Ergoyan's eyes flared and his mouth curled with a smile. "Good. Good. Go on."

"They know everything about your operation," Malmon said, panting as if he'd run a marathon. "They could be here any second. The local police, too."

Cruz's eyes widened and the bartender unconsciously looked around. Ergoyan smiled at his boys like a patient father.

"Now you lie," the drug boss said.

Cruz stepped to the man's side. "How can you be sure?"

Ergoyan's dark eyes burned a hole in Malmon. "Because, if that was true? The feds, the cops, they'd have been here already. They wouldn't let us...*entertain* their friend for so long a time. No, our guest here, he was still in his hotel, waiting. He had not yet made contact."

That seemed to mollify Cruz, but the bartender continued to glance around as if he expected a SWAT team to jump out of the shadows any second.

Behind the trio, Malmon glimpsed motion. Not a SWAT team...just Gonzalez.

Gonzalez, bringing up his pistol.

There was a burst of orange that momentarily erased the shadows concealing Gonzalez, a loud crack, then the bartender's eyes popped as a mist of red erupted from his head. The torturer's blood showered Malmon, sprinkling his face, his chest and bare arms with scarlet raindrops.

Cruz reached under his suit coat, but met the same fate before his gun cleared his jacket.

Ergoyan ducked forward toward the water-boarding table, but Malmon's hand had just enough freedom grab a hank of curly hair and hold the man, who yelled an obscenity in a foreign tongue.

The crime boss batted Malmon's hand loose and straightened, a gun appearing in his hand from somewhere, but a third shot rang out and the pistol slipped from Ergoyan's grasp as the Turk sagged to the floor, then landed with a thud, as if a bag of laundry had been tossed on the cement.

Gonzalez—Superman to Malmon's Clark Kent—was a Native American who could pass for Hispanic, his long black hair tied back in a ponytail, his dark eyes narrow and glittering, his wide face broken into a grin, despite the grisly nature of the tableau his entrance had created.

"You okay, man?" he asked. His black shirt and pants had helped him blend into the shadows.

Lying there, soaked in Ergoyan's blood and his own, Malmon managed a nod.

After establishing that the three men were dead and that no one was lurking about, Gonzalez found some wire cutters and freed his partner, helping Malmon sit up.

Gonzalez called the local cops and for an ambulance, then applied makeshift dressings to Malmon's wounds.

Finally Malmon said, "What took you so damn long?"

"Come on, man," Gonzalez said, "you knew I'd get here as soon as I could."

Malmon surveyed the damage to his body, and he didn't

even want to consider the damage to his mind. Debriefing on this one would not be pleasant.

"Don't tell me you gave up on me," his partner said, making a bandage from the late Ergoyan's white shirt. "You *did* figure I was coming, right?"

"I was getting...nervous," Malmon admitted.

Shaking his head, Gonzalez said, "Jesus, man, you really gotta to learn to have a little faith."

Then his partner knelt and lifted Cruz's limp left arm, exposing the dead man's wrist, where Malmon's watch glinted back at him.

"Of course," Gonzalez said with a grin, "doesn't hurt to have a little luck while you're at it."

LIE BESIDE ME: A John Sand story

John Sand could scarcely believe the unpleasant sensation he was enduring, even though all the evidence at hand and every fiber of his being seemed to resonate with its truth. He had suffered at the hands of the most experienced practitioners of pain -- from bamboo shoots to laser beams, all applied in extremely unpleasant places -- but nothing could compare to this singular agony.

Here he was, just past his fortieth birthday, hair still black with barely a whisper of gray at the temples, muscles still toned from a life of physical activity, a young man by any reasonable standards -- a vital man.

And yet, only two years removed from MI6, he found himself -- for the first

time in a remarkably active, frequently precarious life -- experiencing a sensation surely common to the average man...a category to which he most certainly did not belong...but which he would be damned if he'd abide.

Sand -- who had traded his license to kill for a license to thrill with his beautiful wife Traci -- was bored.

There could be no other word for it. He didn't want to

be suffused with such a sorry state of mind, and until this very moment he supposed he never had been. Nevertheless, there it lay at the core of his being, like a fat, lounging cat, too ennui-ridden even to bother purring -- boredom.

Her auburn hair tied in a loose ponytail hanging nearly halfway down her spine, Traci slipped through the sliding glass doors out onto the patio of their rambling, modern ranchstyle desert home, where Sand sat nursing his vodka martini. The sun was low and throwing cool blue shadows, banishing the dry Texas wind of another hot listless day. Barely six feet away, the swimming pool beckoned, sunlight dancing on its shimmering blue skin -- perhaps a quick, bracing dive would wake him from his apathy... if only he had the energy to climb out of the deck chair. Sand felt the pool's pull evaporate as his bikini-clad wife drew his attention to her.

Almost a foot shorter than Sand's six-three, Traci's one-hundred-ten pound curvaceous frame made the skimpy red bathing suit seem even more insubstantial as the firm yet supple shelf of her bosom threatened to spill out with each step she took. He knew what she wanted, and he also knew that his current mindset left him unprepared to meet that need.

"A pound for your thoughts," she said as she eased her nearly naked body onto his lap.

Sand grinned at her, lazily. "A penny will do -- I'm an American now, you know...by marriage."

Then, striking without warning (which was, after all, his way), Sand pulled her down onto his lap, and embraced her. She smelled of peach soap, an enticing scent to which he was partial, as she well knew. Yet it wasn't working, which only served to help Sand feel more like he was at fault.

"In for a penny," she said, one hand playing with his hair, "in for a pound...."

"You'd be over-paying, darling -- you still don't understand British currency, do you?"

"I don't have to." A playful smile edged into the corners of her mouth; tiny white teeth flashed -- as perfect as Pepsodent commercial, yet exquisitely feral.

"And why is that?"

Pulling back from him slightly, Traci said, "Two reasons. One, I'm filthy rich -- y'got to love my late daddy's oil money."

Sand returned her smile but said nothing.

"And two, I'm married to you -- I'll leave it to you, to deal with that silly British Monopoly moolah."

He laughed at that and gave his wife a long, deep kiss. Sitting sideways on his lap, Traci undid her bikini top and dropped it teasingly to the cement; then her hands began to move through his hair, her breasts, soft but firm, pushing against his chest as she shifted toward him -- he could sense her need for him heightening.

She rubbed against him, shifting, almost squirming, as if trying to absorb him through her skin. The perfect valentine of her bottom seemed to be trying to polish his lap -- yet no cupid's arrow availed itself. Finally, unable to manage either the woman in his lap or his own frustration, Sand let the glass slip from his hand. As it shattered, a small spray of vodka spattered his pant leg.

A giggle welled up, then burst from Traci, as she pulled her lips away from Sand's. "Finished your cocktail?"

"Bottoms up," he said.

Rising, his wife still firmly in his arms, Sand smiled grandly at Traci as he carried her to the edge of the pool.

As she realized what he was about to do, Traci wrestled fruitlessly to free herself from his grasp. "John," she shrieked. "You wouldn't. I just did my hair, please, honey, I..."

Without a word, Sand dropped her unceremoniously into the pool. Her backside slapped the water and the water slapped back, making a huge splash. She sank, rose, and broke the water flapping, yelling, "God damn you, John Sand! I never..."

"Oh, but you have -- and frequently," he said, with a hearty laugh that seemed a balm to her anger.

Soon Traci's shattering-crystal laugh joined her husband's booming one, and she watched from the pool as he cleaned up the mess, then brought them each a fresh drink.

Soon he was stripping off his wet pants and white shirt, to join her at the pool. Naked, he sat on the edge of the shallow end as she stood nearby, water at her narrow waist, her breasts boldly white where the bikini top had shielded them from the sun, beige nipples perked by the cold water; with a casualness that was perhaps too studied, both husband and wife sipped their trademark cocktails.

For Sand, this meant a vodka martini, which had been yet another clue that a certain British novelist had nicked the former secret agent's life as the basis for a series of bestselling spy novels...although that "shaken not stirred" business seemed bloody stupid to Sand.

And for Traci, her specialty was bourbon with a single cube of ice, a concoction she'd dubbed the Titanic. When quizzed on the title, Traci had looked dreamily at the glass and said, "All that bliss and a damned iceberg."

Traci moved languidly through the glimmering water, then leaned closer, her breasts pushing warmly against his legs even in the chilly pool. "You care to tell me what's been troubling you so much lately?"

"It's nothing."

"...is it me?"

"Don't be foolish." Sand gazed into her deep green eyes; but he had to look away -- they were too probing.

Letting her free hand wrap around his back, she said, "We made a promise not to lie to each other."

"I'm not lying," he lied.

She shook her head. "Your lies may have fooled villains world 'round, my darlin'," she said, "but to me, you're this transparent." She was waving the cocktail glass in his face, the cube rattling around, a gesture that was teasing but not unkind. "I want to know why it is every time I come near you, of late, you find an excuse to not make love to me."

Sand still could not meet her gaze. "That's simply not true," he blurted.

"Ah, but it is. When was the last time we...what's that quaint Limey term? Shagged?"

He shrugged.

She touched him lightly on the tip of his nose with a fingertip. "Too damned long ago, that's for sure."

With a curt nod, Traci set her glass on the edge of the pool, climbed the short ladder, and disappeared drippingly into the house.

Sand knew he should go after her, at least call her name, but his pride or some damn thing kept him frozen there at the pool's edge; and she hadn't seemed angry, exactly... perhaps a little hurt. He just sat there, legs dangling in the pool, like a splashing child; he wondered how they had come to such a wretched state of affairs. He'd survived a world war, escaped assassins, rival secret agents, and threats too numerous to list, even to remember, and suddenly his own wife petrified him to his core...although lately the most important part of him hadn't been petrified at all.

Even bored, John Sand was a man of action, however; knowing he had to do something, he climbed out of the pool and strode naked into the house to talk to Traci.

Moving from room to room, Sand called her name but found no sign of her. Had she been angrier than he thought? Had she...left him? He ran to the garage, but found her little Austin Healy convertible still parked there beside the Bentley. Retracing his steps, he slowly searched the house, and as he stepped into the guest bedroom, he glanced at the mirror hung on the bathroom door. Inside the bathroom, he saw the back of a woman in a white bikini, starkly so against her dark tan, long tawny-blond hair trailing down her back, a knife handle protruding from the back of her fist.

Sand's heart leapt into his throat.

He hadn't seen this dimpled backside since his very first mission, but he'd never forget Greta "Honey" Bunsch -- the lushly lovely paid assassin who had very nearly done him in. Questions flew through his mind -- who sent her? how had she gotten in? -- but no time for answering them presented itself: Greta Bunsch, Honey herself, as deadly a villain as she was a beautiful woman, apparently had Traci trapped in the tub, and was about to deliver the fatal blow....

Sand leapt, grabbing the woman around the waist, yanking her back. She gasped in surprise and pain, as he dragged her rudely out of the bathroom, hauling her like a rolled-up carpet. Though he'd tried to see into the tub, he could not, his view blocked by Honey Bunsch herself. They wrestled -- she'd always been an athletic wench, strong as most men -- falling onto the bed, Sand on top, Honey putting up a good fight, her arm with the knife-in-hand extended out, as if she were trying to get an angle to thrust it into his back; but Sand had a lock on her wrist and kept the knife pointed away from him. Despite her strength, he soon gained the advantage and slowly turned the knife toward its owner.

Suddenly she simply loosened her grip on the blade, submitting, her body beneath him, too, ceasing its wriggling. Surprised, Sand looked into her face, obscured by tawny hair, and swept it away from beautiful features...

...and for the first time and realized he'd very nearly stabbed Traci!

"What the hell...Trace -- what are you doing wearing that wig?"

Her smile stunned him even more. "I thought I'd add a little spice to our love life -- by dressing up as one of your old flames."

Sand pushed away from her, his mouth hanging open.

She nodded toward his erection. "I'd say my plan worked out just fine...."

He flopped onto his back, next to her, staring up at the ceiling, breathing hard. "But...but I could have killed you."

She lay on her side beside him, taking his throbbing member in her delicate hand and squeezed gently. "It does look dangerous...but I doubt it's deadly."

"The knife, I mean!"

She shook her fake blonde locks. "Oh, we couldn't have that! That would have wrecked my plan."

Shaking his head, he asked, "Where did that outfit come from?"

Grinning with those tiny white teeth, Traci said, "I've had it for a while. I saw the photographs of the infamous Ms. Bunsch, in that Life article...I knew what that Teutonic twat looked like. I was just saving it for the right occasion. You found me before I was completely ready -- it was supposed to be a surprise."

"That it was," he said. "That it was....Christ, she's still at large, you know. This is no joke."

She was stroking him, gently, pleased at what she saw -- and held. "No...no it isn't!" With her free hand, Traci ran her fingers through the long hair of the wig. "How do you like me as a blond?"

Unable to find any words, Sand merely nodded his approval.

Traci's grin widened as she released his erection and sat like an Indian beside him, sliding the skimpy straps down her arms, exposing her full breasts to him, their full, quivering ripeness, nipples the size of sand dollars, the tips erect. "Tell me, darlin', do you think blondes reallyhave more fun?"

Sand swept her into his arms. His mouth pressed to hers in a passionate kiss, his tongue exploring her mouth. His hands found her breasts first, followed quickly by his mouth, as his hands tugged away her bikini bottoms.

As her husband devoured her, Traci moaned, her left hand around his neck, her right finding him and pumping slowly as she tried to keep him somewhat in check. Easing her hand away, Sand showered her belly with kisses as he moved off the bed. On his knees at the foot of the bed, Sand yanked Traci toward him, his tongue leaping into her wet center.

Writhing, pulling his hair as she held his head in place, Traci screamed in wonderful agony, ecstasy engulfing her, once, twice, and finally a third time before Sand let her up to catch her breath.

"Jesus," she said between gasps. "You sure are makin' up for lost time, darlin'...."

He stood and she rolled over flat on her belly -- as flat as those breasts would allow -- and took him into her mouth, just the tip at first, pausing to tell him how good he tasted, before sliding slowly down his shaft, taking more of him into her mouth, her throat, until he could feel her cute turned-up nose tickling his stomach.

She looked up at him, licking her lips, kicking her legs like a gleeful kid, the perfect globes of her ass forming that wonderful valentine, awaiting its arrow.

"More?" she asked, tongue in one corner of her mouth.

But he turned the question around on her, saying, "Much more," a Cheshire-cat grin crossing his face, as he gently turned her onto her back and crawled around and climbed on her. His mouth found her taut nipples -- the round aureole turned oblong, when excited -- then he slipped down between her legs again where his lips kissed hers and then as she started to come again, he entered her. She moaned and shuddered and wrapped her arms tightly around him, her fingernails digging into his back, her teeth nipping at his shoulder as she encircled him with her legs and bucked wildly against him until, with a great shiver, they each climaxed...then collapsed in a heap and, soon, sleep.

When Sand finally opened his eyes, the guest room was shrouded in darkness.

Traci was gone.

For a moment, he lay there wondering what the hell had happened earlier -- he felt like something his wife had rolled over, however nicely. Evidently, he wasn't quite as bored as he thought. And chances were that Traci would never let him be. That made him smile, and he was still smiling, when he heard the soft metallic rattle at the door.

He could see her outline in the light from the hallway. As she strolled confidently into the room, backlighting allowed Sand to see that she wore a black leather outfit complete with stiletto heels and a headpiece that contained only openings for eyes, nostrils, and mouth. As she came closer, he realized the rattle he'd heard had been handcuffs which dangled from her left hand -- several pairs of them!

So the game play was not over -- not that he minded. She was mimicking the deadly, delirious Fawn De Cets, the albino Basque assassin that his nemesis Jake Lonestarr had sent to kill him three years ago. Fawn was a graduate of the Marquis De Sade school of lovemaking -- an honors student...he still had the scars from the steaming-hot candlewax to prove it. A little mild S & M play might be fun, though his wife could hardly hope to compete with Fawn's expertise in pleasurable pain...or was that painful pleasure?

"Well...Fawn. Striking ensemble -- ever the dominating personality."

Traci said nothing, answering only with a tight smile as she handcuffed his right wrist to the brass headboard.

With his eyes finally adjusting to the soft lighting, Sand saw the pink tips of nipples protruding from small holes in the front of the leather suit. He nipped playfully at one as it moved past, but Traci put a hand on his chest and just shook her head. Taking the hint, Sand lay back quietly as she produced a second pair of handcuffs from somewhere and cuffed his left wrist to the headboard as well. Then his feet were bound to the footboard and Sand licked his lips in anticipation of what would come next.

At the foot of the bed, his captor ran a stray leather-gloved finger over his bare leg, then slowly allowed it to find its way to one of her exposed nipples. She rubbed against it as if trying to massage his warmth into her body. Then, slowly, she let the hand trail up to the zipper at the back of the hood.

"What do you have in mind for act two?" Sand asked.

Unzipping the hood, she let it fall away. When Sand didn't see the cascade of Traci's auburn hair, but instead a close-cropped white cap of hair, he squinted into the dim light and saw the strangely lovely if rat-like eyes in the albino face of the real Fawn De Cets.

"You!" he blurted.

She smiled sublimely down at him, her mouth a pretty pink line. "For act two, Mr. Sand? I will kill you -- very slowly. But exquisitely...your final orgasm and your final breath will be as one."

Forgetting his predicament for a moment, Sand tried to throw himself at her, but his bonds held tight and finally, in exasperation, he stopped thrashing. "What have you done with my wife?"

A cagey grin crossed the alabaster face. "I prefer to torture you with wondering... let's just say, she is unable to interrupt us."

"You heartless bitch!" Sand thrashed, metal cutting his flesh. "If you've harmed her in any way, I'll..."

Fawn took one quick step and slashed out with her gloved right hand, catching his cheek. The slap cracked like a gunshot in the small room. "You'll do nothing, Sand, unless I tell you to."

The warm taste of blood flooded Sand's mouth. Turning his head, he spit it onto the pillow next to him.

"I'll kill you fast, bitch, and the only pleasure will be mine."

For the first time, Sand could see her pinkish pretty-rodent eyes glaring down at him. She dipped her fingertip into the pool of blood and spittle on the pillow, then licked it from her finger and let out a sigh of contentment. "I love the taste of blood, Sand -- especially yours."

Holding her gaze, despite his revulsion, Sand struggled to keep his voice calm. "Where is my wife?"

"My dear Sand, while it is true you have many problems..." Her voice trailed off as a six-inch stiletto appeared in her hand. Slowly, the point of the blade ran down his chest leaving a small white indentation in his skin as it travelled toward his groin. "...but your wife is no longer one of them."

A growl of pure hatred boiled up from within him as Sand tried again to launch himself at his captor.

This time she just laughed at him.

"You are a dead woman," he said coldly, despite the heat of his rage. "So bloody dead..."

Tapping the blade against the lump in the sheets just below his waist, she said, "That doesn't seem to be what you really have on your mind."

Sand tried to will his erection away, but that only seemed to make the problem more prominent.

"I'm going to enjoy this. I've owed you this for a long time, Sand."

As the knife arced down toward his face, Sand froze, welcoming a death that would reunite him with Traci. He didn't want life without her and he wondered how he ever could have allowed boredom to come into their lives even for a moment. As the blade rushed toward him, he focused on the point, willing it to do its job quickly. At the last second, the knife swerved past his skull and Fawn jammed it just above Sand's head, into the wall, where the blade quivered.

Her laughter pealed through the room as she looked down at Sand. "I told you...very slowly, Sand, very slowly. And not before I've had my fun. My orders are to kill you, but 'how' is my business."

He said nothing as she leisurely unzipped the leather suit and stepped out of it. Her white skin offered a striking contrast to the black leather as she tossed the suit aside and moved closer to him. Her body was leaner than Traci's, her breasts somewhat smaller; but it was a body as beautiful as its owner was evil -- pale flesh interrupted only by pink nipples and the wispy platinum of her pubic triangle.

"This too," she whispered as she drew near enough for him to feel her warm breath against his face, "I have waited a long time for."

Avoiding his thrashing head, Fawn explored his chest and stomach with her hands and tongue.

Strangely, as repelled as he was emotionally and intellectually, some physical, animal part of him remained drawn enough to her shapely form for that damned erection -- where it had when he needed it? -- to stand firm.

"Wouldn't it be just...delicious...to be kissed in that most private of ways," she said, lowering her lips above his pulsing member, "wondering when sharp teeth might bite? Might even -- shall we say -- dismember? How long would it take you to bleed to death, I wonder?"

Her lips hovered above the tip of him when Sand heard a sound from the door: a throat clearing.

Fawn's head whirled away from his erection, toward the backlighted doorway.

There -- nude as a grape, blood trickling from a cut on her forehead, a set of handcuffs dangling from her left wrist -- stood Traci Sand.

She glared at the albino killer, bending over the bed.

"Excuse me," she said finally. "I believe that's my job."

Pink eyes gleaming in the dim light, Fawn snarled at her escaped prisoner, just as Traci leapt at her. The two women landed in a tangle on the bed between Sand's bound legs and for just a second the thought struck him that of all the scenarios he'd ever conceived for his demise, having it come while in bed with two naked women would normally have been near the top.

Not tonight.

The two women scratched, clawed and pulled at each other's hair, neither gaining a clear advantage until Traci hammered home a solid right that caught Fawn on the point of the jaw and sent her flailing off the bed.

Traci glanced down at Sand, nodding toward his erection. "You've got some explaining to do, mister."

"Me?" Sand asked. "I didn't invite her!"

Fawn got to her feet and lunged across Sand for the knife still embedded in the headboard. Traci understood the assassin's goal a split second too late, ending up behind Fawn, wrapping her arms around the killer's chest, her hands glued to Fawn's bare breasts, nipples popping pinkly through Traci's fingers.

Both women on top of him, the handcuffed Sand, his voice innocent, said, "We'll talk about it later, dear. I see you have your hands full just now."

Fawn strained, her fingers just a fraction short of the knife handle. Still, Traci found time to toss a glare at Sand for his smart remark. Then, just as Fawn touched the handle, Sand shifted his weight suddenly tossing both women off balance.

Traci lost her grip on the killer and Fawn grabbed the knife, yanking it free from the wall just as Traci regained her balance. Fawn swung around trying to stab Traci with a backhand motion.

Ready for her husband's bucking this time, Traci neatly blocked the thrust with her forearm and plucked the knife from Fawn's hand as the killer went flipping off the bed, over the footboard.

As Fawn -- framed in the doorway -- got to her feet ready for another assault, Traci hurled the knife end over end, the blade disappearing completely into Fawn's abdomen. The killer grunted, then looked down surprised to see the knife protruding from her albino belly, a faint trickle of red sliding down to mingle with her white pubic hair.

"It...it hurts," the killer burbled.

"Enjoy," Sand said.

Even as Fawn slowly and painfully pulled the blade from her stomach, Sand glanced toward his night table. Not needing any more prodding than that, Traci lurched to the drawer yanked it open and withdrew Sand's Walther PPK.

Fawn raised the blade over her head as blood gushed from her now open wound. Traci planted her feet -- she'd been shooting since childhood, Texas girl that she was -- and squeezed off two shots, the first ripping through Fawn's right shoulder, spinning her around so the second bullet caught her in the middle of the back and sent her tumbling out into the hallway, where she sprawled in a lifeless heap of pale flesh.

Traci crossed the room and went out to check the body, to make sure the killer was dead.

Satisfied, she re-entered the bedroom, turning her attention to her trussed-up husband. "Would you like to explain that?"

"I...I thought she was you. More of this fantasy routine. Then she..."

"Oh, John, really, she doesn't look a thing like me."

"Yes, well, that's true, but she was wearing that," he tossed his head toward the leather suit on the floor.

Fists on her hips, like Wonder Woman (only naked), Traci smirked down at her bound husband. "So you let her handcuff you to the bed?"

Sand smiled sheepishly. "It seemed like the thing to do, at the time....And where were you anyway?"

She gestured with her head and the auburn hair flounced. "I'd gone to use the shower off our bedroom; I didn't want to disturb you. That witch jumped me, hit me in the head with something, then handcuffed me to the pipe under the sink."

He smiled, proud of her. "And you took the plumbing apart to escape."

Traci nodded. "Made a hell of a mess on the floor...but nothing like this."

"I presume the keys for these things are in that suit," Sand said, nodding toward the discarded, exotic garment as he rattled the cuffs.

She ignored him and sat on the edge of the bed leaning over him, her dangling hair nearly touching his face. "I'm not sure I want to let you go, just yet. Maybe I wanna brand you, like a steer...."

Sand tried to look serious. "For God's sake, Traci, there's a dead body out in the hall!"

Traci thought about that for a moment, then she went over and slammed the door on the corpse.

"Screw her," she said. Then her expression darkened -- or pretended to. She pointed at her husband. "No, John Sand -- screw you!"

And she did.

Several times -- during none of which did he think of any other woman.

THE HIGH LIFE

Summer had invaded Iowa like a horde of Huns in early June, looting and pillaging through July and most of August. Each week the heat seemed to grow more intense, the crops suffering in the rural areas, everybody in the cities becoming grumpy, then angry, then just plain pissed off.

Now, with Labor Day only a couple of weeks away, the nights still saw temperatures in the high eighties with equal humidity making for heat indexes over ninety and a violent crime rate rising at an exponential rate to the temperature increase. The steep rise in violence had so overtaxed the city's crime lab that the state Bureau of Criminal Investigation, the state lab, located just up the road in Ankeny, had been forced to pitch in on most nights.

In Des Moines, the sweltering community had become so testy that two citizens had been shot to death at the scenes of separate fender-benders in the last two days. One of them not even involved in the crash, merely an onlooker who had spoken up at the wrong time. The capital was supposed to be a friendly, warm-hearted place to live. This summer it had turned into an unfriendly, hot-headed place with suspicious glances taking the place of ready smiles, hospitality swapped out for paranoia, and violence replacing tolerance.

As the cauldron of hate simmered, the concrete buildings of downtown Des Moines worked like a giant oven, holding the heat and insuring that the occupation army of high humidity and even higher temperatures would easily defeat any hint of a cool breeze that might sweep in off the rain-deprived crops of the farmland on the north and west sides of the city. One of these downtown buildings, a new high-rise apartment complex, the Crossroads Towers, had been open less than a year and had been sold to its potential residents as a paradise in the heart of the city. Complete with a full-service mall on the ground floor, including a grocery store, the well-to-do residents would never have to enter the real world again if they could work from home.

Tonight, though, with heat lightning cracking across the sky, the real world had entered the Crossroads Towers where even the twenty-fifth floor didn't seem high enough to avoid the rage that gripped the city. The BCI crime scene team was being called to the scene of an alleged murder-suicide.

Pulling up to the guard shack that protected the entrance to the Crossroads Towers underground parking facility, BCI crime scene supervisor Dale Hawkins, "Hawk" to his friends and subordinates, was loathe to roll down the window to speak to the guard.

Fiftyish with dark hair, graying at the temples and receding faster than he would like, Hawkins didn't want to let the air-conditioning out and the heat in. Slim, rectangular black-framed glasses perched atop a nose that might just as easily have been the source of Hawkins's nickname as was his surname. He wore a black short-sleeved shirt with BCI-

CSA embroidered inside a badge over the left pocket, the word supervisor embroidered beneath the emblem. Black slacks and matching black Rocky oxfords completed the outfit. Cops only wore two brands of shoes, Rockys or Bates. Hawkins had always been a Rocky man. His only accessory was a Glock 21 .45 automatic that dug into his right hip under the seat belt.

In the passenger seat, willowy brunette Krysti Raines tried not to look as nervous as Hawkins was sure she felt. Porcelain skinned with wide-set brown eyes almost as dark as the chestnut locks clipped into a short bob, she was riding into her first crime scene as a CSA.

Four years on patrol with the Des Moines PD, Raines's road to detective was gridlocked by the seemingly endless supply of gold shields in front of her who never retired or got better jobs. Seeing her wasting away and getting more and more frustrated, Hawkins had lured her away to the BCI. He had practically watched her grow up with the PD. Hell, he had even instructed her fingerprint class. She had excelled in several other classes too and Hawkins knew she had the skills to handle the job of Crime Scene Analyst. Now, they would both find out if he was right.

Reluctantly, Hawkins finally pushed the button on the electric window. The glass hummed down, the heat pouring in like he had opened an oven door. The guard stepped closer, his thin mouth a straight-line frown telling Hawkins that he didn't want to be out in the heat any more than the CSA supervisor did. Pushing sixty, the guard could easily be a retired cop, but Hawkins didn't recognize him. The guard's name tag read STUART, and Hawkins briefly wondered if it was a first or a last name as he showed the guard his credentials.

"What about her?" Stuart asked, his voice obviously

ravaged by years of cigarettes.

"She's with me," Hawkins said.

Raines held her own credentials towards the driver's side so the guard could get a better look.

Finally, Stuart nodded them through. "Take the elevator to the twenty-fifth..."

Hawkins pulled away before the guard finished. He knew where the crime was and the guard knew he knew. This had just been Stuart trying to exercise the minimal authority he carried. Hawkins couldn't help but wonder if the guard had been this diligent all evening. He would make sure the detectives questioned him about people coming in and out this evening. As Hawkins wound the SUV through the aisles of the parking garage, Raines remained conspicuously silent next to him.

At this hour, nearly two in the morning, there were no parking places anywhere near the elevator doors.

"Naturally," Hawkins muttered.

Turning to him, eyes bright with curiosity, Raines said, "Pardon?"

"Nothing, nothing."

He turned into a parking place clear across the garage diagonally from the elevators. He kept his face a blank mask as they climbed out of the lab's black Chevy Suburban and marched to the back to unload.

Raines's outfit mirrored Hawkins's, black Rockys, black slacks, and black Polo with the embroidered BCI badge on the breast pocket. Her shirt was a small, compared to his extra-large. She gave up six or seven inches to his six-two and weighed half his two-twenty. Though not as rock hard as he had been even ten years ago, Hawkins was still a long way from doughy. It wasn't enough that her weight was only fifty percent of his, so was her age. Being roughly the same age as his oldest daughter gave Hawkins a paternal feeling about his new assistant.

He opened the vehicle's back doors and they each grabbed a silver, metallic crime scene case, Hawkins choosing to be chivalrous enough to also lug the camera case.

"I can get that," Raines said, hand snaking towards the case.

Whether the offer had been made in deference to his seniority or due to his seniority, Hawkins could not tell. He shook his head. "I'll get it. If you're as good at this job as I think you'll be, you'll have twenty-five more years to lug this thing around."

"There's something to look forward to," Raines said, barely a trace of sarcasm in her voice, as Hawkins closed and locked the Suburban's rear doors.

"Long hours, low pay, no gratitude from the bosses or the clients and on top of all that, if you make a mistake, you lose your certification and your job. What's not to love?"

He referred to the position Raines was going after, Certified Latent Print Examiner. In the state of Iowa, only a dozen people, including Hawkins, held the certification and only a couple of hundred nationwide had attained the status conferred by the International Association for Identification. The price for a single error was the loss of certification. Every member of the small fraternity knew the price of a mistake and it wasn't just their job, it also meant that an innocent person might go to prison, or in some states, death based on an ident they made. In the eyes of the CLPEs, the standards were no higher than the stakes involved.

"You make the job sound so appealing," Raines said as they crossed the silent garage. Though full of cars, there was no one down here at this hour and the place was as silent as church.

They got to the elevators and Raines touched the up button. It lit and they had to wait for only a moment before the doors whispered open. The pair got in with their gear.

"What floor?" Raines asked.

"Twenty-five."

"The penthouse?"

"One of them," Hawkins said. "My understanding is there's four, two on each of the top two floors."

"Probably pricey."

"No 'probably' about it, a cool million apiece if what I heard is true."

"Money's a good motive for murder," Raines said as the elevator lifted them up to the twenty-fifth floor, then eased to a stop.

"Let's not get ahead of ourselves," Hawkins said.

Raines nodded as the doors slid open.

The normally quiet hall bustled with people and noise. There were only two apartments on this floor, one to the left and one to the right, yet the small foyer they shared was jammed with two uniformed officers, two EMTs, a guy from the coroner's office, two civilians, probably the neighboring couple, and Detective Ron Stark, a short, skinny guy with longish, dark hair parted on the left, Hawkins knew Stark was smarter than his more senior partner, but Yackowski's larger personality always seemed to push Stark into the shadows. The kid, he was maybe early thirties, wore a dark suit that seemed too big for him and had inquisitive gray eyes and a hook nose that dominated the rest of his face.

"Been a while," Stark said, his voice quiet but friendly.

Hawkins nodded. "The gang thing over by Drake in April?"

"Yeah," Stark said. "That was a bad one." He looked to Raines. "Hey, Krysti, like the new job?"

She smiled at the detective. "So far."

"Good, you deserve it."

"Thanks."

"What's up, Ron?" Hawkins asked.

"Same shit, Hawk, different night."

"You want to be more specific?"

Stark just shook his head and pointed towards the open door on the right. "You might as well just ask Yack. Ain't no point in you hearing the same shit twice."

"Yack's here?" Hawkins asked.

Stark nodded. "High profile crime, high profile detective. These rich people start killing each other, you know Chief Anderson's going to demand his best man. And you just know Yack can't wait to tell you how he solved the case already."

Yack—Phil Yackowski was, by his own admission, Des Moines' top crime solving detective. Hawkins had known the curly-haired Yackowski for the better part of twenty years and, unlike the public, knew that the detective had made his bones solving the murder of a doctor's wife by her husband by stealing the credit from a beat cop who had actually been the one to find the vital clue.

Gesturing vaguely towards a man and woman huddled in front of the door to the left, Stark said, "Roger and Angela Triplett. They're the tenants across the hall."

Giving them a quick onceover, they both appeared to be about forty, Hawkins was struck by the incongruity of their dress. Mrs. Triplett, an auburn-haired beauty with piercing green eyes and a look of utter confusion etched on her heart-shaped face, wore a gold evening gown cut just low enough to offer a hint of the charms beneath the flimsy fabric. Meanwhile, her husband, Roger, his dark hair short in an almost flattop, wore jeans and a white

Polo and expensive tennis shoes. He had a furrowed brow over brown eyes that seemed dazed by the crowd and the activity. He kept a protective arm around his wife's creamy shoulders and Hawkins noticed a tiny burn on the man's forearm.

"What's their story?" Hawkins asked.

"Mrs. Triplett was downstairs. She was hosting a charity function in the second-floor ballroom. Her husband said he wasn't feeling well so he's been in their apartment all night. He heard the shots, called us."

"You'd think for a million bucks, they'd have better soundproofing," Hawkins said.

Stark shrugged.

"Can I talk to him for a second?"

"Sure."

They approached the couple and Stark made the introductions.

"Mr. Triplett," Hawkins said, after they had shaken hands. "You said you heard the shots."

"Yeah."

"Aren't these apartments soundproofed?"

"Yeah," Triplett said. "Really well. You have to understand, it was very faint. But I do know a gunshot when I hear one. I served in Iraq."

Given the man's age, Hawkins was a little surprised.

"Not this time. Desert Storm, back in '91," Triplett said, answering Hawkins's unasked question. "That's why, no matter how faint, I know a gunshot or, in this case, shots, when I hear them."

Hawkins gave a quick nod of understanding. "And you, Mrs. Triplett?"

The woman seemed to shrink further into her husband's embrace at the mention of her name.

"I was downstairs until Roger called my cell and told me what had happened," she said, a quaver in her voice.

He wanted to ask how she could possibly conceal a cellphone inside that dress, but Hawkins decided not to push it for now.

"What about your neighbors?"

"The Hoffs?" Triplett asked.

Hawkins said nothing. To his surprise, it was Angela who spoke up.

"I knew Carl had a vindictive streak, but I never imagined him capable of anything like this."

"So, they were having trouble?"

"They were separated," Triplett said. "Caroline was living here, Carl spent most of his time away on business."

"What kind of business?" Hawkins asked.

"He was a commercial real estate developer. He had deals going on all over the country."

"Did he have a history of violence?"

Triplett shook his head. "Not that I know of. I had no idea that either of them even had a gun."

"Thank you," Hawkins said. "I'm sure Detective Stark told you we might have more questions later."

They both nodded.

As Hawkins and Raines moved away, Hawkins turned his attention to Stark.

"Hell of a thing," Hawkins said.

"Yeah," Stark agreed.

"And Yack's already inside?" Hawkins asked.

The other two men traded a look, then both nodded.

"Uh huh," Hawkins said.

Stark said, "You two better get in there before Yack figures out that it was a double suicide."

Hawkins turned towards the open door of the other

apartment, Raines on his hip. They stopped long enough to don latex gloves and plastic shoe covers with the word "POLICE" stenciled in the bottom so they could tell their own footprints from any they lifted. One thing Hawkins knew for sure, unless the perp was Peter Pan and flew into the crime scene, he left footprints.

They stepped from reality into fantasy. The living room was huge, probably bigger than any two rooms in Hawkins's house. The floor was a light-hued hardwood, shiny as the sun on a summer day. The wall opposite the door was at least nine feet high and all glass. Hawkins had the thought that maybe someone saw the murders through the window, then, instantly, realized he was in the tallest building in the city and that a witness would have to be in a low-flying plane to see through these windows.

"Nice place," Raines said to no one in particular.

The right-hand wall was made up mostly of bookshelves that ran floor to ceiling and were filled with hardback books that looked like they had been shelved more for their appearance than what was between their covers. A large center section held not books but a big screen plasma television. In front of that a living room set made up of a long, wide sofa, two huge chairs with ottomans and a glass coffee table was laid out atop a white area rug. The furniture was made of white leather and obviously expensive. At the near end of the shelves, a dark corridor led back to what Hawkins assumed would be bedrooms and the bathroom.

Behind the living room, to the left, the large room was bisected by a stone wall that contained what Hawkins was sure was a gas-driven fireplace. There were large openings on either side of the fireplace wall that Hawkins estimated at about eight feet wide. He figured the far opening led to the kitchen while through the near one Hawkins could see a full bar and another uniformed cop who waved.

Before Hawkins could say or do anything, Raines stepped up. "C.J., what's up?"

"Hey, Krysti," the uniform said. He was a tall, broad-shouldered kid with a blond crewcut and an easy smile.

"Jacobsen," a voice growled from a part of the next room that Hawkins couldn't see. It didn't matter, he recognized the cantankerous tone of Phil Yackowski.

The blond uniform turned away from them.

"Does your opening your mouth mean the crime scene people are finally here?"

Hawkins felt his temper rising. Stepping forward and peering around the stone fireplace, he saw Yackowski standing next to a white piano and directly between two bodies that were lying on the floor, one male, one female, a small puddle of blood near the man, relatively little blood around the woman. She wore only a revealing negligee, her breasts clearly visible through the gauzy material. She lay on her back, a small, neat entry wound in her forehead. The male victim lay on his stomach at almost a ninety-degree angle from the woman, his head lying on the left cheek, his eyes open, staring at nothing. He wore a tan Polo shirt, khakis, and expensive brown loafers with no socks. A .9mm automatic lay on the floor near his right hand. He had an entrance wound on the right side of his head,

"Yackowski," Hawkins snapped, his voice sharp as a razor. "What are you doing here?"

The detective, a muscle-bound weightlifter whose biceps bulged beneath the polyester of his navy-blue suit jacket, wore a mock turtleneck that looked more like a tee shirt since he had no neck to speak of. He had a florid face, a nose that had been broken at least twice and a forehead big enough to serve as a solar panel.

"Hawk," the detective growled. Then trying to regain control, he added, "the chief wanted the best on this one."

"So, where's Dearden?"

"Dearden?" Yackowski sneered. "What's he got that I ain't got?"

"Sense enough not to tromp through a crime scene for one thing."

Yackowski's already ruddy face turned crimson as he looked down to see where he was standing. "I...I was studying the evidence."

Shaking his head, Hawkins said, "You were contaminating the evidence, Yack. You think you can get out of there without destroying any more than you have already?"

The detective fumed, but carefully walked over until he was in front of Hawkins, less than a foot between the two, the BCI supervisor at least three inches taller than the detective.

"It doesn't matter anyway," Yackowski said. "This fucker's open and shut."

"Really?" Hawkins asked, his voice mild as he stared into the hateful brown eyes of the detective. "Why don't you tell me how you know that?"

"The woman," Yackowski said, pointing vaguely in the direction of the female victim, "Caroline Hoff, this is her place."

"Rich lady," Hawkins said.

"Not so much. She was married to decedent number two, Carl Hoff. Rich guy with a pretty, little trophy wife. Problem was, it was a stormy romance. They were getting divorced. She had the apartment. He couldn't take it. So, he comes over, they argue, one thing leads to another, bing, bang, boom, murder-suicide."

"Any witnesses?" Hawkins asked.

"Neighbor across the hall said he heard the shots. He was the one that called it in. Besides, what do you care? You're all about the evidence, right?"

Hawkins nodded. "Still, you seem so sure about your scenario, I figured you had an eyewitness."

"I don't need one when they're this easy," Yackowski said smugly.

Glancing at the two bodies, Hawkins moved closer to them. Squatting next to the male victim, Hawkins examined the entrance wound in the man's head, near the backside of his right ear. There was a small, neat hole, not unlike the woman's wound and though there was a smear of blood around the wound, that was all Hawkins saw and it troubled him.

"Yack, nothing would give me more pleasure than to let you go to Chief Anderson with your half-baked theory..."

"Half-baked?" Yackowski interrupted, his face turning red again.

"Yeah, half-baked. This is a double murder."

Yackowski wanted to argue, it was plain on his face, but there was something else there too, confusion. "Not a murder-suicide?" he asked, incredulous.

"If it is," Hawkins said, "Mr. Hoff shot himself from about where you're standing then managed to cross that six feet and beat the bullet here."

"Huh?"

"There's no powder burns, Yack. If he shot himself, he'd have powder burns around the wound. There would probably be a starburst wound from a contact or near contact wound too. That's not here either and to top it off, unless Hoff was double-jointed I'm not sure how he shot himself from this angle. The wound was delivered from almost behind him. Tough shot if you're holding the gun yourself."

Yackowski stood there dumbfounded, mouth hanging open slightly.

"Still if somebody is going to shoot themselves tonight, it might as well be you shooting yourself in the foot when you go tell Anderson your half-baked theory."

"All right, all right," Yackowski said, patting the air in front of him. "I get it. You do the crime scene, then we'll go talk to the neighbor again. Maybe he heard more than shots. He might have heard the killer."

"That's the first good idea you've had in years."

The detective glared but said nothing.

"The second-best idea you can come up with is taking off your shoes and giving them to CSA Raines."

"What the fuck?"

Hawkins's voice remained calm as he shook his foot towards Yackowski. "You don't have on shoe covers. You want us to be able to tell your prints from the killer's or would you just like to confess now?"

Grumbling the entire time, Yackowski slipped off his shoes and handed them to Raines who bagged them.

"How long are you going to have them?" Yackowski asked.

Raines looked a question at Hawkins. The supervisor looked towards Jacobsen, the uniformed cop, and asked, "How long was he in there?"

The young cop looked scared as he glanced at the detective, but he said, "About fifteen minutes."

Nodding, Hawkins said, "Two days per minute, I figure you'll be getting your shoes back in about a month, Yack."

"A month?" Yackowski exploded. "That's bullshit!"

"How many times have you been told not to enter a crime scene without shoe covers?"

The detective grew silent, eyes scanning the floor as if

the answer might be etched in the wood.

"I thought so. Time you learned."

Hawkins watched as Yackowski left, shuffling on the hardwood floor in his stocking feet, grumbling the whole way, Jacobsen trailing him as far as the door.

When the others were out of earshot, Raines said, "You two don't seem to get along very well."

Rising from his position over the body, Hawkins managed a small smile. "I told you you'd make a good crime scene analyst."

"Thanks," Raines said, only a trace of sarcasm in her voice. "Where do you want to start?"

"You do the bodies and the immediate scene. I'm going to look around a little. I want to make sure we can rule out robbery as a motive."

The rookie looked hesitant. "Are you sure you don't want to do the bodies yourself?"

Hawkins took a couple of steps towards her. "You're going to have to do it sooner or later, might as well be sooner."

"But..."

"No buts," Hawkins said. "You're as natural at this as anyone I've seen and you've had good training, Krysti. Trust it."

She took a deep breath and let it out. "Yes, sir."

Shaking his head and turning towards the living room, Hawkins said, "Rufus was right."

"Pardon?"

"Nothing, Raines. Go to work," Hawkins said, strolling away so she could concentrate and not feel like he was watching her every move.

Returning to the living room, Hawkins looked around. Knick-knacks on the coffee table were untouched, magazines were stacked neatly. On a side table next to the front door, a small basket held envelopes that proved to be the day's mail and a set of keys, presumably Mrs. Hoff's. Everything seemed to be in order. He went down the hall. On the left, he peeked into a small bedroom that had been turned into an office. Again, nothing seemed disturbed.

On the right side of the corridor, he entered a bathroom that felt like stepping onto the flight deck of the starship Enterprise. Along the wall to his right, two glass sinks perched atop twin black columns beneath two stainless steel plates and no visible faucets. Beyond those, a small cubicle held the toilet. Against the left wall was a deep, two-person tub outfitted with water jets. Dominating the center of the far wall was a glass-enclosed shower with four brass shower heads aimed at various angles. The glass walls still showed beads of water. In front of the shower a huge, furry, lavender rug covered most of the Mexican tile floor.

Squatting down, Hawkins investigated the rug. It felt damp, but not wet. Someone had taken a shower earlier in the evening. He looked at the towel rack on the wall next to the shower—empty. Maybe Mrs. Hoff had taken the towel, or towels, into the bedroom with her. Getting down closer, his face mere inches from the rug, Hawkins peered at the footprints pressed into the nap. They were already fading away, and there was no way to preserve them, but Hawkins was sure he could see the outlines of at least two different size feet in the damp rug. Mrs. Hoff had been wearing a negligee but Mr. Hoff had been completely dressed. Could they have had a short-term reconciliation that went bad later? Maybe.

Hawkins pulled a short, plastic ruler from his pants pocket. He normally used it to give scale to evidence he was photographing, but tonight he used it to measure the disappearing footprints in the rug. The first print was almost exactly eight inches long, the length of Hawkins's ruler. The second print was at least two inches longer than the first and much wider. A man, Hawkins figured.

Again, he wondered where the bath towels were. Looking at a second towel rack between the sinks, he noticed two lavender hand towels that matched the rug. Rising, he considered trying to photograph the footprints but knew that if he could manage to get the lighting right, they would have long since disappeared.

Leaving the bathroom, he returned to the corridor which held two doors on the left side. The first door led into a small bedroom that had been turned into an immaculate office. A computer desk occupied one corner, the monitor on top was in sleep mode with the power on. This room also looked undisturbed.

Hawkins moved back into the hallway and moved to the last doorway, the master bedroom. Flipping on the light, he noticed this room, too, was immaculate. A tall armoire stood immediately to the right of the doorway. A king-size bed took most of the right-hand wall along with two nightstands. In the corner in front of him, a television and dvd player occupied the top of a dresser. Nearer to him, on the left-hand wall, a double-door closet was closed. Opening it carefully, he pushed back both doors all the way without touching any areas that might contain fingerprints.

What he sought stood against the right-hand wall of the closet, a wicker laundry hamper. Flipping up the lid, he used his mini-MagLite to provide light inside. He moved around a few of the things on the top, but there were no towels. Where the hell had they gone?

He knew that someone, probably two people, had showered earlier in the evening. Why weren't the towels here?

Shaking his head, confused, Hawkins turned away from the closet and let his eyes wander the room as if the towels would suddenly appear in front of him. He was staring emptily at the bed when he realized that there was a wrinkle in the floral bedspread just in front of where it disappeared beneath the pillows.

The wrinkle needled Hawkins. It wasn't that he was an OCD person who needed everything just so, but the obsessive-compulsive who lived here was. That meant that even this tiny wrinkle, something Yackowski probably would have overlooked if he had even bothered to look into the room. To Hawkins, it yapped like an angry little dog. There was no way Mrs. Hoff would have been able to tolerate this affront to her neatness.

Raines appeared in the doorway. Hawkins just looked at her.

"Something's not right," Raines said.

"No shit," Hawkins said.

She eyed him, confusion evident on her face.

"Never mind," Hawkins said, concentrating on his new associate now. "What's not right?"

"There's no shell casings."

Hawkins stared at her, considering that. "There has to be. The pistol's an automatic. The ejected shells are somewhere."

"Agreed," Raines said. "They're just not in this apartment."

"Really?"

"Well, not in the room where the crime happened anyway."

"You've moved the furniture?"

She nodded.

"The bodies?"

Another nod.

Hawkins felt a headache coming on. First the towels disappeared, now the shell casings. Some murder-suicide. He still had a hunch about the wrinkle in the bed. Maybe, just maybe, he could also use this as an opportunity to teach. Glancing at Raines, he asked, “What do you see?”

She looked around the room for a long moment before saying anything. When, at last, she did speak, she pointed towards the closet. “I see the same thing in here that I saw in the rest of the apartment—somebody with serious obsessive-compulsive issues. The hangers all face the same direction. The clothes are divided by her good clothes, her work clothes, and her casual clothes, and within those sections, sub-divided by style and color. Everything has a place and everything is in its place.”

Hawkins nodded his approval. “Good. Anything else?”

Raines looked around again, Hawkins watching her.

Finally, she faced him and shrugged. “I don’t know what it is you want me to see.”

Staying patient, Hawkins said, “Does anything look out of place?”

Her eyes passed slowly over the room again.

Hawkins was about to tell her his theory when she suddenly said, “The bedspread. It’s wrinkled.”

Smiling, he said, “I told you that you would be good at this.”

She blushed a little. “But what does it mean?”

Hawkins shrugged. “Maybe something, maybe nothing, but the small out of place things can sometimes be the most important. Do you have a forceps with you?”

Nodding, she pulled the ten-inch stainless steel tool off a loop on her belt and handed it to Hawkins.

He took it, opened the serrated jaws, got the end of the bedspread between them and locked the jaws, then he pulled back revealing the pink blanket beneath. It, too, was wrinkled. Releasing the jaws of the forceps, the bedspread fell away and he repeated the action with the forceps on the blanket and top sheet. Beneath that, on the pink satin bottom sheet, there was a wet spot the size of a half-dollar near the middle of the bed. Hawkins wondered who had made the deposit.

"Looks like someone had sex recently," Raines said.

"You're going to swab that, right?"

Raines was already moving in, buccal swab at the ready. "Damn right."

She pushed the swab up out of its protective plastic sleeve and gently wiped it over the spot on the bed. Next, she pulled the paper handle so the swab disappeared back into the sleeve. She snapped the small lid on it and then held it carefully as she handed Hawkins a roll of an adhesive tag from her pocket.

Using his Sharpie, Hawkins dated the tag, initialed it, then pulled off the backing and handed it to Raines who placed it over the lid of the swab sleeve, sealing it.

"What have we got?" Hawkins asked.

Raines took a deep breath, then let it out. Holding up the swab, she said, "We have evidence that someone, probably Mrs. Hoff and a partner had sex in this room."

"Her ex?"

Raines considered that, then shook her head. "Doubtful. I used the electrostatic print lifter and got footprints off the wood floor. I think there was a third person here. Another man, this one wearing sneakers."

Hawkins told her his theory about the towels and the wet rug in the bathroom.

"So, there were three people here."

"I think Carl Hoff definitely interrupted something. Tell

me about the shootings."

"Both were shot from a distance of about six feet. It looks like they were both shot with the same gun, about the same caliber anyway, judging from the entry wounds, and the shell casings have disappeared from Hoff's automatic."

"Anything else?"

"The footprints indicate there was a struggle between the man wearing the tennis shoes and Hoff. Hoff was trying to get away when the man shot him. The killer wiped the gun clean of fingerprints then put it on the floor near Hoff."

"Which one of them shot Mrs. Hoff?" Hawkins asked.

"Hoff tested positive for gunshot residue. It looks like he shot his wife, wrestled with her lover, lost the fight for the gun, then tried to get away but got shot in the head."

"What's the first rule about witnesses?" asked Hawkins.

Raines gave him an odd look. "First on the scene, first suspect."

"Good. Now, who called in the crime?"

"The neighbor, Roger Triplett."

"Right. What kind of shoes was he wearing?"

"Tennis shoes."

"Did you notice the burn on his arm?"

"Yeah. It wasn't very big."

"About the size of an ejected shell casing?" Hawkins asked.

"Oh shit."

"Yeah. I want you to go get Yackowski and Stark."

"Right away," she said, turning towards the door.

"Krysti."

She stopped and looked back.

"If Triplett's still in the hall, don't let him know you know. If we're going to convict him, we're going to want the towels and casings. He didn't have time to leave the building. They've got to be here somewhere. Hopefully, he was dumb enough to hide them in his own apartment, but if not, we need to search for them."

She gave him a quick nod and headed down the hall. As soon as she was gone, Hawkins pulled out his cellphone and woke Judge Jonathon Maynard from a sound sleep. The judge was, naturally, livid but once Hawkins explained the situation, Maynard agreed to sign a search warrant and fax it to the security office of Crossroads Towers.

Closing his cell and returning it to his pocket, Hawkins went out to the primary crime scene where Raines and the two detectives waited for him.

"What did you figure out?" Yackowski asked, his tone that of a diner who had just found a dead mouse in his salad.

Not sure whether he was doing it to rub the detective's nose in it or whether he was truly helping Raines get used to doing it, he had the first-time crime scene analyst explain their findings to the detectives.

When she finished, Yackowski said, "You're shitting me."

"Nope," Hawkins said.

"If Triplett got the gun," Stark said, "why shoot Hoff?"

Hawkins said, "Well, for one thing, Hoff now had a witness to him killing his wife. If he got away, Triplett would never be safe. At some point, Triplett's going to claim self-defense."

Stark shrugged. "Could it have been?"

"If it was," Hawkins said, "what was Triplett protecting himself from? Hoff was disarmed and running away. Self-defense is not shooting a man in the back of the head from six feet away. If it was self-defense, why steal the evidence? What we have here is two separate homicides. Hoff shot his ex-wife, then Triplett shot Hoff. The crimes just happened to have been committed with the same weapon."

Shaking his head, Yackowski said, "And you're sure the lab will find what you say they'll find?"

"They'll do all the tests, but I'm betting we'll get a DNA match from the bed, match his shoes to the prints in the dining room, and we can probably get a positive GSR test with the warrant. If we find the towels and shell casings, we'll have a slam dunk."

Turning to Stark, Yackowski asked, "Where's Triplett now?"

Shrugging, Stark said, "I think he and his wife went to bed. I know they went into their apartment. Hell, it couldn't have been ten minutes ago."

Without another word, the quartet moved through the apartment and into the corridor.

A security guard in a Crossroads Towers suit jacket and black slacks waited for them. He held out a small sheaf of papers. "Which one of you is Mr. Hawkins?"

Stepping forward, Hawkins accepted the papers. They had their search warrant. "Thanks."

Yackowski was the one who knocked on the Tripletts' door. There was no answer.

Turning to the security guard, Hawkins asked, "How many elevators are running at this hour?"

The guard said, "Just the one. Security. We lock down the others."

Yackowski pounded on the door again.

"Was anyone in the elevator when you got on?" Hawkins asked.

The guard shook his head.

The apartment door opened and a teary Angela Triplett opened the door.

"We need to speak to your husband," Yackowski snapped.

"She took an involuntary step backwards. "H...He's not here."

"Where is he?"

The woman was crying again now. "The stress of all this was too much, he went out for a pack of smokes. He knows I hate it when he smokes so he won't do it here."

Yackowski turned towards the elevator.

Hawkins stepped forward. "Mrs. Triplett, this is important, how long ago did he leave?"

"Not even five minutes ago," she managed through ragged breaths as she dabbed a hanky to her eyes.

"Was he carrying anything?"

The woman looked puzzled, her handkerchief now being twisted between her hands. "How did you know?"

Ignoring her question, Hawkins asked his own. "What was it?"

"He said he was going to drop the garbage down the chute," she said pointing at a small door recessed in the wall between the apartments.

Hawkins turned back to the group as Yackowski punched the elevator button. "He's in the stairwell!"

Yackowski stood frozen for a second, but Stark hit the stairway door and started down. The burly Yackowski came out of his trance and tossed a walkie-talkie to Hawkins. "Stay in touch," he said as he went through the door behind his partner and sprinted down the stairs.

"Follow them," Hawkins barked to Raines. "He might just be dumb enough to ditch the evidence in the building's trash bin."

With a curt nod, Raines disappeared through the door and down the stairs after the two detectives and the suspect.

The elevator dinged and the door slid open. Hawkins stepped inside.

"You want me to come with you?" the security guard asked.

"No," Hawkins barked, holding the door open. "You stay here. Are you armed?"

The guard nodded and held up a small can of pepper spray.

"You stay with Mrs. Triplett. Make sure she doesn't warn her husband."

"Yes, sir."

"If Triplett comes back, you don't hesitate, you don't warn him, you just spray the hell out of him and call 911. You understand?"

"Yes, sir," the guard said.

Hawkins expected the guy to salute and snap his heels together, but, thankfully, the doors whispered shut and the elevator started its descent. Hawkins had pressed the button for the parking garage, figuring that was where Triplett was headed. As he rode, Hawkins pulled his pistol and clicked off the safety. Triplett had left Hoff's gun at the crime scene, but that didn't mean he didn't have one of his own.

As the elevator eased to a stop, Hawkins dropped into a shooter's stance. He knew he was ahead of Raines and the detectives in getting to the parking garage, but he probably wasn't ahead of Triplett. If the killer was waiting for him when the doors opened, well, Hawkins had seen The Departed and he wasn't going out that way.

The doors silently slid open and Hawkins arced the gun across the opening. He saw nothing in the darkness. Stepping out into the concrete dungeon, Hawkins waited a few seconds as his eyes adjusted to the dim light of the garage. He listened carefully to the silence. A sound, any sound, the scraping of a shoe on the concrete, the click of the safety of a gun, the clunk of a car door, anything that would tell him where Triplett was.

Creeping forward, pistol at the ready, Hawkins strained

to see into the cars on either side of him as he moved down the middle of the aisle. He wished he had thought to ask Mrs. Triplett where their parking place was. This was slow going, one car at a time, first on the left, then on the right, then back on the left.

Sweat ran down Hawkins's back, his hair matted to his forehead as he inched forward. The garage was cooler than outside but only a little and the heat pressed in on Hawkins as he searched the Lexus, then the BMW, then the Jaguar.

Still there was no sign of Triplett.

To his left and behind him Hawkins heard the scraping of a door and it occurred to him that maybe he had beaten Triplett to the garage and the killer was now behind him. Spinning, Hawkins trained his pistol on the doorway and saw a 9mm Glock coming through the door first. He increased the pressure on the trigger. Just as he was about to squeeze off a round, Hawkins saw the burly frame of Yackowski follow his pistol into the garage.

A car roared to life and Hawkins spun away from Yackowski as a gray Lexus zoomed out of a parking place, tires squealing as it hurtled towards him.

Steadying himself, even as he heard Raines scream behind him, Hawkins took aim and squeezed the trigger, once, twice, three times. The car continued towards him even as the first shot tore through the windshield. The other two bullets followed the leader through the spidering glass as Hawkins dove for cover between two cars.

The Lexus heeled to the left, scraping against a concrete pillar, sparks flying as the car smashed into a parked Cadillac.

Even before the sound of the crash had fully died away, Hawkins was on his feet, running towards the smashed Lexus, his gun in front of him. The air bag had deployed and Triplett was trying to get out from under it as Hawkins aimed his pistol through the shattered passenger side window. "Freeze!"

Triplett stopped battling the bag and raised his hands. Yackowski, Stark and Raines came running up. Yackowski and Stark yanking the suspect out of the car and cuffing him.

When Hawkins backed out of the car, Raines reached through the window, picked up a white garbage bag and carefully shook the broken glass off it. She laid the bag on the concrete floor and, wearing latex gloves, opened it. She pulled out two lavender bath towels that Hawkins recognized as a match to the ones in the Hoff apartment. Raines also removed two shell casings.

Stark read Triplett his rights.

Triplett said, "He shot Caroline! I was just defending myself."

Hawkins pointed to the bag. "And this?"

"I panicked. I didn't think anybody would believe me."

"That's funny," Yackowski said. "Because we don't."

Triplett's eyes widened in surprise.

"He was running away from you," Yackowski said. "You didn't have to shoot him. You had the gun, why didn't you just call 911?"

Triplett's eyes dropped to the floor and he said nothing.

Stepping forward, Hawkins said, "Because he knew. That's it, isn't it?"

Triplett stared at Hawkins. So did Yackowski.

"Knew what?" the detective asked.

Hawkins's eyes bored into Triplett until the suspect finally looked up at him, then glanced at Yackowski.

"He knew about Caroline and me," Triplett said, his voice barely above a whisper.

"You witnessed a man kill your lover, his ex-wife, and then you shot him because he found out about your affair?" Yackowski asked, incredulous.

Triplett managed a lame shrug. "The money's all Angela's. If she found out about Caroline and me she would have divorced me whether Caroline was dead or not."

Yackowski was shaking his head now. He looked over at his partner who shrugged and rolled his eyes.

Stepping forward, Hawkins laid a hand on Triplett's shoulder. "You know what you did wrong to get caught?"

The suspect shook his head. "Everything."

"I thought it would look like he killed her then killed himself," Triplett said glumly.

"Yeah," Hawkins said, glancing towards a suddenly uncomfortable Yackowski. "Except suicides don't pick up the shell casings and take them with them."

Yackowski asked, "Why the hell did he do that?"

Hawkins pointed at the burn on Triplett's arm. "The ejected shell casing was hot and burned him. He probably figured we could get DNA from that."

Triplett nodded.

"Nope," Hawkins said.

The suspect sagged.

"But he didn't know which casing burned him, so he took them both."

"I still don't get it," Stark said. "He's going to do life over an affair with a dead woman?"

Hawkins grinned at Triplett. "The lowlife didn't want to give up the high life."

MY LOLITA COMPLEX

On my second night in the house, sitting in the hot tub with Kelly, I agreed to kill her father. Sweat poured down my face and whether it generated from the steaming water, Kelly rubbing against me beneath the surface, or what I had just promised to do, I couldn't tell you.

Her arms still around my neck, her heart-shaped face inches from my spade-jawed own, her breath sweet and warm, her pert young breasts pressing hard against me, she said, "Uncle Joe, you're a lifesaver. I can't tell you how I've prayed for this moment." Then she kissed my cheek, her lips lingering a second too long.

The shit I was getting into, like the water I bobbed in, was about neck high. My first day in that brick mansion had been slightly less eventful, but as I thought about it, murder had been in the wind even then.

I'd made the trip to Davenport, Iowa, for the funeral of my sister, Rachel Forlani. Two years older than my forty, Rachel had still had that jet-black mane even if my Beatle mop had already begun to gray at the temples. She was one of those women who aged slowly and well...and now she would never look old.

A freak accident, her husband Jason had told me on the phone; Rachel had somehow gotten drunk while bathing and drowned. Jason Forlani and Rachel had been each other's second spouse. Stepdaughter Kelly's mother -- a woman I never met and Jason never spoke of -- had divorced him years before he met my sister. Rachel's history had been little better: her first husband, Peter, had dropped dead of a heart attack ten years ago while still in his early thirties.

Peter, a successful investment banker, had left Rachel with a great deal of money. I knew Sis pretty well and she would have traded the whole pile to have him back. The world doesn't work like that, though, and Rachel seemed to be searching for Peter at the bottom of every vodka bottle on the planet. That was pretty much the story until she met Jason Forlani. Somehow he broke through her vodka fog, and before long Rachel turned up at my front door and to my surprise, she was sober.

She stayed a couple of days and told me everything about the new man in her life. At the end of the visit, Rachel invited me to come to Iowa for their impending marriage, which I did. My sister seemed genuinely happy and I liked Forlani immediately. Affable and low key, he appeared the perfect bearer of the quiet life I thought Rachel needed.

Now, barely two years later, Jason was meeting me at the front door of the brick mansion they had purchased in an old money section of the town that lay in the crook where the Mississippi ran east and west.

Several inches shorter than me, Jason stepped out onto the stoop and put his arms out. Laptop slung over my shoulder, I let my suitcase drop to the ground and accepted his embrace. A frail man, he seemed to be hanging off me, his weight sagging against me as if he had used the last of his strength to attach himself to me.

"Joe, I'm so glad you're here," he said, his voice a hoarse whisper in my ear.

I stood there patting his back awkwardly.

"Rachel could always depend on you," he went on. "She'd be happy to know that you came so quickly."

Still locked in the clumsy embrace, I said, "We all loved her."

That broke whatever emotional damn still remained for Jason. He sobbed into my chest, arms gripping with more strength than I would have given him credit for. He was small, but damn strong. His tears soaked into my shirt, and I felt like a fool standing at his doorstep for the whole damn neighborhood to see.

"Maybe you should go in and sit down," I said, trying in vain to steer him through the door.

"I'm just so glad you're here," he blubbered between sobs.

"I know, I know, me too."

Slowly, Jason allowed me to lead him inside the house. A wide foyer opened to the heavy oak staircase that led to the second floor. Doors to the right and left led to the living room and dining room respectively. I helped Jason ease down onto one of the lower steps and returned to the porch to retrieve my bag, kicked the door shut and turned to face the emotional wreck that was my host.

I hadn't seen Jason in about six months, since Christmas, and in that time he seemed to have aged twenty years. His skin sagged, almost as if his face were melting. His eyes, red-rimmed and bloodshot, bugged behind Coke bottle wireframes. I knew Jason was diabetic, and that he took insulin shots, but he looked like an old man. Barely seven years my senior, strangers could have mistaken us for father and son.

"You look like shit," I said, adding a grin as punctuation.

He flashed a weak smile. "You don't pull any punches, do you? Rachel liked that...."

"How much sleep you getting?"

"Some."

"Not much, you mean."

"Not much," he admitted.

I sat next to him on the stairs. "Find out anything else?"

Shrugging a little, Jason said, "The coroner's ruled it an accidental drowning. She was drinking in the hot tub, coroner's opinion, fell asleep and drowned. The vodka bottle was still on the floor next to the tub."

I shook my head. "She'd been sober for what..."

"Almost five years, since we first started dating."

"Damn," I said. "Had she been depressed? Stressed?"

Jason thought for a moment before answering. "I don't think so -- anyway, she seemed fine to me. I thought we were happy. But you knew her, Joe -- Rachel kept a lot inside."

I nodded. "She was always hard to read."

We got up, Jason absently brushing off his butt despite the fact that the stairs were immaculate. "I'll show you to your room."

He reached for my suitcase, but I got there first. "Better let me get that," I said. "I brought my anvil collection."

Nodding, he led the way up the stairs. "The first bedroom is Kelly's, the second one'll be yours. Bathroom's right across the hall and I'm down at the end."

I remembered the layout from the single night I'd spent in the house right after Rachel and Jason were married.

He opened the door, and I passed him and entered the

bedroom.

"You need anything else?" he asked.

I shook my head.

"Go ahead and rest up, then -- dinner will be about seven."

"Sounds fine," I said.

Jason started to go, then turned back. "I'm sorry we lost her."

He wasn't going to let this be easy. He seemed to need to wallow in it every second. "Me too."

Jason nodded and shut the door behind him.

Not quite claustrophobically small, the bedroom had about as much personality as a Holiday Inn room. The hardwood floors peeked out from under the edges of a massive area rug that created a beige island in the middle of the room. A chest of drawers with a twelve-inch TV on top sat against one wall, a double bed with a pastel floral print comforter squatted against the opposite wall. On the wall to the left of the entrance was a sliding door that hid the closet. The final wall contained a window that overlooked the back yard. Beneath the window a low bookcase held Clancy, Parker, Grisham, Cornwell, and even a couple of my books.

I pulled River of Death off the shelf. A small-press true crime book I'd done when I first became a full-time writer, the copy looked as though someone had actually read it. I leafed through the title page where I found my inscription to my sister, "Stay on land and avoid the River of Death -- your lovin' brother, Joe."

What had seemed cute at the time now seemed macabre.

"Reading your own book?" a voice chirped from the doorway.

I jumped halfway out of my skin. I hadn't even heard the door open, yet Kelly, Jason's seventeen-year-old daughter, stood there as nonchalantly as if it were her own room. Something inside me stirred as much as I tried not to let it. Five-five, maybe five-six, her longish blonde hair bleached from time spent in the early summer sun, Kelly sported a tan that made me wonder if there were bikini lines beneath the denim short shorts and the tight white tee shirt that accentuated the firmness of perky breasts and allowed just a teasing glimpse of tan stomach and belly button.

"Hi, Kelly," I managed.

She swept into the room, brushed by me, lifting the book from my hands on her way by, and plopped onto the bed. "Am I interrupting?" she asked.

"Nope, I just got here."

Sitting up straighter, her eyes met mine. "I'm really sorry about Rachel, Uncle Joe."

"Thanks."

"I know you two were close."

I nodded. "Has it been hard for you?"

Kelly looked down at the book in her lap, studying it for a long moment. "Even though she wasn't my real mother..." her voice trailed off as tears rolled slowly down her high pink cheeks.

"I know," I said, then she was in my arms.

She'd set the book aside, gotten to her feet and hugged me before I knew what was happening. "It's just that I miss her so much already. She was so cool, so good to me."

"I know," I said patting her shoulder.

"And Daddy, she was always good to him whether he appreciated it or not."

"What?"

"I'm sorry," she said, backing away, blinking her big blue eyes. "I shouldn't have said that."

Kelly practically left a vapor trail she left the room so

fast. She left my door open, and before I even completely realized she'd gone, I heard her door close.

What the hell had she meant, "Whether he appreciated it or not"?

Plopping onto the bed, I picked up the book and settled back. As I read the dedication, "To Rachel, my sister, my hero," I felt tears pooling, then spilling. And to my dismay, I noticed that I could still smell the sweet aroma of Kelly where she'd pressed against my chest. I shifted the erection in my pants and willed it to go down.

The next sound I heard was a soft rapping on the bedroom door. I awoke slowly, my tongue thick in my mouth, my eyelids heavy, my throat dry. "Yeah?" I croaked.

Kelly opened the door and stepped into the dusky bedroom. I could barely see more than an outline, but she seemed to be wearing a short dress now instead of the tee shirt and shorts. "Daddy says dinner's ready."

"Okay," I said. "I'll be down in just a minute."

"I'll tell him," she said, then disappeared.

I got to my feet, ran my fingers through my hair and decided I better make a stop across the hall before I went downstairs. As I crossed the room, I again noticed Kelly's sweet scent hanging in the air.

The aroma of dinner filled the first floor. Coming down the stairs, I found Kelly waiting for me at the bottom. She leaned against the newel, her long blonde hair now pulled back in a loose ponytail, a very short floral dress showing off her tan, slimly muscular thighs. I tried not to notice.

She looped her arm in mine and led me through the door into the dining room. Jason sat at one end of the table, and a short broad Hispanic woman trundled in and out of the room, carrying dishes in from the kitchen.

"Joe, I hope you like baked chicken," Jason said, waving me to a chair at the end of the table.

I nodded my approval as Kelly let go of me and took the chair to my right between her father and me. I looked at the table awash with dishes. Steam rose from the huge plate of baked chicken, as well as from a bowl of mashed potatoes, a tureen of gravy, and a huge bowl of corn. Two kinds of rolls and a huge bowl of tossed greens completed the setting.

"Expecting company?" I asked. "Like maybe the Oakland Raiders?"

Jason smiled. "Conchita comes from a large family. She cooks a lot. We've always got leftovers in the fridge, so help yourself. You're family, Joe -- what's mine is yours."

"Thanks, I'll remember that."

The food was excellent and we ate mostly in silence. We avoided talking about Rachel and had little else to discuss. It wasn't until the plates were cleared and dessert, cherry pie ala mode, sat in front of us, that Jason finally got around to bringing up my career.

"Working on the next great book?" he asked.

I knew he was trying to be upbeat, but considering the condition of my career, it sounded like sarcasm. Those first two books, River of Death and Torso: Catching The Chainsaw Killer, had each sold moderately well in the Midwest, where the crimes occurred, but stiffed throughout the rest of the country. There'd been a few magazine articles and some freelance newspaper work, but for the most part, it had been my teaching job that allowed me to write at all. Then, when I lost that, handouts from Rachel had become my meal ticket.

I shook my head. "Working on an article for a magazine," I lied. Truth was I had no jobs, and an equal number of prospects.

Jason's eyebrows raised with interest. "Really? About what?"

Fuck, I thought. I put on my tap shoes and continued the lie. "Uh, it's a follow up to River of Death."

"Really?" Jason asked.

"Yeah, you know, interview with Lane five years later."

Jason nodded.

Donald Lane, the man who had drowned his entire family in the Mississippi, had been the subject of my first book. He was now serving a life sentence with no possibility for parole in Iowa's maximum security prison at Ft. Madison. Saying it out loud, it really didn't sound like a half bad idea. I wondered if I could peddle it. I looked up to see Jason and Kelly staring at me. Obviously, one of them had spoken and I'd been caught not paying attention.

"Sorry."

Jason repeated his question. "Have you spoken to Lane yet?"

I shook my head. "Still doing the preliminary background and trying to get past his lawyer."

This sounded so good it was beginning to feel like I wasn't lying. I definitely had to look into this story.

"Do you think he'll even talk to you?"

"Can't hurt to ask," I said with a shrug.

The conversation sort of petered out then as we settled in to work on our pie and ice cream. After dinner, we moved into the living room. Kelly excused herself to go upstairs and phone a friend. Jason and I sat mostly in silence, pretending to watch some show on television. After the local news, he too excused himself and went up to bed.

I was drifting off to sleep somewhere in the middle of Letterman when I felt a warm hand running down my cheek. I opened my eyes, blinked several times and finally focused to see Kelly standing over me. She again wore the white tee shirt and denim shorts.

"You were asleep," she said her voice soft and sweet as marshmallow.

"Just resting my eyes."

She smiled. Her teeth were large and white, her lips soft and a deep red, with just the tip of her pink tongue showing through. "You always snore when you're resting your eyes?"

I chuckled. "If you want to really get rested you have to snore, didn't you know that?"

She laughed too, the sound bubbling up from inside and coming out rich and captivating.

I stared at her fighting the desire to take her in my arms. Kelly reminded me a great deal of Heather, the student I'd lost my job over.

That was what I got for trying to relate to my kids, being too close to them, too friendly -- who else my age listened to Christina Aguilera and Brittany Spears, for Christ's sakes? Thirteen years of teaching high school shot to shit because some well-intentioned counseling got too personal.

Which is horseshit, right? Boils down to, I couldn't keep my hands off one of the students. The affair had cost me my wife as well. Marion hadn't even bothered to listen to my side. As soon as I admitted the truth, she tossed me out on my ass.

Now I was having those same feelings again, with my niece, my goddamn niece! Of course, she was only my niece by marriage, and legal in this state; but still, I didn't think that would fly with Jason -- and it sure wouldn't have with Rachel, if she were still alive.

Which, of course, she wasn't....I shook my head trying to clear away those thoughts.

"You okay?" she asked.

I nodded. "Tired."

"Too tired to go for a walk?"

She turned and looked up the stairs like she was afraid Jason would hear us.

"I think so," I answered, not wanting to tell her the truth, which was that I was afraid to be alone with her.

"I need to talk to you," she said her voice turning breathless as she again glanced toward the stairs. "It's important."

This seemed like a really bad idea, but Kelly seemed seriously troubled about something and maybe all she needed was someone to talk to -- somebody older who could listen, and help.

"I'm your uncle," I said. "You can always talk to me."

Once we were outside, down the front walk and strolling through the peaceful neighborhood, Kelly seemed to relax a little, though she still hadn't said a word about what was bothering her. The June night air contained a little more bite than I'd anticipated and I wished I'd brought along a sweater. Glancing at Kelly, I couldn't keep myself from noting pencil-eraser nipples poking under her top. Getting to the corner of her block, Kelly took a right and I stayed even with her allowing the silence to continue.

Finally, she turned to me, her hands on my biceps stopping my progress. "He killed her, Uncle Joe," she said -- her voice so hushed I figured I hadn't heard right.

"What?"

"He killed her," she repeated her voice a more insistent whisper.

"Who killed who?" I asked searching her face. The streetlight at the corner was behind me, my head keeping her face in shadow as if I were part of an eclipse of her face.

When I tried to move to one side she followed. When I moved the other way again she stayed in front of me. If any insomniacs were looking out their windows, we probably looked like a drunken dance team.

She bounced now, still holding my arms, her frustration strangely electric; but she kept her voice low. "Daddy killed Rachel."

"Bullshit," the word leapt from my throat unbidden.

"It's not," she said her voice high-pitched, urgent.

I shook my head vigorously. "No way," I said, struggling to keep my voice low so as not to alert the neighbors. "No fucking way. That's not funny, Kelly. That's a bad, bad joke."

Her face grew pinched, her grip tighter, her eyes pleading. "It's not a joke, Uncle Joe. He did it."

"I'm not going to listen to any more of this," I said.

And I tore myself from her grip and marched away.

She followed close behind. "Joe, I can prove it."

I stopped, spinning to face her, anger rising in my voice. "How?"

Kelly almost ran into me, took a step back, then looked up at me with the eyes of a scared animal. "Wuh...well," she stammered, "I can...can't exactly prove it."

"Why would you even say such a thing about your own father..."

She grabbed my face in her hands, our eyes locking. "Joe, he makes me have sex with him."

My hands went to wrists to pull her hands away, but I paused as I looked into her eyes. Something I saw made me think that somehow these unthinkable things she was saying might be true. Her eyes never wavered, no sign of anything but innocence and honesty on her face.

"He's been doing it ever since...you know, since my boobs came in."

"Kelly...you can't say these things unless -- "

"They're true, Uncle Joe. He's been raping me and raping me and I can't do anything about it, he looks scrawny but he's so strong...."

Slowly lowering her hands from my cheeks, I said, "We've got to take this to the police."

She shook her head. "They'll never believe it."

"Sure they will. You'll talk to doctors, and counselors, and -- "

"No one will believe me. My father is an upstanding citizen, and I've been in all kinds of trouble...and I've been with a lot of boys. If they investigate, I'll be the one that looks awful."

I didn't know what to say.

"We should head back," she said.

"Wait a minute," I said, grabbing her shoulder and stopping her. "Let's say I believe you...at least about the incest. We've got to do something!"

"There's nothing to be done," Kelly said, her voice as matter of fact as if she were ordering drive-up at MacDonald's.

We walked, and I said, "Tell me why you think he killed Rachel."

"Two reasons. First, I finally told her about him, what he'd been doing. And she believed me. I think she suspected, before."

"When was this that you told her?"

"The night before he killed her."

"Shit!"

"And then there's the other reason -- her money."

"You know about the money?"

"Yeah, from her dead first husband -- my dad and Rachel sat me down and explained about it. She thought it was important that I know about stuff like that, you know, just in case."

I nodded. Truthfully, Rachel had given me the same speech, or at least something near it.

"How did he do it?"

"Kill Rachel?" Kelly trudged wearily toward the house, pondering my question. "She was crying, all upset, and drinking...she must've conked out and he injected her and put her in the hot tub."

"Injected her? With what?"

"Shit, Uncle Joe! He's diabetic! The easiest thing in the world for him to get is insulin."

I tried to wrap my brain around the words that Kelly spoke. Quiet, unassuming Jason, the man who had wept in my arms earlier this afternoon, a rapist and killer? He'd seemed so broken up when I'd arrived -- was it possible he'd been play-acting? But if it wasn't true, that meant that Kelly was lying and what possible motivation could a seventeen-year-old girl have to lie about her father raping her?

The rest of the night passed in fits and starts as I tried to sleep and failed. I just couldn't stop thinking about what Kelly told me and the more I considered the accusations, the less sense the situation made.

When I came downstairs, dressed in my best (and only) black suit -- since we were, after all, about to go to my sister's funeral -- Jason and Kelly were already at the dining room table, although neither of them seemed to be eating. Jason nursed a cup of coffee, his own suit a dark gray pinstripe, his shirt white, the tie a conservative gray with narrow stripes the color of dried blood.

"Morning," I said, fighting to keep both my voice and face neutral. I wanted to shout at Jason, "What the hell are you doing fucking your own daughter?" But I didn't say it. If I confronted Jason about the incest, I'd get tossed out on my ass, and Kelly and I would never get the evidence he killed Rachel. Yet I still couldn't believe Jason had killed my sister...though if he did, I was determined to see him put away for the rest of his life.

"Good morning," Jason said, his eyes downcast, studying his coffee.

Kelly glanced up from her glass of juice, an untouched saucer of toast in front of her. She didn't smile, she just met my eyes for a moment, then looked away.

We got through the funeral somehow -- that's all you can do with any funeral. Jason seemed more in control than he had when he'd met me at the front door yesterday. Tears trickled down his cheeks, mine too for that matter. The minister said some nice words about Rachel. I spent the entire service looking at only two things: Rachel's casket sitting in the center aisle to my left; and Jason's profile two seats away from me.

Kelly sat between us. I touched her knee with mine and she glanced over at me. I mouthed the words, "We need to talk," and she nodded.

After the service, we hosted a church luncheon for Rachel's friends, most of whom I didn't really know, and members of Jason's family, none of whom I knew. I had many conversations with many people that afternoon, but it's all a blur in my memory; hell, it was a blur, then.

Anyway, as soon as we were back in the house, Jason bid us good night, even though it was barely five p.m., and he disappeared into his room.

Kelly knocked on my bedroom door around seven and we went down to the kitchen where she made us both chicken sandwiches from last night's leftovers. She nuked the remaining corn and mashed potatoes and it served as a decent enough dinner. I started to broach the subject of Rachel's death, but she shooshed me and told me we could talk about it later when she was sure her father was asleep. I agreed and retired to my room.

She came to fetch me shortly after ten. The white string bikini she wore filled in most of the small holes my imagination had left about Kelly's figure. "Why don't you put on your trunks," she said. "We'll go down to the hot tub -- it always relaxes me."

I shook my head. "No trunks."

Pointing at the dresser, she said, "Top drawer."

I opened the drawer and pulled out a pair of black trunks that looked to be approximately my size, and held them up. "Where'd these come from?"

Kelly shrugged. "I think Rachel bought them for when you visited. You just didn't visit."

"Oh," I said.

I pulled off my shirt and looked up to see Kelly still standing in the doorway, an appraising smile settled on her pretty face. I guess I was in pretty good shape for an old fart.

"I...I'll meet you downstairs," I said and eased her out of the bedroom, closing the door behind her.

When I arrived downstairs, Kelly was nowhere in sight. I remembered Rachel phoning me in early March to tell me about their installing a hot tub in the backyard. Quietly, I made my way through the house and went out the backdoor. The yard was surrounded by a seven-foot privacy fence which the neighbors weren't close enough to see over the fence from their bedrooms.

Kelly had already entered the water. She floated in the huge tub, hair streaming and drifting on the surface like blonde seaweed, her head leaning against the edge, her arms bracing her against the bottom as the rest of her body shimmered through the torrent of bubbles and rising steam. "Come on in," she said, her voice turning into that husky whisper again.

I got into the water slowly, the heat coursing deeper inside me with each step down.

"Feels good, doesn't it?"

Nodding, I eased myself onto a seat across from her. "I can see how this would help you relax."

"Best thing," she said. "I love it here."

"About your dad," I began.

Suddenly, she sat up and moved closer to me, pushing against my arm until I raised it so she could huddle against me, my arm around her, her soft flesh against me. "What do you think we should do?"

"I think we should go to the police."

Kelly pulled away, her mouth open, her eyes wide. "We can't."

"Trust me," I said. "No -- trust them. They'll get to the bottom of whatever's happening."

Shaking her head, she rushed back into my arms. "Don't make me tell the cops. They'll never believe me and...and the humiliation..." Her voice trailed off.

"We've got to go to the police," I said, trying to sound adamant even though I could feel Kelly against me, every inch of where she touched on fire with desire.

"There is another way," she said, her voice practically a purr, her head resting on my shoulder.

I pulled back a little to see her face. "What other way?"

"You could take care of it for me."

The look in her eyes didn't allow me to mistake the intention of her words. But still I asked, "Take care how?"

"Do to him what he did to her."

"No fucking way! What are you, nuts?"

"They'll never believe me, and if they do, I'll be this dysfunctional incest person, to everybody in the world, for the rest of my life -- you gotta take him out, it's the only way."

"No chance."

She moved closer, her warmth infiltrating me, her arms around me, her tongue flicking my ear. "I would do anything to repay you, Uncle Joe...just anything."

Nothing on earth would have given me as much pleasure as saying yes at that moment. If she was right about her father murdering Rachel, I would do it happily, joyfully, even -- I glanced down at the tan body in the water next to me --without such a generous reward. Still, I managed to say no.

"We've got to try my way first," I said. "It has to be right."

Soft tears trailed down her cheeks. "You're right, Uncle Joe," she said. "You must think I'm horrible and evil for even thinking such a thing."

I patted her shoulder, wiped away the tears, ran a hand through her blonde hair, moving damp tendrils off her face. She still cried softly, tilting her face to mine. I kissed her softly on the forehead, then both eyes. Kelly looked at me for an instant, her face an unreadable mask, then she pressed her lips to mine -- softly at first, then more urgently. Her tongue slid into my mouth, then mine into hers. Immediately, we tore off each other's bathing suits and my kisses moved from her mouth to her long neck to her supple breasts.

Beneath the water, her hand found me, stroked softly, her legs moving around down there until she straddled me. Our heat rocketed through me as she guided me inside her.

We rocked and bucked, water slopping over the sides of the hot tub, her moans like music....

As we lay in each other's arms, she said, "The only way we can be together is to have my father out of my life --forever."

"That's what jail will do."

She shook her head. "What if he's found innocent?"

"We'll still find a way."

"Do you love me, Joe?"

The question took me by surprise but I nodded.

"I mean, did you love me before this, tonight?"

"Sure, Kelly, you're a very special young woman. I've always seen that. Of course I love you."

I mean, she was my niece.

"You believe me, that my father's been fucking me?"

"Kelly...."

"Do you believe me?"

"Yes."

"Did you believe me when I told you all of this last night?"

I shrugged.

"Did you?"

Slowly, I shook my head.

"Then what makes you think strangers will believe me?"

Damn it, she made sense.

She reached into a towel wadded up next to the tub and came out with a small caliber automatic pistol. "This was Rachel's gun."

"Rachel's gun...."

"It has to be now, Joe. While he's still asleep, before he can hurt me again. You heard terrible sounds and caught him raping me and you went nuts and got your sister's gun and...and that's what happened."

Things were moving too quickly. I jumped out of the hot tub, staying as far from the gun as I could.

Climbing out carefully, making sure not to get the gun wet, Kelly followed me. She stood before me, the moonlight bathing her nudity in an eerie white light.

I wanted to tell her she was crazy, that this whole idea was fucking insane, but I just kept staring at her body there in the moonlight, not saying a word.

Then she pressed against me again, her body hot, her kiss ardent and eager.

I felt her press the gun into my hand. "Just this one little thing and I'll be yours forever. You can do anything, anything you want."

She pulled away then and like a zombie I walked toward the house. I couldn't believe I was doing this. I went in through the back door and climbed the stairs. My nudity didn't even feel out of place. This would be pure, just me and the man who had killed my sister, raped the woman I loved. I crept down the hall, even as a voice in my head shouted, "Stop, this is insanity!"

I continued to move forward, silently twisting the doorknob. The room, pitch black, felt cold, the air prickling my naked skin. I eased forward, Jason's breathing coming from just ahead on my right. He slept soundly, his breathing even and regular. Each time he exhaled I moved another step closer. On the fourth breath I leaned over his bed, his body a lumpy silhouette in the bed. His face, upturned and placid, showed no shadow of the guilt he must feel for his crimes.

Letting my hand come forward, I softly touched the barrel of the pistol against Jason's temple. At that precise second, just as his eyes popped open in shock, I heard a siren in the distance. I don't know why I heard that when I heard no other sound save for Jason's breathing. The breaths came faster and shallower now that he was awake. Just as his eyes found mine in the darkness, I pulled the trigger.

The report did not explode, as I expected, but sounded more like a cap gun going off. My arm jerked slightly from the recoil, and a small clump of Jason's brain blew out the far side of his head. It wasn't at all like these things appeared in the movies. Of course, having written true crime I knew that; but it still surprised me a little.

Jason's blood appeared black on his skull and the pillow. I said nothing, just turned and walked out. When I got to the end of the hall and looked down the stairs, Kelly stood at the bottom, a flimsy robe clinging to her damp skin. She seemed to be watching out the small window next to the front door.

What was she looking for, lights going on in the neighbors' houses?

I came down one step, the gun dangling from my hand.

"We...we have to get our stories straight," I said.

Suddenly, Kelly jerked open the front door and two policemen entered with their guns drawn.

They saw me and the bigger one, a rangy white kid who looked like a college linebacker, pointed his nine-millimeter at me and yelled, "Drop it now."

His black partner dropped to one knee, aimed at me while sweeping Kelly behind him out of the line of fire.

"He raped me," she screamed. "And he murdered my father."

Then it all became clear. Now I knew that Rachel really had been murdered -- injected with insulin, all right; it was just that Jason hadn't been the one to do it.

"Wait," I said, my hand coming up automatically in a stop gesture. I realized I was still holding the gun just as the first bullet ripped into my chest. The force knocked me backward and I was about to fall, my feeble hands trying to toss away the pistol, then the second bullet hit higher than the first and I crumpled to the floor.

It would have been better if I'd died then, I suppose. Certainly better for Kelly, who would have inherited not just her father's share of my sister's estate, but the portion meant for me as well. Instead, I'm in Ft. Madison, serving a life term, in the company of two murderers I wrote books about. My presence amuses them.

Anyway, this is the book proposal. It would flesh out easily -- I could do a whole section on being a teacher and the girl who seduced me. And if we want to go for a cheap irony, I could do a few chapters about prison life, and how one night in a hot tub led me into hundreds of nights of terrible sex in the showers.

Not that I'm complaining. They're letting me write in here, so at least I can still pursue my craft; and I'm over my Lolita complex, even if I can see the warden's daughter from my high barred window.

OUT FOR BLOOD

2:42 AM, Friday, NOVEMBER 4, 1960

A Cheshire Cat smile blossomed on the craggily handsome face of Lieutenant Cliff Hunter as he stood shivering in the cold night air.

The shiver was only marginally weather-related—mostly it came from the thrill of a chase successfully concluded...even if he'd not been there himself at the finish line.

Hands in the pockets of his black overcoat, hatless to reveal close-cropped gray-tinged brown hair, Hunter might have been a tall, angular scarecrow, if that scarecrow had been given a damn good stuffing of hay. Standing in the back yard of Coach Michael Massey—whose shredded corpse lay at his feet—Chicago's nastiest homicide dick damn near whooped and hollered for joy.

Instead, Hunter stood stoically, studying the bustle around him, a team of uniformed cops under work lamps digging around the yard—seven graves had been at least partially open when the Homicide lieutenant arrived. All seven girls were cheerleaders, some missing for as long as three years, the latest one—lucky survivor, Bonnie Larkin—having disappeared not quite six weeks ago.

A scrawny young uniformed officer named Jensen sidled up next to Hunter. "There's a reporter at the roadblock. We told him to bug off, but he claims you called him."

"That would be Mr. Grayle," Hunter said with a smile.

"It's Grayle, all right. Sticking his nose in again."

"Laddiebuck, the fourth estate has its uses. Go get him."

"Yessir," Jensen said, rolling his eyes, but doing as he was told.

Hunter yanked a pack of cigarettes from his coat pocket like a gun he planned to fire at a fleeing suspect. He shook out a Lucky Strike, pulled out his Zippo, and cupped a hand against the wind as he lit up. He took a deep soothing drag, then exhaled its blue cloud as he watched the reporter coming around the house.

The detective hadn't called the TV stations—they would love to have this for their morning broadcasts, lovely breakfast background for their viewers—or any of the other papers or even a radio station or two. But Grayle he trusted, at least as far as any reporter could be. So only he got the call. Let the other newshounds do their own work.

Grayle was accompanied by a scrawny bespectacled photographer, Kenton, who was practically dwarfed by his flash camera. To his credit, Kenton marched in the reporter's shadow and didn't immediately start snapping away. The photog had been around long enough to know that Hunter would bust up a camera if he felt his territorial rights had been violated.

Blond and blue-eyed and boyish, the husky Grayle had been mistaken for actor Troy Donahue by more than one autograph seeker. Hunter had no idea what the initials in C.T. Grayle stood for. Like everybody, he called the reporter "Digger." Beyond that, the cop knew little about the *Chicago Daily Journal's* top police beat scribe, other than that Digger Grayle's investigative pieces had helped topple the last two corrupt administrations, and the guy wasn't even thirty yet.

As the reporter and his cameraman neared, Hunter blew out another gray-blue cloud and nodded toward the two men. "Digger. Kenton."

They nodded and said, "Lieutenant," so simultaneously they might have rehearsed it.

Taking the lead, Grayle said, "Lt. Hunter, what goes on here? Looks like a treasure hunt."

"Not exactly." He gestured vaguely toward the looming Victorian monstrosity behind them. "Maybe you'd like to interview the owner of the house."

The reporter and photog traded puzzled looks, but then followed as Hunter walked a few steps, then pointed the amber eye of his Lucky Strike down at what was left of their host.

The reporter sucked in a quick breath and the cameraman took an involuntary step backward. They had seen plenty, but this was an especially grisly one….

*****

9:17 P.M., Thursday, NOVEMBER 3, 1960

When Rusty was alive, she didn't believe in God.

But Madeline "Rusty" Naylor had long ago begun to have doubts about her doubts—*long ago.* The petite, slender, red-haired beauty with the ghostly pale flesh had been twenty-eight when she died. But what that meant in the context of her age now, well, she would have to look it up and do some math (ha!) to give you an accurate count.

Moonlight brushing her black silk ivory, jumpsuit, she crept along the edge of a row of high bushes, approaching an old Victorian home right out of Charles Addams. The man who lived in that house was a human devil—not in the supernatural sense, but a devil, all right. And that was what got Rusty thinking about God.

She had encountered so many devils over these long years, they simply *had* to have a big boss, right? A top devil? Like the mob guys in Chicago, a big boy? And if Satan existed, didn't it stand to reason a Higher Power was working the other side of the street, too?

But which side of the street am I *working, anyway?* she wondered.

Still, there was no doubt which side of the street Michael Massey worked.

Massey—a "consulting coach" who traveled among Chicago's public high schools helping cheerleaders—was a prime suspect in a string of disappearances among the teenage girls he had taught. The police had investigated him for months, but come up empty. Her pal Cliff Hunter on the detective bureau had suggested to the Larkins—the distraught parents of one missing girl—that they try Tooth & Nail Inquiries on Rush Street.

Tooth and Nail was Rusty and her longtime partner, Max Mantooth, and their small office was above the Rusty Nail Bar on Rush Street, out of which the two also worked—Rusty singing, Max noodling the eighty-eights. She owned both businesses. A little jazz/blues club with a couple of P.I.s attached—just like *Peter Gunn* on TV.

Almost.

Rusty only worked nights. Max worked days and the occasional night, but they met with clients together, at the Nail, between sets. They had listened to the troubled parents for only a few minutes before taking on the case. Max—whose stumpy, frame hadseen him underestimated by more than one unlucky devil—had been digging into Coach Massey's life ever since. Her partner had put most of the story together, and tonight had phoned Rusty to say that he had verified their suspicions about the popular coach.

Now, it was Rusty's turn to get into the case.

It was cold enough that she might have been able to see her breath—if she still drew breath. The moon hung high and full, a killing moon they called it. A wintry blast off Lake Michigan had turned this Northside Chicago suburb into a veritable ghost town...and Rusty knew where the bodies of those ghosts were likely buried.

This far north, there weren't many houses and the one she surveilled stood well apart from its few neighbors, woods buffering it on three sides. A two-story gothic, it reminded her of the spooky hilltop house in last summer's Hitchcock flick, *Psycho.* The killer in that movie would have felt perfectly at home residing here.

She was downwind of it. Massey wouldn't know she was there, but even twenty yards from his lair and through its wood and mortar walls, Rusty could smell his cheap aftershave—but all the Old Spice in the world couldn't cover up the smell of corruption that oozed from that dark old house.

That was one benefit of her weakened powers—the smell of Massey and his aftershave might have overwhelmed her, had her senses been as sharp as her incisors were right now. She had not fed, really fed, for months. Her arrangement with a contact in the local blood bank allowed her to get expired blood, which did the trick (if barely), though the taste of the stuff was hardly gourmet.

For the real, fresh thing, she relied on cases like the Massey one.

Rusty Naylor's biggest problem was her conscience. She had never been comfortable feeding on the innocent. She could only live with herself (so to speak) if she dined on the guilty. But there hadn't been that kind of case, that kind of monster, available for some months now.

As with humans, the quality of a vampire's health was determined by the nutritional value of their food intake. Tonight—to her—a healthy, adult male in his early thirties would be like a juicy rare filet at George Diamond's to a day dweller. The fact that Massey was a vicious, shrewd, resourceful, physically fit specimen, who would probably put up a good fight, well...that was a bonus of sorts. Though Rusty never gained weight—being dead was a real benefit to a girl trying to keep her figure—she still needed to keep her muscles toned.

In the wooded area to the right of the house, she perked, her nostrils flaring in recognition of another scent, this one more—her partner. Keeping an eye on the house, she made her way around to that dark patch of woods. By the time she entered the tight tangle of trees, Max had moved on. He would be getting into position behind the house.

The reason he had drawn her here, however, was immediately obvious—*the aroma of death tinged the air.* Not enough so that humans might smell it; but she caught it right away, a foul scent that grew stronger as she moved forward to where she could see a grave that lay open, as if an animal had dug up the body that was buried there.

But the face that stared up at the night sky belonged not to a corpse, but the missing Larkin girl.

Alive.

Wild eyes—daring relief at seeing someone who wasn't Massey—saucering up at her over a slash of duct-tape gag. The girl's wrists and ankles were similarly duct-taped, and she could wriggle down there but not much else.

Who could say what horrors this young woman had endured before her captor had finished with her and deposited her in a hole in a backyard where—Rusty shivered to think—he would likely bury her alive after having done with her?

So many monsters in this world, she thought.

That was why the smell of death had been so muted. The Larkin girl lived! But nearby, other graves had been scratched open by the claws of an animal...an animal that had somehow resisted attacking Bonnie Larkin...and if Rusty had held any doubt that Massey was their man, that doubt vanished into the moonlit night.

This was a graveyard—the graveyard of a mad man.

Well, she thought, as matter of fact as a plumber about to begin an unpleasant but necessary job, *it's time for Massey to pay for his crimes and for me to get a decent damn meal.*

*****

2:45A.M., Friday, NOVEMBER 4, 1960

The seasoned copper supposed he would have preferred that the system had been able to take care of the sadistic, perverted coach. But though they'd suspected Massey from the start, the Homicide Bureau had never been able to tie Massey to the disappearances, much less bring him to justice. And among his students at various schools around the area, Massey had been a popular, charismatic figure.

The coach? Do something bad *to those girls? Why, that's crazy—he's an All-American boy, a man's man, everybody's favorite.*

Right now, the rescued girl was in the hospital—she had been beaten and sexually assaulted, apparently kept prisoner all this time, the plaything of the dead monster at Hunter's feet. The girl was in shock and had said very little, but even when she came out of it, she would give them jack squat about the exact nature of her rescue—this much Hunter knew.

And that was fine with Hunter, because it was his recommendation of the Tooth and Nail Agency to the child's parents that had put Coach Michael Massey on a collision course with rough justice.

Hunter had no doubt about who had settled the score for those girls, but so far no evidence indicated that Rusty Naylor or her fat-ass partner Max were anywhere near the crime scene. Of course, if there *had* been any such evidence at the scene, Hunter would have made damn sure it went undiscovered.

It didn't hurt that the surrounding neighbors had already been quickly canvassed, and no one had seen anybody around these parts resembling either of those two rather distinctive-looking private eyes.

Hunter didn't give a damn if Naylor had killed Massey or if Max had done it, or even if it had been the animal attack it appeared to be. In the past, the villains he'd sicced Tooth and Nail on had just...disappeared. But this time—because of the missing girls—it had been necessary for the coach's evil to be exposed.

Why the Tooth and Nail duo had chosen such a brutal, bloody and even savage method of concealing their actions, Hunter couldn't hazard a guess. He would talk to them about it, suggesting in the future so gruesome a cover-up might not be the smartest way to fly...though truth be told, Hunter flat out didn't give a damn what had been done to the coach in this charnel house of a back yard.

Whatever had happened to beloved Coach Massey had been too easy—because the son of a bitch had earned the kind of fate the state was just too damned genteel to mete out.

*****

9:21 P.M., Thursday, November 3, 1960

Rusty helped the child out of the hole, the girl obviously astonished that her slender female rescuer could lift her so easily. Like a groom carrying a bride over the threshold, Rusty transported this precious duct-taped cargo to the bushes where she deposited the still-frightened girl to relative safety.

All Rusty did was raise a "shush" finger to her lips and go.

Given the situation, she saw no reason to bother with stealth. Although Massey seemed to like blondes, a petite redhead turning up on his front porch might just arouse his attention. She unzipped the jumpsuit enough to give herself some cleavage and headed for the front door.

Light shone in several downstairs windows, presumably the living room, and another in a room in the back, maybe the kitchen. She climbed the stairs, the wood creaking even under her slight weight.

She knocked.

Nothing.

She knocked again, hard, insistent.

Footsteps echoed hollowly within the old house, growing louder until the door swung open and she stood face to face with a muscular man nearly a foot taller than her five-five, and easily a hundred pounds heavier than her one-ten. His immediate, chillingly charming smile conveyed his certainty of a huge advantage over her in size and strength.

Wouldn't be his first mistake, but possibly his last.

He had a square-jawed, dark-haired Rock Hudson look, his dark brown eyes poring over her like pawing hands. Let him try something like that and she would break every single finger, then his hands, forearms, and so forth, and relish every moment.

But she doubted he was so crude, so early in a relationship.

"Well," he said. "Hello."

His collar was open at the throat, black chest hair curling, carotid pulsing. He wore jeans and a plaid work shirt, giving him a lumberjack air, and they were a little dirty, as were his clodhopper boots. He'd been digging, after all.

"Hello," she said.

"Car break down?"

She smiled without showing her teeth and fought the urge to rip out his throat where he stood. But the light was on over the porch and the house wasn't *that* remote.

"My name is Madeline Naylor, Coach Massey, and I wondered if we might talk. It's something important."

Perhaps reading her for a fellow teacher or possibly parent, he dialed his smile down and creased his brow. "Do come in, Miss Naylor. If you think you have something important to share, of course I'm interested."

Massey moved aside and gestured for her to enter.

"Sorry I'm a little messy," he said, grinning now as if they were old friends. "I was doing some late-night gardening."

"Moon's right for it," she said.

The living room was bright, welcoming, masculine in

an anonymous manner more typical of apartments than an old Victorian home. It gave no hint of being the lair of a molesting murderer.

He motioned her to a comfortable-looking leather sofa, and took a seat on a nearby chair, his attention focused on her with well-practiced professional concern.

"So, what brings you to my door, unannounced, at this late hour, on such a cold night?" Now it was just half a smile, and he conveyed just a hint of displeasure. "Without a phone call first? I'm in the book."

She leaned forward slightly, giving him a good look at her cleavage. Rusty was a permanent twenty-eight, and wondered if she was too old for Massey. If he could have guessed her *real* age, well, she'd *really* be too old for this lethal Lothario...

"Coach Massey, it's about the disappearance of Bonnie Larkin."

His eyes left her breasts and found their way to her face, and then he let out a long, slow breath. "Very distressing thing. Sweet child. Lovely girl."

"Yes."

"I didn't have much contact with Bonnie."

"No?"

"No. And I'm terribly surprised."

"You are?"

"Yes, from what I saw, she didn't seem like the type of girl who would just...run off like that."

"Oh. So you assume she's a runaway, then?"

He mimicked sadness and shook his head. "It's a terrible trend. It's the loosening of values. I would never dream of blaming the parents, but...well, if they were doing their job, this kind of thing just wouldn't happen."

"Actually, she didn't run away."

"Oh? You seem convinced of that."

"I am. I *know* the circumstances of her disappearance."

He frowned in deep interest, leaning forward a little, cocking his head. "Really? What...?"

"It was more an abduction. A lot of these mass killers gain the confidence of their victims...ask them for help, or offer a ride home...often someone they know. That they trust. An uncle perhaps. Or a teacher."

Something flickered across Massey's face. *Was it fear?* Hard to tell, because almost instantly the monster's mask of concern was back in place. "It's an interesting theory. Have you shared this with her parents, or the police?"

"I could, but it's not a theory, and, anyway, that isn't what I was hired to do."

He shifted on the chair slightly, sitting more forward, a concerned teacher who was actually a predator ready to pounce. "You were...hired? You're not a counselor, or another teacher? Though as familiar with the area school system, I think I'd have noticed if you *were*..."

"No. I was hired to get her back."

"You mean...like negotiating with a kidnapper?"

"Not really. You see, I'm a detective...not police, private. This is a missing persons case, and the parents didn't feel the authorities were getting the job done...so here I am."

Eyebrows lifted and dropped. "Ah. I see. But, as I say, I really didn't have much contact with that poor girl."

"Right."

His expression turned openly lascivious, as he allowed his eyes to travel her tight jumpsuit again. "What's a nice girl like you doing in a job like that? You don't look like a...private dick. Can't pay that well."

"I don't charge particularly high fees."

"Then why go into such a rough line of work?"

"Because of the perks."

"What kind of perks?"

She shrugged a shoulder. "Well...sometimes I get to take bad people off the street."

He was enormously amused, the teeth in his grin huge. "Really? A sweet little pussycat like you?"

She nodded, and—like an accountant giving a client the bad news about his taxes—coldly stated, "You had your fun and were about to bury the girl in the backyard, when I showed up and interrupted the party. Did you bury them *all* alive? That's a pretty sick kink even for a bastard like you."

Massey sat in silence for several moments. "How much, honey? How much to take a walk?"

Now it was Rusty's turn to smile, still careful not to show her teeth. "You think you can *buy* your way out of this?"

"If this isn't blackmail, why bother with the visit? I'm willing to pay. Big."

"You *are* going to pay," she said. "Big."

He leapt.

*****

2:46 A.M., Friday, NOVEMBER 4, 1960

"Who *was* he?" Grayle asked the detective, pale as a blister, his voice raspy.

"Now don't you go puking on my crime scene."

"I've seen worse."

"I doubt that, laddie."

"Who was he, Cliff?"

"Michael Massey," Hunter said, not minding the informality.

Grayle's gaze met Hunter's. "Your suspect in the missing cheerleaders case. Coach Popularity."

"Well, apparently not popular with everybody."

The reporter shook his head, bared his teeth. "I should have gone with that story. Why did I listen to you and not run the damn thing?"

"Because the coach mighta sued your ass. We weren't sure it was him."

"You're sure now?"

"Those holes being dug up? The boys ain't plantin' flowers, bucko. And they ain't lookin' for truffles. Them's graves."

The reporter and photographer took a slow look around, then their eyes returned to the bloody body at their feet.

Grayle asked, "Have you identified any of the victims?"

"Just the survivor, whose name we're withholding for now."

"Well, it has to be the Larkin girl."

"I didn't say so. But the surviving child hasn't even given a statement. She's getting medical treatment. And probably a head shrinker'll be called in, too. She had a rough few weeks."

"And you're sure these others are the rest of the missing cheerleaders?"

"Some of 'em, anyway. All of 'em, we hope."

"How can you know that, without being able to identify them?"

"The good coach was thoughtful enough to bury 'em with their cheerleader uniforms on."

Grayle shuddered. "Sick."

"Maybe so. But he's taken the cure."

Blinking behind big lenses, Kenton asked, "How so? I mean...what the hell *happened* to him?"

Hunter shrugged. "Until the coroner gets here, and scoops him up for an autopsy, your guess is as good as mine."

*****

9:28 P.M., Thursday, NOVEMBER 3, 1960

The blow was a right that landed flush on her cheek and would have subdued any living human half her size. In Rusty's anemic state, she felt slightly stunned. Pressing his advantage, Massey grabbed an arm and flung her off the couch and onto the floor. She let out a soft moan.

He threw himself on top of her, pinned her to the floor, and his fists rained blows on her slender body, blows that should have turned her bones to kindling. She gave no resistance, and he did not notice the lack of crunching or breaking of those bones.

Assuming she had been properly subdued, Massey sent his hands to her throat and she could hear his breath accelerating with passion. He was enjoying himself. Did he intend to kill her, or merely black her out and have his way, and then she, too, could be deposited in a grave and have dirt shoveled in her face, to suffocate in terror?

As he squeezed harder, she opened her eyes, then parted her lips.

And gave him a good look at the distended fangs.

"Hell!" he blurted, and let go as if her throat were a hot stove, then scrambled off her.

At first he back-pedaled, then he turned and ran, heading for the back of the house. She was right behind him, not having to work at it at all. Even weak, she was twice as fast as any living human.

She caught up with him in the kitchen, where he had opened a drawer and pulled out two forks. He held them toward her in the form of a cross.

Rusty laughed and threw a tiny fist squarely into his

sternum. The sharp little punch shot him back into the counter, his forks flying in opposite directions, clanging to the floor.

"It only works when we believe," she said, jerking a thumb at herself. Then she pointed at him like Uncle Sam on the poster. "Plus, *you* gotta believe. And I'm pretty sure you don't."

Like a dancer, she kicked her pointed boot into his stomach and drove the air from him. He dropped to his knees.

He looked up at her in shock and pain. "What are you? What *are* you?"

"What do you think I am?"

"A fucking vampire!"

"Got it right off the bat. No pun intended."

He gulped air and managed to struggle to his feet.

"I'm dreaming," he said. "I'm hallucinating."

"Yeah. That's probably it."

She lifted him by one arm and threw him against his refrigerator, knocking his teaching schedule and the magnet that held it to the linoleum floor.

Massey picked himself up and his face tightened as he studied this creature who, whatever her ungodly powers, was so much smaller than he. And now he bared his own teeth, flew at her with a growl and delivered a left-right combination that stung a little, even knocked her back.

Then he scrambled for the back door.

She followed him, with no sense of urgency. She felt weaker, having really exerted herself. At least the odor of his cheap aftershave had been blotted out by the scent of fear.

The full moon illuminated the dead grass of the backyard, making Massey's plaid shirt practically glow as he ran toward the woods, past the open grave and over the graves of other victims. He glanced in terror over his shoulder and saw her advancing, in no apparent hurry.

As he neared the woods, she could sense his relief at the chance he might actually lose her in the thick brush. This was geography he knew, and that this intruder did not.

Then the coach paused involuntarily as he heard the snarl of an animal—*a dog?*

She could hear it, too, though she wasn't near him yet. She smiled.

No, not a dog.

When she saw the coach next, he was frozen in his tracks, until he spun toward her, wondering if the animal sound had emanated from her...

A howl ripped the quiet night in half, so loud, so terrible it might have torn the moon in two.

Now Massey turned to her, his handsome face horror-struck, his voice pitiful: "Something's out there."

"Yes," she said. "But it's not after me."

His clasped hands reached out. "Please help me. I'll...I'll turn myself in. I'll give the police a list of all the names. The parents can have some peace of mind!"

"Ah. Peace of mind. That *can* be comforting."

His eyes bugged and he held his palms out in front of him, like a crosswalk guard, as if that would stop her.

"*Please*," he said.

Almost strolling now, moving ever closer, she asked, "Did you make those girls beg? Beg for their lives?"

"I'm sorry," he moaned, the fight out of him now. "It's something...something I can't control. Something inside me."

"I know the feeling. But with that kind of sickness, you have to channel it, Coach. Channel it into something constructive, or at least not *de*-structive."

"I'll do anything you want..."

She was close enough to kiss him now. His breath was in her face. What was that, Sen-Sen?

"I know," she said gently.

"*Anything* you want...if you just...don't *hurt* me."

She smiled and embraced him, pulling him tight against her body. The human felt so warm to her, it was like hugging a furnace.

The enormous wolf, larger than any man, came out of the woods on all fours, then reared up onto its hind legs, and walked several steps, as if that were the most natural thing in the world. The creature stood not far from them, his cold red eyes staring at Massey hungrily, the saliva dripping from fangs that made hers look meager.

The coach made no effort to pull away from her, as if they suddenly were friends, even lovers.

"A wolf," he whispered. "Around *here*?"

"Not just any wolf."

Massey swallowed. "That can't be...that's not a...a..."

"Werewolf? Yes. He's with me."

"What?" Massey blurted, finally trying to pull away now, if only to see her face better in the moonlight.

"That's my partner—Max. Max, meet the coach. Coach, meet Max."

The wolf took a big step forward.

Massey seemed suddenly to have forgotten all about being in a vampire's embrace.

To the werewolf, she said, "Stay, Max. Not yet. You know the rules. Now, *sit!*"

The werewolf sat, its demeanor cooling, its tongue lolling, like a big Irish Setter.

Massey looked incredulous. "How do you manage *that...*?"

Her answer was to sink her incisors into the coach's

carotid artery. Arteries were better than veins, the blood more oxygenated, the flavor more full, the spurting liquid thicker and hotter—or at least it seemed that way, flowing freely and reminding her how hungry she really was.

The coach didn't even have a chance to scream, though his mouth was wide, as were his eyes. He was learning what it was like to be violated.

*****

2:48 A.M., Friday, NOVEMBER 4, 1960

"Looks like an animal attacked him," Grayle said, stating the obvious. "But it's almost like that animal got...interrupted. If it *was* an animal, it would have, well...*finished* its feast. And if the creature had kept at it, there'd be nothing left but bones that might get scattered. Or if the beast were doing someone's bidding, maybe...buried?"

Chuckling, Hunter said, "With that imagination, maybe you oughta go on *Shock Theater* and help introduce the horror flicks."

Grayle ignored the crack. "You don't think it's odd, a wild animal attack so close to the city?"

"I suppose," Hunter conceded.

"Whatever it was must have surprised him."

"Yep," the detective agreed. He wasn't about to help Grayle on a fishing expedition.

"You know," Grayle said, eyes narrowing, a hand on a hip, "three other really bad people—guys *you* weren't able to bring in—have disappeared in the last six months. There was that cheating husband suspected of killing his wife. That Outfit guy who you figured burned down his restaurant and got three employees killed. And that nightclub guy whose ex-waitresses had a bad habit of dropping off the edge of the earth. Now, *this.*"

"I don't see a connection," Hunter said.

"You don't think they could be related?"

The detective shrugged. "Hadn't much thought about it."

"Three guys who the Homicide Bureau couldn't bag just... disappear. And now a mass murderer, who's similarly evaded your grasp, suddenly gets attacked by a rabid dog or a bear or God knows what, in his own backyard? And you don't think they might be related?"

Hunter was starting to regret that he'd given Grayle the nod tonight; but they didn't call the guy "Digger" for nothing.

"We'll look at this thing from all directions," Hunter allowed. "But isn't this enough of a story for you without dragging in some half-assed theory?"

A tiny smile made a half-moon curve on the reporter's surfer-boy face. "Okay then, Cliff. Let's stick to the story. How do you explain an animal attack like this, essentially inside the city?"

"Son, we're standin' in the last suburb on the edge of civilization," Hunter said. "If this hadn't been related to an ongoing missing persons investigation, I wouldn't even be here."

"But you *are* here, and the local cops are out setting up sawhorses in the street, and keeping back the rubber-neckers."

"Gives 'em something to do."

Grayle shook his head. "So it's a suburb—that doesn't make it Yosemite National Park. Let's face it, suspected killers don't usually just disappear, *or* get mauled by bears in the city limits."

"I'll grant it's unusual," Hunter said, and he placed a fatherly hand on Grayle's shoulder. "But Digger—I didn't call you out here to let you indulge that wild-hair-up-your-tail imagination of yours."

The reporter was shaking his head. "Look, Cliff, this is a fresh kill—how the hell did you even hear about it so soon?"

"The girl who might or might not be the Larkin girl got free, then managed to find her way to the nearest neighbor's house. They called the locals. When they saw the graves, they phoned me and I called you."

"Why *did* you call me?"

"I called you and *only* you," Hunter said, gesturing toward the graves, "because these girls need Digger Grayle."

Bodies of sad skeletal cheerleaders were now visible all around them, washed ivory in the moonlight, an eerie tableau with work lamps creating spotlight effects on each grave.

"You," the detective said, "can give them peace...them *and* their parents. Tell your readers that the killer of these kids is dead and that he won't be killing anyone ever again. You can quote me—to hell with 'alleged.'"

But Grayle wasn't fully onboard yet. "What, and I should just say that justice was wrought by a wolverine?"

Hunter moved closer to the reporter and this time when he settled a hand on the man's shoulder, he squeezed a little.

"Sonny boy, write it up however the coroner tells you to. The important thing to remember is that a killer of young girls is off the street—for good."

Hunter drew back.

Grayle brushed his shoulder like Hunter's hand had left dirt there. "You think that's all there is to it? A killer gets killed, so justice is done, and who cares how?"

"Think of it as an early Christmas present, bucko. St. Nick come a month early this year."

Then Hunter walked away from the reporter and his photographer, to check in with his other team of diggers.

*****

9:34 P.M., Thursday, NOVEMBER 3, 1960

Rusty followed him to the ground and fed for a good long time, hunkered over Massey, savoring the meal. There was nothing delicate about it, and she knew she was a beast, like Max, at feeding time.

Speaking of Max, nearby he was growing impatient, scratching an ear with a clawed paw, as if any flea would dare travel on that fur. Finally he began pacing, a lion not liking being caged.

When she had finally drained their host of everything that had made him human—well, as human as a monster like the coach could be—she rose over the withered corpse, and gave the werewolf a nod.

Max needed no more invitation than that.

Having a werewolf for a partner had its advantages. Once she had fed, she couldn't exactly leave Massey's body lying around on the ground, with two big punctures torn in his throat. That was where Max Mantooth came in.

First, she fed.

Then, he ate.

And for such a bad man, Massey had been delicious.

With his wounds now camouflaged by even more massive injuries, the killer was barely recognizable; yet he could still be identified. Rusty looked sternly down at the wolf, raising a finger. "Enough, Max."

The wolf continued to chew on the corpse, tearing scraps of meat off bone. He lingered over the ribs, his favorite cut.

"*Max*," she said sharply. "Enough!"

Grudgingly, the animal stopped chewing and took a slumped-shouldered step back.

"Now, heel."

Max crept to her side like a scolded puppy and she scratched his ear for him. If she hadn't been undead, the werewolf would have torn her flesh off every bit as quickly as he had Massey's. Only part of her P.I. partner, the genial Max Mantooth, remained accessible within the werewolf. But in her state of unliving, she was able to help mediate and moderate Max's behavior, and summon the man inside the beast.

That was who she spoke to now.

"Max, the families of those girls deserve to know that their daughters' killer isn't out there anymore."

The wolf just looked up at her. Simple commands Max easily understood when the wolf took over. More complicated thoughts, that varied greatly. Still, she felt the need to try to explain why she had called him off.

"Getting their girls' bodies back will give the parents some peace...and being able to know their killer is dead and not merely...vanished...*that* will give them a different kind of peace."

Max nuzzled her hand.

"Good boy," she said, and scratched his neck.

The werewolf loped off into the woods. Max's car was somewhere on the other side, waiting for sun-up. There was no danger to innocents, not when he had fed so recently and well.

She went into the *Psycho* house to freshen up—to get the blood off her face, and clean off her jumpsuit, the silk cloth of which cooperated nicely. She looked at herself in Massey's bathroom mirror—her incisors had withdrawn. She was sated.

Then she went to the bushes where she untied the Larkin girl.

"Who are you?" the girl asked, smiling and crying.

"No one. I wasn't here. Understand? You crawled out of that grave yourself and got away."

"But—"

"It has to be that way. You'll hear that something terrible happened to Coach Massey—"

"Good!"

"Yes, but you know *nothing* about it."

The girl's eyes were wide. "Well...well, I don't."

"Bonnie—who am I?"

"I...I don't know."

"Could you tell a sketch artist what I looked like?"

"No."

"Who saved you?"

"Uh...no one. I...I crawled away by myself."

She patted the girl's shoulder. "Good girl. Give me a couple of minutes, and then find the nearest house with a light on. Tell them to call the police." Rusty pointed to the west. "Go that way, it's not far to the neighbors."

"Oh...okay. Thank you!"

"Pleasure is mine," Rusty said, and ran off into the night.

*****

11:13 P.M., Friday, NOVEMBER 4, 1960

Many hours later, when darkness had once again fallen, Digger Grayle—pulling his red Studebaker Avanti into a Rush Street parking space—wondered if he'd done the right thing, filing a story that said an animal attack had ironically taken out the animal that Coach Massey had secretly been.

What better exclusive could a reporter ask from his cop contact? When the *Journal* hit the street tomorrow morning, the news of the backyard graveyard, the surviving cheerleader and the mauled murderer would have the city talking—hell, screaming. The good citizens of the Windy City would bemoan the loss of the young girls, celebrate the escape of one lucky survivor, and applaud the death of a madman—his readers caught up in a fever as animalistic as Massey's demise.

Still, Digger felt he'd dropped the ball—he hadn't allowed himself, in his front-page byline story, to speculate on the possible connection between those other recent disappearances of human monsters. It was just too thin, too much of a reach, and anyway, this was not a story that needed any extra window-dressing.

Maybe in the days and nights ahead, he could dig. Maybe he could find the connection. If there was one. But to do that, he needed more than what he had now.

What he *needed* now was a beer. The Rusty Nail—whose red and yellow neon sign with its flashing hammer-and-nail extended toward Rush Street like an invitation, or maybe a threat—was just the spot for that.

The club stayed opened till four a.m., and it was after two now, but the small, intimate piano bar was at near capacity. The entertainment here never changed, yet it always drew a healthy audience—Rusty Naylor singing, her pal Max Mantooth at the ivories, a combo that locals and tourists alike couldn't get enough of. Why she worked her own little room like this, and nowhere else, never going on the road, was a mystery that eluded the city's star crime reporter.

Digger stepped into the smoky club, nodded to George

behind the bar and got a nod back, the pug-faced bartender immediately drawing a glass of beer for the reporter.

A sea of little round tables faced the tiny platform stage with brick-wall backdrop; perched on a stool next to the piano, Rusty was singing "Cry Me a River," in a sexy, breathy style that Julie London herself couldn't best. A pale vision of beauty with bright red lipstick, she wore a black sheath with side slits almost to heaven, her diminutive yet buxom form caught in the single fixed spot like a fog light glowing through the cigarette haze.

Digger got lucky and caught a stool down toward the end, fairly near the stage, and George was right there with that frosty glass of Schlitz. With Rusty's voice in his ear whispering, "*Cry me a river*," and a cold beer at his lips, Digger suddenly found life less horrible.

When Rusty finished the tune, the audience applauded, only the out-of-towners really slapping their palms, while many of the hipper locals snapped their fingers, not clapping. Digger smiled at that. The beat scene was making inroads everywhere.

Then Rusty did a very smoky "That's All," and Digger had to admit that Max, the stocky piano player in the baggy brown suit, somehow lent a deft, nicely jazz touch to everything Rusty sang, even if his fingers did look like sausages. More applause, more finger-snapping, and Rusty slid off the stool, flashing lovely white limbs, blew a little kiss to the crowd, and stepped down from the stage.

One of the oddities of the Rusty Nail was, you never knew what nights Rusty would perform, you never knew what time she'd begin, what time she'd end, even how long a set was, or whether she'd be back for another. It was her place, after all, and the spirit had to move her. Digger dug that.

Then she was standing beside him. "Buy you a drink, handsome?"

"I should buy *you* one. You're the girl. I'm the boy."

An eyebrow arched. "I could tell that right away. But I own the place, so I do the buying. Come sit."

Though the dialogue varied, this was a ritual. He would come in almost every night about now, and if she were singing that night, she'd come over, they'd flirt a little, then she would lead him to the private booth in the corner that always had a RESERVED sign on it.

They sat across from each other.

"Coffin nail?" he asked her, offering her a cigarette.

"No. I quit." She'd brought along her standard Bloody Mary.

"Yeah, they're saying it's bad for you." He fired his up. "But I smoke filter tips. It cuts the risk. Not that I care."

She sipped the drink. "You're in a mood, aren't you?"

"Am I? Maybe I'm wondering when you're going to go out with me. I mean, night after night, we sit here, and I get the feeling that you...well, that you like me okay."

"I do like you okay."

"Then how about lunch tomorrow? The Berghoff?"

The blood-red lips smiled and showed off very perfect white teeth. "You know I don't go out much in the day. It's my condition."

"You're sensitive to sunlight."

"More like allergic."

"It's fall. Damn near winter. They predict clouds to-morrow. Let's get lunch."

Another sip. "No. I need my rest, Digger. I need my sleep. As long as we both work nights, it's gonna be tough, getting to know each other any better. It's a nice friendship. A nice flirtation. Don't mess with it."

The reporter sighed. "Can't blame a guy for trying."

The red lips formed a sexy little smirk. "I'd be disappointed if you stopped. But what's wrong, Digger? Something's different tonight. You've got a weight on your shoulders."

Digger shrugged. "A man died last night. Or really this morning."

"Men die every night. Was he a good man?"

"No. A very bad one. You know those missing girls?"

"Ah—the cheerleaders? I read about that—a trusted coach behind the disappearances. Seven dead girls."

"That we know of," Digger said. "That one girl got away is a blessing, but..." He blew a wreath of smoke. "... Kind of a lousy world, isn't it?"

"You're a crime beat reporter in Chicago, and you just noticed this? The news is mum about how this coach met his fate...if I may be so flip about it."

Digger sighed. "The coroner calls it 'death by misadventure.'"

"Well, that's a little vague."

"Animal attack...coyotes...according to the ME on the scene."

"Was this in the city?"

"Up north," Grayle said. "Suburb right where the city turns into the country."

"So God decided to step in and balance the ledgers. Does that bother you?"

"You sound like Cliff Hunter." Digger shrugged again. "It's just...too many coincidences lately. Three other bad guys disappeared in recent months—maybe *they* had 'misadventures' too."

George brought Rusty another Bloody Mary.

She sipped it casually and asked, "Gonna do a story on

these 'coincidences'?"

He finished his beer, then nodded. "Think so. Gotta dig some, first."

She thought about that, then said, "I'm going to do one more set, if you want to hang around and talk about it."

Digger shook his head. "Naw, I need some sleep."

"Then, uh...how about that date tomorrow? Still up for that?"

"Lunch at the Berghoff?"

"No, how about a pizza at Gino's, down the street. Meet me here at seven, and we'll walk. I'm not going on till about ten tomorrow, so we'll have plenty of time to talk."

"Cool."

Another little red smirk. "Do me a favor, would you? Round up Max—he's up at the bar. Tell him I want to go over the set list with him. Then you go home and get forty winks."

"Sure. But it'll be like fifty winks. I am *beat.*"

He slipped out of the booth, winked at her and got one back for the effort, ran his errand, then headed out into the cold night. But he felt better now, knowing that he'd finally wrangled a date out of Rusty, though he had no clue why tonight had done the trick.

He was pulling his Avanti out of its parking place when he noticed the car waiting to pull in was a familiar one, an aqua-blue Thunderbird.

Couldn't be two cars like that, he thought, and as he pulled away, he glanced in the rearview mirror and saw Lt. Cliff Hunter step from the car and head toward the Rusty Nail, his footsteps keeping time with its pulsing neon.

But a voice from somewhere back in his skull whispered: *Time to start digging, Digger. Time to start digging....*

Digger Grayle didn't see the lovely young woman, who was not really young at all, shooing the homicide detective inside only to linger beneath the pulsing Rusty Nail sign, watching the reporter's taillights recede.

Rusty Naylor didn't want to have to make a meal out of this good man. Maybe she should just bring him deeper into her world. He was smart, tenacious, resourceful, and would make a better ally than an enemy.

And he was certainly taken with her, and she knew that getting him to, well, neck with her would be easy enough.

Anyway, he already worked nights, didn't he?

“Murderlized,” first appeared in *Hollywood and Crime*, copyright 2009, Max Allan Collins and Matthew V. Clemens.

“A Pebble for Papa,” first appeared in *The Mammoth Book of Roaring Twenties Whodunits*, copyright 2004, Max Allan Collins and Matthew V. Clemens.

“Devil’s Face,” first appeared in *Crime Square*, copyright 2012, Max Allan Collins and Matthew V. Clemens.

“The Two Billys,” first appeared in *Worlds of Edgar Rice Burroughs*, copyright 2013, Max Allan Collins and Matthew V. Clemens.

“East Side, West Side,” first appeared in *Murder and All That Jazz*, copyright 2004, Max Allan Collins and Matthew V. Clemens.

“Mystery Train,” first appeared in *Pop the Clutch*, copyright 2018, Max Allan Collins and Matthew V. Clemens.

“A Little Faith,” first appeared in *Dark Faith: Invocations*, copyright 2021, Max Allan Collins and Matthew V. Clemens.

“Lie Beside Me,” first appeared in *Flesh and Blood: Guilty as Sin*, copyright 2003, Max Allan Collins and Matthew V. Clemens.

“The High Life,” first appeared in *At the Scene of the Crime*, copyright 2008, Max Allan Collins and Matthew V. Clemens.

“My Lolita Complex,” first appeared in *Flesh and Blood: Dark Desires*, copyright 2002, Max Allan Collins and Matthew V. Clemens.

“Out for Blood,” first appeared in *Hardboiled Horror*, copyright 2017, Max Allan Collins and Matthew V. Clemens.

A Look At:
An Eliot Ness Mystery Omnibus

A FAST-PACED, ONE-TWO PUNCH OF CRIME AND DROP DEAD SUSPENSE.

Legendary lawman Eliot Ness goes solo… In 1929, Eliot Ness put away Al Scarface Capone and became the biggest living legend this side of law and order. Now it's 1935. With The Untouchables and Prohibition behind him and the Great Depression falling darkly across the nation, Ness arrives in Cleveland to straighten out a crooked city.

An anonymous ring of bent cops is dealing in vice, graft, gambling and racketeering, over lorded by a mysterious top cop known as the outside chief. But between corrupt politicians, jealous colleagues, a parasitic reporter and two blondes with nothing in common, Ness has big troubles pulling the sheets off the bed of blue vipers.

"For anybody who loves crime novels, Max Allen Collins is the gold standard."

An Eliot Ness Mystery Omnibus includes: Dark City, Butcher's Dozen, Bullet Proof and Murder by The Numbers.

AVAILABLE NOW

About the Authors

MAX ALLAN COLLINS was named a Grand Master in 2017 by the Mystery Writers of America. He is a three-time winner of the Private Eye Writers of America "Shamus" award, receiving the PWA "Eye" for Life Achievement (2006) and their "Hammer" award for making a major contribution to the private eye genre with the Nathan Heller saga (2012).

His graphic novel Road to Perdition (1998) became the Academy Award-winning Tom Hanks film, followed by prose sequels and several graphic novels. His other comics credits include the syndicated strip "Dick Tracy"; "Batman"; and his own "Ms. Tree" and "Wild Dog."

His innovative Quarry novels were adapted as a 2016 TV series by Cinemax. His other suspense series include Eliot Ness, Krista Larson, Reeder and Rogers, and the "Disaster" novels. He has completed twelve "Mike Hammer" novels begun by the late Mickey Spillane; his audio novel, Mike Hammer: The Little Death with Stacy Keach, won a 2011 Audie.

For five years, he was sole licensing writer for TV's CSI: Crime Scene Investigation (and its spin-offs), writing best-selling novels, graphic novels, and video games. His tie-in books have appeared on the USA TODAY and New York Times bestseller lists, including Saving Private Ryan, Air Force One, and American Gangster.

Collins has written and directed four features and two documentaries, including the Lifetime movie "Mommy" (1996) and "Mike Hammer's Mickey Spillane" (1998); he scripted "The Expert," a 1995 HBO World Premiere and "The Last Lullaby" (2009) from his novel The Last Quarry. His Edgar-nominated play "Eliot Ness: An Untouchable Life" (2004) became a PBS special, and he has co-authored (with A. Brad Schwartz) two non-fiction books on Ness, Scarface and the Untouchable (2018) and Eliot Ness and the Mad Butcher (2020).

Collins and his wife, writer Barbara Collins, live in Iowa; as "Barbara Allan," they have collaborated on sixteen novels, including the "Trash 'n' Treasures" mysteries, Antiques Flee Market (2008) winning the Romantic Times Best Humorous Mystery Novel award of 2009. Their son Nathan has translated numerous novels into English from Japanese, as well as video games and manga.

*****

MATTHEW V. CLEMENS is a writer and teacher whose first book was a non-fiction true crime title, Dead Water: the Klindt Affair (1995, with Pat Gipple). He has co-written numerous books with Max Allan Collins, the pair having collaborated on over thirty novels and numerous short stories, as well as the much-lauded non-fiction work, The History of Mystery (2001). They also contributed an essay to the Edgar-nominated In Pursuit of Spenser (2012).

In addition the duo has produced several comic books,

four graphic novels, a computer game, and over a dozen mystery jigsaw puzzles for such famous TV properties as CSI (and its spin-offs), NCIS, Buffy the Vampire Slayer, Hellboy, and The Mentalist, as well as tie-in novels for Bones, Dark Angel and Criminal Minds. A number of the team's books made the USA TODAY bestseller list.

Matt also worked with Max on the bestselling "Reeder and Rogers" debut thriller, Supreme Justice (2014), and shared byline on its two sequels, Fate of the Union (2015) and Executive Order (2017). He has published a number of solo short stories and worked on numerous book projects with other authors, both non-fiction and fiction, including R. Karl Largent on several of the late author's bestselling techno-thrillers. He has also worked as a book doctor for numerous other authors.

Matt lives in Davenport, Iowa with his wife, Pam, a retired teacher.

Made in the USA
Middletown, DE
28 June 2021